MY CARAMEL

ANGELY KAHN

MY CARAMEL

Copyright © 2023 by Angely Kahn Ltd
Cover and internal design © 2023 by Angely Kahn Ltd
Cover and image design by Banastudios

All rights reserved. No part of this book may be reproduced in any form or by any electronic or mechanical means, including information storage and retrieval systems— except in the case of brief quotations embodied in critical articles or reviews—without permission in writing from Angely Kahn Ltd.

The characters and events portrayed in this book are fictitious or are used fictitiously. Any similarity to real persons, living or dead, is purely coincidental and not intended by the author.

All brand names and product names used in this book are trademarks, registered trademarks, or trade names of their respective holders.

ISBN: 9798866931460

MY CARAMEL

For my own Mimi, my backbone,

forever, my parents

and my grandmother, my entire world.

MY CARAMEL

CHAPTER ONE

AIDEN.

I see her again.

She looks conspicuously graceful tonight, her emerald dress, her smile, and her humility guarding her. Everything about her seems as if she's something I've only ever read about in great novels; the way she glides through the crowd with decorum, it was hard to take my eyes off her. The way she walked, her brown eyes unfathomably deep.

Her.

Just *her.*

Mystery is fickle and dangerous. Here I am, falling in love with a stranger, yet I am *'in love'* with someone else.

Our eyes meet each other.

Aiden, do not do this.

Ah shit!

"Hi, I'm Amala." She says softly.

I looked around to see if my date was near, already feeling guilty- of what? She's just saying hi.

"Hi, Aiden." I keep it short.

She runs her eyes on me quickly, "So, where's this Gatsby fellow, anyway? Seems kind of rude not to greet your guests, don't you think?" She smiles.

"Actually, I'm Gatsby?" I smile at her strangely; she's *a reader*, I think to myself.

She smiles at me one last time; that is all it takes. One epic smile, how do our hearts decide who it deserves? What makes it blush, beat, or burn? *God.*

Every weekend is robbed and replaced by parties and not even the kind I want, *'Galas.'* Grown people traipsing around in expensive garments celebrating something or the other. Tonight, it is because the mayor won his re-election, a small private celebration for his family and friends, yet all I can think of is, *who is she? This woman whom my heart has taken a liking to. Who is Amala?*

MY CARAMEL

"Dad is looking pretty good up there," Amelia says, admiring our father.

"After everything we went through, I'm just glad he is living, breathing, and smiling," I reply.

"Four more years, Aiden, and then we can return to being a family, but for now, he needs us."

"A lot can happen in four years, Amelia heck, a lot can happen in a year," I say, regrettably thinking.

The room glitches, jolts, or maybe it's my eyes...my thoughts. The Oak Room feels small, my focus shifts- I feel as if all the windows are shut, every seal closed, and the air sucked out. I need some air. I feel the oxygen slowly leaving my body, my breathing becoming more profound, and my thoughts darker. *Aiden, you need some air.* I step outside to desperately distract my inner thoughts from the endless possibilities of what-ifs...

Alas, air.

New York City in all her glory, the lights, the hustle and bustle, the coolness in the air, she masks your worries with her charm and beauty; in essence, she is the allure of mystery...damn its fickle and danger.

"Hey." A soft voice speaks, bringing me comfort.

I turn to look at her, and I watch her, watch the night sky. It's her again. *Amala.*

"You should come to May's Cupcake." She said while still looking up, trying to find the stars. Her eyes reflected all the colors of the city lights.

"Urm, okay."

"It's over on the 22nd." She keeps it short.

"I'll check it out, I guess," I reply slowly.

I stare at her a little longer, with curiosity, before I return my gaze up at New York. In silence, we both stare at the night sky in awe, as if tonight is the first night- we witness the beauty of New York City.

A thought violently interrupts the peace, *'I should go back inside.*

STILL CHAPTER ONE
THE VERY SAME NIGHT, THROUGH A DIFFERENT LENS

AMALA.

Greyhound Day is what you feel at these events: same circle of people, same obnoxious food, same strapline of gossip. Congressmen this, and congressmen's daughter that, and oh, divorce. I stand in the corner of this low-lit ballroom and observe from the distance. Every flute glass sparkles and glistens, that if you step back and unfocus your vision, everything from the debutante women to the older men twinkles like diamonds. Except one, one rough diamond amongst them all. He stands tall, with broad shoulders but not muscley, a neat stubble, his eyelashes thick enough to make any girl jealous. He's wearing a pressed black Dolce suit with satin strips on the side. An emerald pocket square perfectly aligned in a perfect shade that matches my emerald dress.

Life has a funny way of drawing people together in the most organic way that almost blinds them. Curiosity gets the best of me. Why didn't he sparkle like the rest? Is he broken? My grandfather's mantra is, *'Too much of something and you become numb to it; too little of something and it's desired,'* but I don't know what is numb to me and what is desirable. I quickly peek around the room and question if they all know. What do they secretly want? My thoughts on a conveyor belt taking me back around to what I secretly want. An adventure? To experience adrenaline without compromising myself and have everything lined up for me after graduation. To fall in love, to experience both the beauty and bitterness of it. To feel! And through my internal affairs, I thought back to the moment I felt a flicker, for the first time, a glimmer of something when I first saw him.

My parents swam through the crowds to greet everyone as if they hadn't seen the same people on some other occasion last week. It's not that I hate being here; at times, I love it, it's like having the upper hand in chess-the sheer privilege of being in the same room as some of these people. Talking of privilege,

MY CARAMEL

"Hello dear, how are you?" Mrs. Mimi Margaux asks; she is one of the very few women in this room I enjoy talking to, and she radiates the room—a woman who can be both graceful and a goodfella, indeed a rare talent.

"I'm well, and how are you? Oh, your trip, how was it?"

"Extraordinary, handsome Moroccan men. You must go some time."

"I might just…but not without you!"

"It's a girl's trip." We both laugh. She squeezes my hand and lights her whole face with a smile.

I see my mother walk towards me, a group of women following behind like ducklings, my mother turns her head, she moves left, they observe, she looks in my direction, and they look, waving at me. I turn around, walk in the opposite direction, and find myself walking into a crowd of strangers. I walk until I'm outside, and I jump at the sound of cars beeping, one setting the other off, the horning forcing me to turn around to shelter my ears from the loud sound, or maybe life is nudging me into a different direction- I thought when I turn to see Aiden tugging on his tie. He looks distressed, as if he's trying to catch his breath. It is a feeling all too familiar; at times, life pushes it onto us when moments feel insufferable, but occasionally, all that is needed is a sweet distraction.

The Next Morning

Monday morning, breaking away from the world of fancy clothes and polite conversations, a world of making enough money to pay for the weekends. Today, I'm back to feeling more like myself. The incessant need for an adrenaline-fueled adventure shouldn't have surpassed its expiration date (when I was sixteen), but it remains to occupy my thoughts and now my dreams. Last night, I dreamt of cruising down the highway in a dark green 68' Mustang with Don Corleone and his cat on his lap. We were driving out of Manhattan to try to convince Michael of something (though in my dream, Michael wasn't Al Pacino; he was Aiden.) I barely paid attention to it since I had been reading Mario Puzo's The Godfather before I drifted off to sleep.

I'm the first to arrive in class, not because I'm studious, but because my professor is scary. The type that repeats the same cycle of predictable catchphrases, '*news can't wait but sleep can*' or better than that, '*You're in the best university America has to offer for Journalism, so don't just do exceptionally be the omission,*' and as she is the one marking my final piece this semester, I cannot afford to get on her absolute worse side. No matter what I do or how hard I try, she's never impressed, but for some reason, I continue to impress her, as if her validation is the only one that matters.

Despite Christine Amanpour or my father commenting on my 'brilliant' work highlighting *'what the American Dream is really about'* but when my professor read it, she moaned that it was not politically censored nor was it suited for the 'real world'; she said it's dangerous and ill-advised to think I can write freely. She rambled on about reality, and how dare I tarnish her name by advising people I wrote it under her supervision. She believes journalism is what you're paid to write about, irrespective of your beliefs or ideology.

"As you are aware, your deadline is fast approaching; you're required to write a profile interview about a known person in the media. Their story and no more than 2000 words." My professor says in her grating voice.

Sara raises her hand, "Professor, does it have to be someone in the social spotlight?"

I glaze a look over to the crowd, to everyone, and watch them all tense up at the thought of the professor's response.

"Sara, remind me, what field of Journalism do you aspire to work in?" The professor responds with a sinister undertone to her sarcasm.

Sara, feeling panicked, almost forgetting her field, "Urm... I... urm want to be a... field reporter." Instantly regretting her question.

"Well, then listening would be a useful tool in your arson? Does anyone have a real question?"

Everyone keeps their hands firmly down, either sitting on their hands or holding their other hand down, protecting it against stupidity. The look on Sara's face is crushing; the industry is cutthroat, and we're at the most competitive journalism school in America. I know, to an extent, the professor is trying to 'prepare' us for the world, but I truly believe she does not care about any of us. She's collecting a handsome paycheck and nothing more. She continues her lecture, moving on to the theory of gratification. Before I realize I've joined the entire cohort of students in a daydream, I try to imagine what Don and I would get up to next: do we share a cannolo?

Luckily, we only have her till the end of the semester, and then it's summer. Every year, my mother visits her family back home in Oman, and every year, she pleads for me to join her, but my father is always busy, and I never want to leave him. He has all the good stories. Maybe, this year, I'll finally go.

CHAPTER TWO

AIDEN.

Talks of the summer make me nauseous; for my father, every free time is an opportunity to learn something. We argue every summer about what he wants vs what I want.
"Either option sounds shitty, Dad." I snap.
"Watch your tone. Plus, I think an internship will be a good distraction. Get your head out of this funk you've been in." My dad snaps back.

This summer, like every summer, we move into our beach house in the Hamptons, but my father wants me to stay in the city to intern at a law firm. We haven't been to the beach house in two years due to my father renovating it. The walls got really messed up, and he decided to change it all around. I guess it'll be kinda nice going back.

What I really want to say to my father is that I'm too tired to give a crap about anything. Since he won his re-elections, it's been nonstop bullshit. My mom is impossible to deal with. She treats me as if I'm fragile but expects me to remain her backbone and to remain strong. She can't have both; either I'm protecting, or she is. I try so hard with her, for her to let go of the past, but I can see worry seep out of her pours, like one of those squishy toys- no matter how many times you squeeze and pull it, it'll return to its original shape as if new; unaware of how many times it's been stretched. Maybe it's the village woman in her or the ethnicity, but sometimes it seems impossible. At least I have my Amelia, my savior. My father gave me till the end of the week to make my decision.

Like many things, law school was my father's idea; I didn't mind, I mean, I don't mind, but like I said…I don't care for any of this, for anything. I just want to switch off, to not always be tired. Present enough to be able to finish my essays. I can't even seem to start my torts paper. I type …

~~It is recognized when…~~

~~A negligence claim is established by…~~

~~Negligence claims are reputable when…~~

Argh

I sit at my desk, gazing at my laptop, thinking about this summer and what I want to do. Seriously, what is it? What do I want to do? What is it that any of us want to do? To hit the pause button for a little while without the concept of a 'future' chasing us down a corridor, forcing us to gamble on which door we choose to pick. I hear my bedroom door creak open and the faintest knock.

"Hey, Aiden, can we watch the new Marvel movie tonight?" Amelia asks.

"Urm, do we have anything on tonight?"

"I'm not sure, but it's the Multiverse of Madness, and we only have eight weeks before I go to camp this summer." She replies with her puppy eyes.

"Wait, camp? This summer?" There is no way I'll be spending summer alone.

"Yes, remember the NASA summer camp? Oh, and I was reading up on it, and I think I might actually get to meet him," she squeaked, her eyes beaming with joy and excitement.

"Meet who?"

"Urm, the best astrophysicist in the world... Neil DeGrasse Tyson."
"Yeah...I don't know who that is, but anyway, Marvel, I'll check with Ma if we have to be anywhere."

We both make our way downstairs, and before I could even ask, Ma shrieks at the sight of us. "Oh, my babies are here. Don't forget we have that dinner party tonight!"
Amelia shoots a look at me, and enough was said in that one brief eye exchange.

"Whose dinner party? and do we really have to go, Ma?" I say exhaustively, emphasizing the *Ma*.
"You know the Ali's; they are throwing a party for..." Ma looks at us and laughs (it's flashes like this; I treasure brief glimpses of joy). She explains how she wasn't paying attention when the Ali's invited her. It triggers a laugh from Amelia, and my father walks in, laughing at the sound of my mother snorting.

I don't want to move, but my father leaves to return some emails, and my mother picks her car keys up to collect her dress for tonight.

"Is your girlfriend coming tonight?" Amelia asks, biting on her avocado on hashbrowns.

"She's not my girlfriend. Our moms want us to get to know each other." I quickly snap back.

Mention of her made me realize just how little I thought about her. Everything is just a little too much for me to handle, not that she adds to it; she seems sweet, but she doesn't deserve the minimum from me.

"And I'm not sure, but I'll give her a call," I answer Amelia's question.

I hate feeling guilty, but I hate being lost in my thoughts more,

"Amelia? Wanna go shopping?"

"For?"

"You know, shit, I mean stuff…a gift," I half smile. I'm not sure if Amelia is fond of her just yet- I'm not even sure if I'm ready for anyone in my life right now.

I picked out the dress she reserved at Bergdorf Goodman and rushed back to her house. Her mother let me in, and I placed the dress on her bed with a pair of heels that Amelia picked out for her. I wait like the gentlemen I am, in a town car downstairs, holding a bunch of pink peonies. I just know everything about this makes a girl's heart glow; it's just a shame we don't do this every day…make them glow.

"Aiden," She whispers, standing outside her front door…glowing.

I smile at her and open the door for her, feeling…proud that I made her smile.

"Thank you, Aiden." She said, smiling and…glowing. Uncomplicated joy.

We arrive outside the Palace Hotel, and in the courtyard, people are dressed exceptionally spectacularly. The Ali's are renowned for their parties, each one more unique than the one before; last year, they had animals imported in from all parts of the world: camels, lions, birds, and elephants. We walk towards our table. I look around, searching rather than looking until I see her; in between the huge, fresh, flowered centerpieces, she caught my eye, and it made my heart warm. *Is that her?*

CHAPTER THREE

AMALA.

Nothing shy of complete magic... everything avant-garde. Grand, white-flowered chandeliers drooping from the high-rise ceiling, each swaying with its own scent that complements the one next to it, amber-hugging rose. This sensual, warm, but fresh scent takes away the low-lit ballroom. The warm golden tones harmonize with the guests as if they, themselves, are props. Tonight, we celebrate the Ali's daughter's engagement to someone with deep pockets, who's the son of someone with deeper pockets. The Ali's only surround themselves with certain people, think Frank Costello. If you're in politics, a partner at some big firm, or have profound wealth, you know the Ali's. It's not as if the Ali's are part of the New York Five, but they unquestionably knew people and kept their circle tight-fisted. My father, on the other hand, isn't a corporate tycoon; he doesn't belong to any circle. The only arson my father has is that he's a successful, well-known writer, and if I've learned anything from him, it is, *'you control people's perception of others through two ways: 1. writing and 2. Media.'*

When *'they'* need a profile written for them, in the New Yorker or The Times, they'll call my father. Two years back, a major scandal broke out, and the Ali's were accused of covering up a murder and ruling it as suicide; my father's article rewrote their entire image, from hate to empathy. That's the power of words.

My parents and I are shown to our table; we walk down the ballroom towards our table. My father makes small talk as he passes by friends and colleagues, and my mother runs into a couple of her book club friends. Before I knew it, I was standing alone in a room full of people. As I look around the room, people are conversing, laughing, even making acquaintances, and all I really want is to go home, which frustrates me, not because I am here but because all I dream about is this big adventure and when faced with the faintest opportunity for an adventure I run away. There are people queuing, paparazzi camping outside to get exclusive pictures of socialites and Victoria's Secret models, and here I am in the middle of a page-five scandal, but I couldn't care less. I take a seat and discreetly reach into my bag to take my book out.

"The universe is under no obligation to make sense to you," someone whispers to me.
I look up, and this teenage girl with big, brown, beady eyes stands eagerly in front of me.

"Hi," I smile at her and put my book down.
"Sorry, I'm just a huge Neil DeGrasse fan."

"You've read this book?" I ask surprisingly.
"Yes, I love it. I got into the NASA summer camp, so I'm hoping to meet him."

"Get out of here!" I eek with excitement, and I pull out a chair for her.
She takes a seat, and we talk and talk about Max Planck, the black hole, and Einstein's theory of relativity. We speak about time travel and if it is possible. We touch on how much of space do we really know. How does God come into it, or does God come in at all?

The more you learn about space, the more you dive into the vortex of physics, and the more you come to understand that not a single atom or nebular explosion happened without the will or power of God; nothing more or nothing less. Despite what anyone thinks or how educated they may be...God is the creator. We both take a moment to appreciate the depths of our conversation. Sighing with relief, we smile at each other, and the young girl excuses herself to return to her family.

"You're going to be the exception at NASA." I say, "Wait, sorry, I didn't catch your name."

"It's Amelia." She smiles.

"Amala." I return the smile. I turn to continue reading my book.

I hear a familiar voice.

"There you are." I look up, and I feel a flicker, the same flicker I felt last weekend. Aiden stood tall and handsome, his broad shoulders in a suit.

See, life and its funny ways of drawing people together. I wasn't sure why I felt this way, but some things in life do not always require an answer...so my father says.

"Hi, Amala... right?" He says with a gentle smile.

I nod gracefully.

"You came here alone?" he asks, looking at my empty table.

"With my parents, they're here somewhere," I respond, slightly embarrassed that I was the only one sitting alone.

MY CARAMEL

"You wanna take a walk?" he asks, gesturing his head in the opposite direction.

It's not like I'm having much luck reading my book anyway.

"Aiden, aren't you forgetting about Grandma?" Amelia said strangely, but it sounded like code for something else.

"Grandma went home early. She had a headache." He said, smiling, but behind that smile was a different response entirely. I am under the impression there is no grandma.

I decided to walk with him. Amelia left us something about a Belgium chocolate tiramisu.

"So, how's school?" he asks, not wanting us to sink into an awkward silence.

I look at him with a slight frown, *how's school?* That's something my father would ask me, actually, *no*! My father and I have a relationship. Maybe my father's colleagues; I guess school is all we really have, other than each other's names, we don't know much about each other. He sees the regret of his question on my face, "I'm sorry," he chuckles. "I just…I guess we don't know much about each other." he smiles, looking down.

"I'm struggling with my final report. Not so much struggling. I'm trying to find the right person." I jump straight in.

"Tell me about it, and you never know I could be resourceful." He says, smiling, showing all his teeth.

"I have to write a profile interview about a known person in the media or social spotlight." I fill him in about what's required, and we walk around the ballroom, passing the carefully placed garden in the center.

"So, you're in journalism?"

"Oh yeah, that's my major."

He grabs a couple of soft drinks from the waiter walking past us, "Okay, well, that's easy," He hands me my glass. "Look around us, Amala. People in the social spotlight surround us." He takes a sip and points to a few people.

"All yesterday's news, Aiden. I need something new and intriguing, something that's not been written before." My voice is full of passion and frustration. I can feel his eyes on me as I dive deep into what makes a story unique.

"It's just for your professor? No one else will read it?" he asks.

"Yes, I guess why?"

"Write about me." He says with strength, underlined with vulnerability.

I take a moment before I respond, thinking carefully about what his story could be. More so, why is he trusting me with his story, which takes me back to what his story could be? Did he cheat? Did he break the law? Did he kill someone? Far fetch, I know, but anything is possible. We continue circling the room; I think we've made our third round.

"Are you sure? It requires a few interviews and very personal questions." I emphasize the personal.

"Yes, I am sure," he says, nodding his head with reassurance.

"Why?"

"Why what?" he asks confused.

"Why are you doing this for me?"

"I don't know. You seem nice, and it'll be a good distraction." This time, his smile fades a little, but enough to notice. "How about we meet at that cupcake place you mentioned." quickly snapping out of his blues.

"May's Cupcake on 22nd?" I smile, "okay, I'll see you Monday at 4 p.m.?" I say, not sure what his schedule is like.

He nods and throws me one last smile before he excuses himself. I return to my empty table, smiling to myself; I take my book out of my bag and resume my reading.

CHAPTER FOUR

AIDEN.

I cannot stop thinking about Amala, for the first time in a long time- my thoughts.

    Feel *quieter,*

        less *obtrusive,*

            less *dangerous,*

but not too quiet, that thoughts can slip back in like an alarm clock waiting to go off.

            It's nice.

On Sunday mornings, I walk Amelia to her Space Club, and I spend that hour playing basketball with Omar. The evenings are reserved for family dinners, and my mother would lose her shit if I decided to cancel our family dinner. Once, I was out with Omar, and we were in an intense game against a couple of other guys. Only ten minutes had passed, and she started blowing my line and then Omar's, but that's Ma. She jumps to the worst-case scenario. She wakes up early in the morning to prepare the lamb. It is always her famous rice with a leg of lamb for just the four of us. Sometimes, we have people join us, like my father's friends or mine or Amelia's, and they all fall in love with it.

Dad works for an hour in the evening, ready for Monday; Ma sits and spends an hour talking and catching up with her friends while Amelia and I watch a movie. Amelia somehow loves anything old like Casablanca or anything Hepburn, and then for days, she walks around quoting famous lines, "Hey Aiden, here's looking at you kid," over and over. Thankfully, I get to pick today, and I'm in the mood for something old, too, more like the Bronx Tale or Donnie Brasco. We settled for the Bronx Tale, a tale of a hardworking father pushing his son to be educated and earn a good living, a son who thinks his father has no idea about the world they live in, and they clash until they both learn a valuable lesson. It always takes something crazy to happen for people to learn a lesson.

The credits roll up onto our screen. I look over at Amelia, who is practically asleep; my father checks in on me, the usual how's this and how's that? I know he genuinely cares, but it's a tug of war between time, so I spare him the drama and tell him everything is good.

I jump into bed feeling sleepy after the movie and all the lamb. Thinking about tomorrow about meeting Amala, my mind gets distracted, so I pick up a book (I bought a year ago but never got the time to read it), *'You Get So Alone At Times That It Just Makes Sense'* by Charles Bukowski it reads,

'Some men never
die
and some men never
live
but we're all alive
tonight.'

Food for thought. The original, 'You either get busy living or get busy dying.'

The Next Morning

I haul a cab to midtown, and from Columbia, it's a twenty-eight-minute drive; I pass by the city's landmarks, forgetting how many times I pass by them and forget they're there. I arrive outside the 'famous' May's Cupcake World, it reads she left the '*World*' part out.

I look around until I see her sitting in the corner, wearing a brown Ralph Lauren sweatshirt on top of a white shirt, her head deep into her book.

I walk towards her, "Hey."

She hits pause on her phone and takes her air pods out, "Aiden, hi," she replies softly.

"What shall I get us?" I ask.

"I'll come with you." she gets up, placing her book to the side.

"No, sit; just tell me what you want, and I'll get it."

"Aiden, picking the right cupcake with the right drink is serious business." She said with so much appetite it made me smile.

"Yes, ma'am, lead the way." I step back and allow her to take charge.

She ordered a popcorn pop cupcake with a caramel latte for herself and ordered me a hazelnut cupcake with a chocolate cappuccino; not what I would have ordered, but she seems to be the expert.

"That'll be $36 dollars." The lady behind the counter said. I pull out my card, tap it onto the card reader, and we walk back to our table in the corner.

MY CARAMEL

I watch her smile to herself and lean forward before taking a sip from her steaming hot latte.

"I'll let you in on a secret." She said suspiciously, looking around the café. Intrigued, I play along and look around us before leaning toward her to listen to the secret.

"Sip the hot coffee and quickly take a bite of the cupcake; that way, the cupcake will melt into your mouth, and you'll forget that you burnt your tongue."

"Seems wise, on the count of three?" I signal her by lifting my drink in one hand and the cupcake in the other hand. Following my lead, she does the same, "ready," she signals back.

We both laugh at our stupidity, laughing carelessly until my thoughts slide in one by one, casting a foggy cloud, doubt followed by guilt, followed by anger, followed by sadness.

What are you doing, Aiden?

Focus.

Calm down; it's okay.

It's okay, Aiden,

Shit

I shouldn't be here.

Aiden?

Calm down.

Hey

Look around you.

Focus on Amala.

Caramel and cupcake

Okay.

"Aiden?" Amala says softly, "You, okay?"
I feel all sweaty, and part of me wants to walk out, already feeling embarrassed, but another part of me feels too paralyzed to move. Flashbacks flood my mind, almost drowning me.

"Sorry," I dimly laugh. "I, um, was thinking about my torts paper, sorry."
"It's okay…hey, Aiden, it's okay." She smiles at me, her eyes brown and kind. Silence with the right people allows you to have a whole conversation without words.
I don't know if I can share my story; I don't want to break her hope at the same time. If I can't even trust my own thoughts, then how can I trust another person, a stranger? Although she didn't feel like a stranger from the moment my eyes found her.

I smile at her, "What is the king of cupcakes?" attempting to change the conversation.

"Oh, it's a secret." She smiles at me.

Her smile.

I feel a little calmer.

"Okay, let's dive in," she says, setting aside the cupcakes.

She takes out her notepad and pen and starts by writing the date, time, and venue before 'click,' and the sound of the old tape recorder runs around in circles.

Feeling curious, I ask her, "Why the old tape recorder?"

"Why not a tape recorder?" she replies nonchalantly until she looks at my unsatisfied face.

"It's my father's; he used it in all his big pieces." She adds.

"Even the one he did with John Gotti?" I ask her. A proud smile arose on her face; her father sat across a criminal sensation, "the very one." She beamed. "Let's start with the basics. Your full name?" She asked formally, switching to her journalistic voice.

I reply equally formally, "Aiden Hakeem Sancar."

"What is your Major and why?" she moved on.

"I study Law at Columbia because…can I say because my father wants me to, which is true, but I also want to leave my mark… I guess…is that what I'm supposed to say?"

She looks up at me, "Only if you believe it, Aiden."

"What is the hardest part of being Mayor Sancar's son?"

"Expectation to always do right." I lied.

It's partly true, but I am so accustomed to it that I can't say it's the hardest part anymore, maybe the forced growth, and if that's the case, I don't want it.

"Have you always done the right thing?"

The question I dreaded.

I force my mouth to conjure up an answer, but it is as if my brain is stopping my mouth from speaking the truth; somewhere deep down, I'm protecting my ears from hearing about it again. Just *open your mouth and speak; what is the worst that will happen?* I scream in my head. I reach over and press the pause button on the tape recorder, and it makes this sound as if it's reached and surpassed old age. Amala looks up at me, confused.

"Is something wrong?" she asked.

I take a deep breath, "the truth?" I don't know this woman, yet I feel compelled to tell her something that has been eating away at me. "I want to tell you, and I know you're riding on this for your final, but right now, the words aren't coming to me so easily."

She looks confused and a little sad. She looks at me and replies, "Okay."

"Okay?" I repeat, annoyed and feeling a little vulnerable.

"Aiden, I can't expect you to dive in on your first interview, but you know how important this is to me; if you think it's too much, then I will stop and find someone else."
Say no, you know you don't have it in you just back out, she's giving you a free pass.

"You're right, but I'm good. We can keep going," I reply against every thought that is screaming in my head.
She suggests taking a break, we pack up and head out.

I reach into my pocket, take my phone out, tap on my screen to check the time, and see that we have killed three hours.

"Chocolate praline cupcake," Amala says, smiling.
I look at her confused, "The best cupcake."
I make a mental note.
Not sure why, but I do *Chocolate praline cupcake.*

We circled around the block, talking about likes and dislikes, our parents, Islam, college, life after graduation, and the list went on until we built up an appetite.
"Now it's my turn to show you a good spot for food."
She looked hesitant, "Aiden, I have to get home."

"Amala, this place is a must; I promise to drop you off at home as soon as we're done."
She smiled but gently refused my offer.

"Now, wasn't you saying how you really want an adventure, but you're afraid of it?"

She tried to cut me off, "I know what you're going to say, but the answer to every single excuse is, you won't know until you try... right?"

I give her a quick moment to second guess her thought of going home before I come back in with, "Right, you will never know, Amala. You can't be afraid of everything that comes your way. Do you want to sit opposite the next John Gotti? Then guess what? You have to be willing to do what it takes to beat the other thousands of people with a notepad and pen."

"And dinner with you will change that?" she snaps back sarcastically.

"Yes, an adventure is exploring unknown charter. You'll never know what we'll see or what will happen." I smirk because I know I've just hit the home run.

She looks at me, smiles, and replies, "It better be one heck of an adventure."

CHAPTER FIVE

AMALA.

I hit the big, faded button and watch the tape recorder spin around and around; I lay back on my bed and listen back to my recording with Aiden. Drafting my essay in my mind, where to begin, not that he gave me much to go with, but I feel there's a story here. This profile with Aiden will be my movie moment acceptance for my professor, starring the hardworking individual and the impossible boss, a movie rerun a thousand times. I feel this profile will be my moment - unique, gripping, and full of page-turning emotions.
I feel it.

MY CARAMEL

Baba walks into my room holding a poorly wrapped box with an enormous, silk, red bow placed on top, "For you... for so many reasons, but to think of one you've worked so hard in school, but more importantly, because your pieces are beautifully written that I thought it's time for an upgrade." He stands, extending the box towards me.

I jump up, grab the box, intrigued, and touched all at the same time. I place the gift on my desk, turn around, and kiss him on his forehead.

I pull on the delicate bow, and it unravels for me as if enchanted. "Your very own typewriter." He said, proud and smiling.

"Thank you, Baba." He leaves the room, and I press rewind on the tape recorder, sit back on my bed, and listen to the tape again. Understanding where to start your story is the hardest part of writing. Finding the story is equal parts of fun and stress enough for a mild adrenaline rush; with every piece I write, big or small, I need to feel a subterranean of passion, deep, full of emotions I need to connect to it. I need to feel my sixth sense tingle with excitement, and I feel every bit of that with this piece. Aiden and I are meeting again today at May's Cupcake World. The past two weeks with Aiden have been...nice. Just hanging, talking and eating. I know to some people, it's embarrassing to say, '*I don't have any friends,*' but I genuinely don't care; it's not that I can't make friends, it's just that I've always preferred to stay in and read my book or watch my Gilmore Girls reruns and besides when you have a father as awesome as mine-who needs friends? I guess Aiden has been a nice distraction from my usual company.

Last night, we met up again (strictly for food). He wanted to show me this old diner in Little Italy. It still has most of its old interior, with its wooden tables and wicker chairs. The aroma of fresh basil cooked in hours of hand-picked tomatoes; the place was quiet. There was a group of old guys in the corner talking and laughing. An elderly couple opposite them sat near the window; they watched people walk by on the streets of Mulberry, the restaurant workers pulling customers off the streets, trying to convince them their restaurant was the closest to a slice of Italy. Others are doing mob bits with each other, *'You talkin' to me?'* each of them getting louder, sounding more and more in character. You can see the faces of those who are genuinely scared, having no idea it's all but a bit. We sat on a table closest to the kitchen and far away from a window. At that moment, I almost forgot we were just sitting on Mulberry Street.

Aiden nudged me to look under the table, and I was confused as to why because I couldn't see anything. He looked at me to tell me it was okay…*trust me,* and oddly I did.

We were both leaning to the side as low as we could to look under the table; I reached my hand under the table to feel around. I was scared I was going to find old gum, but instead, I felt something cold, hard, and metal. I asked him what it was, and with a big smile, he replied, "It belongs to the Gambino crime family."

Wait a minute! I reached for the object again, "what belonged to the Gambino crime family?"

"The gun...don't worry, it's not functional." He laughed.

A gun. Under the table. A mobster's gun. Oh my God. I can't believe it.

"You have a whole story here you could write about." I was at a loss for words; I only ever sat in my room reading about stuff like this, reading my father's articles and books, but too afraid to come and explore it all myself.

I couldn't believe he did this for me. Which made me question it, but I threw the thought out as fast as it came in. Aiden started divulging a little about his story, but I know whatever it is, it's painful. He struggled to get past the first few words, but he seemed determined to open up to me, to me. I'm not sure why.

"Bye, Baba, I'm heading out; I'll be back around 7/8 p.m." I kiss him on his forehead and head out. My journal, my pen, my tape recorder, and spare batteries. That's all I need.

'Just got here, want me to order you a drink?' I text Aiden.

Like clockwork, I take my book out, it's new, *'Original Gangster by Frank Lucas.'* He said something that stuck with me, *'I am a businessman. I am anything I need to be at any time.'* isn't that all of us? We're all trying to be someone for one reason or the other. Each not sure if what we're doing is convincing enough, I guess. I keep reading; each page is gripping and fast-paced, like his life, and I get lost in the book. I bury my head deep into it, wishing I could step into the late 60s and 70s, throw on a $30,000 mink coat and observe his life as if invisible. Walk the streets of Harlem in full color, pass the Cotton Club observing the crowded action, and listen to Etta James and Nancy Sinatra shake the room with their voices. Lost in the sugar-coated grapefruit of the 60s. Every time period is covered with glitter and sparkle, a blanket over havoc.

"Excuse me, would you like to order something?" Snapping out of the book back into a different world...May's Cupcake World, to be precise. A young woman approaches me with her own mini notepad and pen. "Sorry, I didn't mean to startle you."

"It's okay." I smile. I tap my phone, realizing half an hour has passed by, and there is no sign of Aiden. I look around the café, and I can't see him. "No, it's okay. I'm waiting for a friend."

I check my phone, and the only message I have is from,

Momma: *Picked out a beautiful dress for the Hamptons dinner.*

Getting slightly worried, I call him. It goes straight to his machine. I try again, but nothing. I'd like to know what I should do, how long I should wait, or if I should even wait. I try him once more.

'Ring'

'Ring'

'Ring',

"Hello," he answers. I instantly feel relief, and my emotions swap from worry to confusion.

"Aiden, where are you?"

Silence. My heart already knew what he was going to say, but I still eagerly listened, hoping for what I wanted to hear, thinking he wouldn't do that to me. I'm more than just a reporter interviewing him, I'm his friend. "Amala... I'm sorry... If I could, I would."

"Aiden." I want to yell at him. I want to question how I will find someone this late. Wanting to cry at the thought of my professor flipping her lid, when she finds out, I have to submit a new proposal after just approving Aiden. Wanting to beg him. Instead, I take a deep breath and say, "Thank you for your time, Aiden."

I sit staring at the rows of different cupcakes, getting lost in all the different shades of brown. Not even lost in thought, just lost in silence, the ambiance in what I imagine disappointment to truly feel like.

No raw emotions of anger

      or sadness,

just this...

        Silence.

I don't have time to fall into silence. I have to think, who can I interview in the last hour? I pack up my stuff and take a coffee to go. I need inspiration, and where better to get it than the streets of New York?

I walk and walk, having a conversation in my head: what about this person and that? What about Sandra, the model?

But no one I really wanted, none that made me feel passionate about writing. I turn to the corner of Prince and Sullivan Street and see a little newsstand that catches my eye: papers and magazines for every genre. Poorly tucked behind Vogue, I see '*Butera the Baron of New York*' by Ahmed Emami Zidane' Baba, I whispered to myself. I pick the magazine up and begin to read the magnitude of my father's words.

'*Butera The Baron of New York*'

A communication of desire and endurance meticulously painted on a hot canvas, that is otherwise known as a plate...

My father, I think to myself, the two-time Pulitzer winner, is who I'll write about. Not that I have a choice, but at least I feel passionate about it, if anyone has an interesting story, it's my father. More importantly, at least he can't disappoint me, perhaps the only man that won't.

Whilst I wait for my ride, I stroll into a café to make notes. The sun has long set, and the air is turning crispier, a slightly warmer but vehement cold. Sparkling with possible ideas of what to write, how to start, and what angle to write from. I'm desperately trying to push past my annoyance and frustration with Aiden.

Later in the evening, after dinner, my father and I sat for hours going over the art of what makes a profile interview. He spoke about his irksome journey as a young journalist. He dived into his stories about John Gotti and how he got to interview him in the first place. It involves spaghetti sauce with walnuts, is all he can tell me. He gave me a step-by-step layout of how to write my piece, which felt like cheating. I love reading my father's work, and it maybe biased to say he is my favorite writer, but we have two very different writing styles. I wonder if I have his talent or if I'm even half as good as him. I tap my phone to check the time. It's reaching close to nine p.m. I'm afraid if I sleep, I'll lose my passion, so I take my new typewriter out and hit away at the keys.

'Life is bound by three fundamental principles that we all chase: **Money, power, and love.**
Each had its own binding controversies, but that wasn't enough for Ahmed. He chased stories not fastened by fairy tales or protected within the confines of safety; no, he chased something much more organized than the government...the New York Five bosses.'

I'm not sure about the government comment. I know my professor would tell me not to get political, but I'm in a rhythm, and I didn't want to break it. I keep writing, tapping, clicking, remembering to slide the carriage back and forth, remembering to look up once in a while. I'm writing, writing with passion. It's not as interesting as whatever Aiden's story might have been, but this is just as good…I'm hoping. Not that I have a choice.

My weekend was planned out with Aiden. After our interview, he wanted to show me this cute café that serves the best hot ice cream sandwich, followed by my favorite pizza spot. I wanted to watch The Godfather (the first one) with him and Amelia before I had to leave for the Hamptons in a week. I guess it'll be just me, in for a wild night with my ice cream tub.

"Honey, we're about to head out to get some desserts. Are you sure you don't want to join us?" my father asks, giving me a pitiful look.

"I'm good, Baba. I just want to watch The Godfather."

"Maybe see what your friends are up to; it's the weekend." My mother chimes in on the pity train. I smile and nod because the truth is I keep myself to myself, not because I'm a weird loner. I have plenty of acquaintances. I get invited to all the cool parties, but I know it's because they think I'm someone I'm not. They think I'm Amy March, but I'm far from it. I'm a little like Jo, maybe even a little like Beth outwardly, ambitiously shy in every aspect with a desire to succeed and explore. With Aiden, I don't know, I felt like Jo, I felt like Amala… I felt like me.

I feel my eyes getting heavier. I fight desperately against it; I want to watch Don Corleone get shot for the 100th time. My feelings of shock and sadness rise to the surface all over again as if it's my first time, or maybe my emotions have been sitting on the surface, waiting to come out.

Saturday Morning

I wake up feeling optimistic and back to my normal self and decide to take my parents to May's Cupcake World for brunch. My father will hate it, and my mother will say it is too sugary, but I talk about it so much they want to check it out.

"Amala, hurry, mama, your father is waiting." My mother calls out.

Rushing to find my book, I yell, "I'm coming."

'Argh,' where did I put it? I remember reading it at May's Cupcake World, Ah! Forget it, I'll find it later. I grab my sweater and head out.

We arrive at the café and take a seat near the window. We have a good view of everyone minding their own business outside, pacing and racing, carrying their own stories in their heads. I can already see my father shake his head at the menu, repeating what is this nonsense. My mother reads the extensive tea list and says to my father, 'When did cafés become medicinal?' and then turns to me and asks me the same question. The same woman approaches me, the one with her own notepad and pen, "Oh, hey, it's you," the woman points out.

I smile, "It's me." Not sure what else to reply with.

"You left your book here the other day, and I gave it to your boyfriend." She says while pointing to the corner of the café, pointing to Aiden and some girl. I feel my mother's eyes burn into the side of my face; I turn to face my father and explain to him why Aiden has my book. Oh, dear God, nothing is worse than someone taking a book you're hooked on.

"May you please get my book from him? He's not my boyfriend." I try not to sound too desperate or annoyed.

"I'm sorry that would be weird, but I can take your order." She replies.

"It's just a book, sweetie. We'll get you another one." My mother shrugs it off because she's ready to order.

She's right, I guess… it is just a book.

It's not, though; it's not just a book. It's my book. A place I can step into, be nosy into other people's lives without them knowing I'm there, reading their inner and deeper thoughts, so no, it is not just a book, mother. My Frank Lucas book was warm, with a slight crack down the spine, and what? Now I have to get another cold book. It doesn't feel right. Frank just bought his mother a big house, and I need to know if he stays in the game or not. God damn you, Aiden. Not that I can do anything about it other than pick up another book; well, actually, no, I have less than three days to submit my final. Just the thought of my professor turns my stomach. I try so hard to push past it, but she has an extremely telling face, a face that does not hide emotions; I don't think she even tries to hide it. Whenever I pitch an idea, her face turns sour, which makes me doubt my ability. Am I wasting my time? *A scary thought:* do people really have the power to make you question your dreams, or do we give them too much power over us? I'm meeting with my professor on Monday, so I have the whole of Sunday to polish and perfect my piece.

Monday

She did not like my piece, not a single word, font, angle, word size, paragraph, or the paper it was printed on.

Not a single punctuation.

Nothing.

She was furious, *"You took the easy way out; not everyone has famous, interesting fathers that can swoop in the last minute. This is not what was in the proposal you submitted, nor is it what we spoke about, and if you think Condé Nast will see anything different, then maybe you're not cut out for this. Part of this final was putting the grit work in; why do you think I especially said someone in the media or social spotlight? Because it is not an easy task to do."* She went on and on about how the biggest part of being a journalist is being tenacious enough to go out there and how she thinks I do not have that. *"So, I'm afraid you've failed your final."*

Worse than disappointment, this feeling of crushing sadness.

CHAPTER SIX

AIDEN.

I wish I could tell her why I let her down, but if I'm wishing for things, I wish I could make it all stop: the constant spiraling. The guilt spilling over in my mind like a narcissistic person who waits for a moment of peace before causing havoc again.

My parents, so easily, were able to slip back into the world of sparkles and hide their sorrows with fake smiles. How can I then ruin it and blurt out my inner crimes…my pain? I wish I could tell her that I really did want to tell her, perhaps in a world where I am much more courageous. Where I'm not ruled by fear and guilt; instead, I live in a world where I trained my broken self to bury everything. *God,* I've tried so hard to shut this overflowing box; I keep burying it deep within another box and another that I'm scared of the monster that's grown in it. I'm scared of the very real reality of what happens when you try to force a box shut. I cannot open it for her, for anyone. I know I shouldn't have agreed to help her in the first place, but *God,* for a moment around her, I felt calm. *Damn.*

Sometimes, just getting out of my head is exhausting; it feels impossible, and once I'm here, in my head, I spiral. It takes so much in me to tell myself it's going to be okay…for everything, and at times, I can't even convince myself it'll be okay. But recently, I've had this new distraction… a new girl, Amala, who, for some reason, makes me feel so calm. I know I told Ma I would get to know her friend's daughter, but with Amala, there is no expectations. She's someone who doesn't know my history, isn't dazzled by the fact that I'm the mayor's son and my sister likes her. My mind spirals until I reach the conclusion that I have to make it right; I need to apologize to her. I can't jeopardize the little calm I have. I reach over and grab the Frank Lucas book the waitress gave me. I know she'll want her book back. I flick through the book, intrigued; I would never have guessed she read crime fiction books. Flipping page to page, reading about Frank but my head starts to hurt, and switch to the movie instead.

I gaze into my screen, sinking deeper into the story. Damn, I kinda feel for Detective Richie Roberts; he's about to lose everything, he's pleading with Laurie, *'Don't punish me for being honest.'* He's not wrong. Amelia barges into my bedroom, startling me, chomping on a bag of chips, talking about something, "So, are we going?" She asks.
I ask her to repeat, her mouth full of chips,

"Are we going to the Hamptons this weekend for that dinner?" I completely forgot about the Hamptons this weekend, but this is perfect. I know Amala's mother hardly ever misses out on these events. I nod my head and tell Amelia we're going.

I tap the space bar on my laptop and continue watching Detective Richie Roberts beg Laurie back. He's pulling all the strings, which makes me think about Amala. I can't expect that she'll be willing to talk to me; I don't know her enough to know what type of woman she is when she's mad. If she's anything like my mama, then Lord have mercy. Some are graceful even when they are mad; some are crazy, some are quiet, and some pretend like everything's okay because they can't show emotion or vulnerability. But every woman has a soft spot for something, and I think I know what Amala's is. The weekend is still two days away, which means I've got shit to do and to buy, I feel a boost of energy, and my mind feels hopeful. I don't fight against it, thinking back to moments I've felt serene and carefree.

I remember when Amelia and I were younger, I was about twelve, and she was ten; my father took seven whole days off. It was epic, but this one moment, in particular, is what sticks with me—a hot, sweaty, sticky summer day in the great sunshine state. We were staying with my aunt, and on our fifth day, my mother fell ill. We spent two days locked up inside my aunt's condo, feeling cramped with Florida's humidity, placing us in a chokehold. My father had enough and literally picked my mother up and carried her in the car; he told us to get in, too. We had no idea where we were going; the only person who was kicking up a fuss was my mom, but my father ignored her. We drove and drove until all we saw were big, wide-open roads; we eventually stopped at this old 50's diner off Route 19. My mother refusing to leave the car, Amelia and I were getting hungry thinking about fries and shakes, and my poor father sat patiently trying to convince my mother to grab a bite and she'll feel better; of course, she wasn't budging. We were getting irritated, but my father remained calm until something beautiful happened. A gift of coolness, it pelted it down with rain, thick droplets of rain. We've never seen rain like that in New York. It was as if the sky itself was banging on the car door, all for my mother to open the door. My father turned around to look at us and smiled. He unlocked the door, and we just ran. Our legs moved faster than our bodies out of excitement; it felt like Disney World, but the stars were my family; we glided and skated up and down the car park, the rain running down faster, almost dancing with us. We laughed. We fell. We were drenched. And then the moment my mother came out and joined us. Complete serenity.

To be young and feel complete serenity again.

Charity fundraiser dinner in the Hamptons

I slept the entire ride to the Hamptons. My eyes stretch up at my Uncle Z's house; since our beach house is still getting its final touches, we'll be staying over at Uncle Z's this weekend. I still can't face to be back here; quickly, I shake my thoughts off and focus on Amala. I'd be lying to say I wasn't nervous, so much so that I haven't replied to the girl I'm getting to know ...*I know,* but I can't get into that right now. I have everything ready for Amala; I have her gift and her book.

My Uncle Z's a cool guy, but he has a short fuse and needs your undivided attention when you're talking to him. This guy will actually tug on your arm to grab your attention, especially if he sees it slip away, but oddly enough, he's not like that in return unless it's important. Unlike my father and grandfather, Uncle Z didn't jump into politics. He took his trust fund and tripled it at the right time with the right investment. I like him; he's the uncle who gives good advice, and he has a soft spot for my mom; he treats her more than just his brother's wife. When the political life tackled my father, Uncle Z would take my mother to her appointments and help around the house.

I pick up my mother's bags from the trunk and take them into the house. We haven't been here in a while; I forgot how nice his place is. I head straight into his games room. He was telling me how he's upgraded the room in the last two years with old arcade games. I secretly glance at Uncle Z's face- it looks worn out. I can't imagine what the past two years have been like for him, how he has the strength to stand there and entertain us.

MY CARAMEL

After my nap, I walk around to check up on everyone; my father and Uncle Z are in a private meeting. Uncle Z's office door is shut, but it reeks of Monte Cristo. Ma is still napping, and Amelia took her bike out for a ride. Just me, bored out of my mind, I open the fridge door and close it; I walk into the pantry, look around and walk out. I walk back over to the fridge, look around, and close it. I check my phone.

Amelia: *I forgot my purse. Can you bring it to me?* Amelia messages me.
Me: *YES! WHERE R U?*

Thankfully, I have something to do: I take my uncle's bike out (mine comes up to my knees), circle the town, and pass by the locals. Mrs. Mimi Margaux recognizes me, I'm surprised. "Aiden? My gosh, you've grown handsome."
I laugh and ask her how she's doing.

"Oh, sweetie, I'm doing just fine. I expect I'll be seeing you tonight?"
"Yes, ma'am."

"Oh, goody, I want to introduce you to someone. You're single, right? Oh, it doesn't matter anyway. This young lady is darling." Mrs. Mimi Margaux, once she's set on something, you couldn't fight her on it.
"Here I was thinking you were finally about to ask me out."

She laughs and throws her garden gloves at me, "You, young man, are trouble." She smiles, shaking her head.

I continue riding towards Amelia, her purse in hand, until I arrive outside Softy's Ice Cream…of course, she would be here. I take my phone out to let her know I've arrived.

"Aiden?" the voice soft and subtle.

No way, it can't be. I don't have her gift or her book, and I'm sweaty. I turn around, and it's Amelia with an ice cream cone the size of her head, and with her is Amala.

"Turns out I didn't need you; look who I ran into, Amala." She points excitedly.

Silence overtakes the moment. We stand and stare at each other. I should really be the one to talk first, to break this silence. Amelia looks up at us and says,

"Seems serious. I'll leave you guys to it; I'll be over there." And walks off, licking her gigantic ice cream.

Standing there looking at me, her eyes deeply brown, I push myself to break the silence,

"I didn't expect to see you here. I'm -" But she cuts me off by turning her head to Amelia, says bye to her, and walks away. I feel anger swell up inside; why is she angry? Why is she this hurt? God damn it.

Uncle Z ties my bow tie for me and briefly asks how I'm doing; we're both still not ready for *'that'* conversation and stick to scripted replies. I arrive at the charity dinner with her gift in hand. I'm hoping tonight will go a little different to earlier. I need her to hear me out, and clearly, I have to do the same.

It's the annual 'Ivory party' (It used to be the 'white party,' but no one really wore white, so the desperate housewives of the Hamptons changed the name to The Ivory Charity Dinner, The ICD'). At first, I thought it was an organization to save elephants, but I was wrong. Mrs. Mimi Margaux walks in and immediately becomes the focus of the party; all eyes are on her. She's Hampton's royalty. People walk over to greet my father before bombarding him with politics; my mother called in sick to this event, the nap turned into a fever, and she's sleeping it off. Amelia runs over to her friends; more like her acquaintances, the girls at events like these, more often than not, are socialite dolls. Amelia has zero interest in becoming another doll.

I circle the party casually. I can't seem too desperate to find her, nor do I want to surprise her again. I rerun my lines in my head, trying to remember the essence of my apology despite still feeling annoyed and angry - is that just my male ego getting hurt? I need to stay calm-headed. I shake it off. I can do this; I'm the Mayor's son, I'm Aiden Hakeem Sancar. Who better than me to charm her? I'm going to shit this up. I circle around the party again until I see her. Surrounding her are the mini, desperate housewives to be. She fakes laughs at their jokes; I know because her real laugh is like a four-year-old, carefree and unafraid. I lay my eyes on her; she looks beautiful in her white dress. I walk over, trying to be something I'm not; the mini housewives see me approach and fix their dresses and their hair, applying on a new layer of lip gloss, but Amala looks up at me and stands perfectly unphased by my appearance. The walk now seems incredibly long; instants like this make you forget how to walk. I keep my cool, well I try to. Not thinking about how exactly I would execute my plan to take Amala away from the pack, what if she refuses to come with me?

"Girls, hi, may you excuse Amala for a moment?" The girls smile, their eyes twinkling. They turn to Amala, but she seems hesitant. "Amala, it's important…Please," I say softly, not trying to sound overly desperate. Emphasizing the important words only, *'Amala and please,'* she stares at me and then through me, all while excusing herself from the girls with a smile. We walk in silence, moving further away from the 'ICD.' I gently call her name to inform her that we've moved away enough. We're no longer in the vicinity of guests. Their voices and laughter are distant muffles now. Gift or speech, which one first? I think to myself; the gift drops her guard down. I reach into my jacket pocket for her book, but as I do, she says my name so softly I feel something in my gut. I feel warmth and comfort; why did I rob myself of her presence?

"Aiden, what makes you think I'm angry?"
"Because I disappointed you?"
She shakes her head and smiles, but it quickly fades, which makes me feel uneasy. If it wasn't that, then what did I do?

"I'm not sure what I did to upset you, which is even worse, but I know I'm sorry. I pushed an idea knowing I wasn't ready, knowing you had limited time." I expand on my answer, trying to fill the empty air of awkward silence.

"Aiden, did you ever think of me as your friend?"
"Of course," I respond quickly.
"I'm not angry at you because you canceled. I mean, yes, I was annoyed, but more so because I thought we were friends, and you didn't even bother giving me a reason."
I tried cutting her off, but she wanted to get more off her chest.

"You saw me at Mays; you couldn't even say hi? You couldn't even give me my book back because of what?"

I reach into my pocket and pull her book out; I hold it out to her, and she grabs it, but I don't let go. I need her to listen.

"I thought you were mad at me, I didn't... I figured you didn't want to see me. I'm sorry I didn't pick up the phone sooner; I do care-"

"Aiden?" I turn to the voice that's interrupted us. It's her, the girl my mother wants me to get to know, standing there watching Amala and me in a book tug of war. I'm not sure how much of that she caught, but she doesn't look happy.

"I haven't heard from you in two days," She breaks eye contact with me and looks at Amala.

Not being one for drama, Amala wins the tug of war, wrenching her book from my hands, and walks away. The girl is standing there with countless scenarios running around in her head. I stand...processing another situation I have to fix; I stand still, dazed, until she walks away, too.

CHAPTER SEVEN

AMALA.

I hold on tight to my book. I feel as if I know Frank Lucas much better than any other person at this event. He's completely, organically transparent. What does he have to hide? I mean, after everything he's done and seen, what is there to hide from? He's not the nicest guy, but he wasn't trying to be, merely a means to survival, as he puts it. Of course, I disagree there should always be a fine line between what you're willing to do to reach your dreams, but then maybe people's acceptance of you is overrated. Frank is no different from politicians; they, too, are just trying to make a quick buck or two…a means of survival, as they put it.

After the encounter with Aiden, I would rather be left alone. Besides, it looked as if it was only going to get messier. I have my book. I nod to myself for reassurance, holding it close to my chest, but it only makes me feel sad. Seeing Aiden makes me think of how badly my professor graded my final. Not forgetting the agitation of waiting to hear back from the twenty companies I applied to intern with this summer. Four have already politely rejected me. I'm pushing all my negative energy onto Aiden, all the what ifs; they should put this level of stress on college brochures, *'halls of success and anxiety.'* The stress is turning me into something I'm not. Okay, think, what has Baba taught you, 'In *life, there's never just one door; sometimes you have to walk through an empty door to find another.'*

I scan the room to see if anyone of importance is here; I take a page out of Aiden's book. I see the desperate powder puff girls in the corner; I quickly break eye contact and turn around, hiding in plain sight, and resume my scan of the other side of the party. I see a friendly face, Amelia. The girl who loves astrology, physics, and not to forget giant lumps of ice cream on her cone. We smile at each other, and she mouths I'm sorry, I respond with a confused look, and she mimes for me to open my book. I do so; written on the inside of the cover, *'rational thoughts never drive people's creativity the way emotions do.' N.D.T.*, I look up, slightly confused, but smile at her. I'm not entirely sure what she means by it, but nonetheless, I'm sure it will serve me purpose. I see Mrs. Mimi Margaux, and she has her mischievous face on, heading in my direction,

"Darling," she says with a smile that consumes her face.

I smile back, trying to match at least half of her smile.

"Do join me for a walk,"

We circle around the party, and she fills me in about her new hobby, coffee beans. So much so that she bought a farm that grows coffee beans. She wants to make the smoothest, velvety coffee ever. She told me about a young man who she thinks is well suited for me; of course, knowing her, she'll try to play cupid or even host a dinner for us so we can be 'well acquainted.'

"Ah, here comes the young man now, isn't he just darling child?"

Of course, it was none other than Aiden Hakeem Sancar; I excused myself and made up a lie that my father was looking for me. I walk past Aiden straight into the house, through the kitchen, and I'm hit with the smell of sautéed mushrooms and garlic with a hint of thyme. It smells like home; Father makes these divine mushroom hors-d'oeuvre, and once, perhaps every month, we cook them and watch a classic movie and call it mushroom popcorn. My mother thought we were doing drugs once because we were watching, Who Framed Roger Rabbit and were uncontrollably laughing at the scene when Judge is holding him back and Eddie's demanding him to *'drink the drink',* and we do the bit back and forth. It's remarkable how a single unit of smell can bring back a rush of memories, so I stop and turn to face Aiden and think to myself, it's my time to *'drink the drink.'*

"Hey, can we try this again? Please," he asked, slowly approaching me.
I smile and shake my head.
"Tell me about the domino effect I caused." He said, willing to listen.

I tell him everything about my professor and what she said; I tell him how it made me question myself as a writer and what if I'm not cut out for it. I tell him about the four companies who rejected me and how bailing on our friendship made me feel. He stands and listens attentively, and with each story, his facial expression grows sadder.
He sighs, "Amala, I got you something. Just wait right here; I'm hoping it'll cheer you up!" He turns around to see if I've moved and gestures like an excited golden retriever to wait.

The kitchen staff are in complete congruence, unaware of Aiden and me. The onions sliced, garlic crushed, lemons squeezed, spinach sautéed; I love hiding out in the kitchen during big events, simply because you become invisible, not a single staff out of sync, the art of attention. I simply watch and observe them move in unison. I believe when you're born with creative tendencies, you bear witness to everything through the lens of art, which is truly magical. Just as a businessman sees the profit in everything, I see the beauty in things, be it in this kitchen or stuck in brutal traffic on 42nd.

"Amala." He says, panting a little.

I turn around to see him smiling at me at the mere fact that I'm still standing in the kitchen. He extends his arms out and hands me a matcha-colored box. I place it on the kitchen worktop; inside is a small box of mixed praline-filled cupcakes, a new book, a new tape recorder, and articles about a mob shakedown that went wrong. Between two crime families, one of whom was a member of the Gambino crime family, but they could never locate the weapon, and he got off. I look up at him with a mixture of feelings: awe, confusion, a tingle in my gut that I ignore.

"Aiden," I look up at him.

"I know, I know you like your old tape recorder, but I thought you might need a backup. Oh, and the article, remember the old diner and the gun?"

"The one under the table?"

"Yes, well, after three days of harassment and a pack of some very expensive cigars, I got an old, retired mobster in a nursing home to talk a little, and he pointed me to the diner." He looked down at his shoes, and his brief moment of proudness quickly fades to sorrow. "I really am sorry, Amala; I know I cost you your grade, but maybe you could write this story up."

"Aiden, you didn't have to do this." I'm not sure what to say or how to feel.

"How about we just start over? So long as you don't get me to unravel my deep dark secrets?" He finally laughs.

I shake my head, agreeing with him, "cupcake?" I offer him. We both stand in the corner of the kitchen, eating the best cupcakes, forever a sweet distraction.

CHAPTER EIGHT

AMALA.

Next Morning

I lay all night conflicted. Should I spend my time with Aiden chasing an old, retired mobster, or should I volunteer for the college newspaper? Summer is officially amongst us; I feel the change in the air and in the people, which only coerces me to make a change, too. Do I play it safe for the millionth time, or do I go on what might be a worthless journey? In seventh grade, I was too shy to enter the school writing competition. In tenth grade, I entered the competition but failed to submit my paper because the winners got to go on a young writer's retreat.

The thought of spending a week with people I didn't know hauled me out of my comfort zone. In twelfth grade, learning from my past mistakes, I entered a poetry competition and won but failed to collect my prize because I would rather be at home finishing my book. But this time, I want to win, big with a big shiny office at some big journalism company with my name on the door.

Two Weeks Later

This morning, I was up with the same contemplation running around. I tap my phone and see a notification from Aiden and Sara (the girl my professor obliterated.)

Aiden: *Have you decided? Are you playin it safe or taking a risk?*
Sara: *Hey girl, have you decided if you're joining us this summer on campus?*

I swipe the notification clear; I'm too tired to scroll mindlessly through Twitter, so I pick my book up to finish the last few pages of Mr. Frank Lucas. I open the cover and see Amelia's note, 'Rational *thoughts never drive people's creativity the way emotions do'* NDT. How will I ever spark creativity without adventure? I immediately think. I need to experience what I read about, or I will never know, not actually. I truly will never know how it feels to fall in love, to experience heartache, to experience adrenaline, to experience shock or fear, to be in a hostage situation or something I could tell my grandchildren (like the stories my father has and all his battle scars-both physically and metaphorically) I will never know, not from my bedroom, not from here not unless I get up and go.

Sent to Aiden: *I'm in!*
Sent to Sara: *Sorry, I won't be.*

I lay in bed for a moment or two, daydreaming about my summer; it's almost humorous how I envisioned writing stories for the New York Times or handing out coffees in big board rooms. I imagined getting my foot through the door this summer to have something to look forward to after graduation instead of months or years of applying or waiting for an opportunity to rise. I think the worst part of having a burning passion for something is for it to be wasted. Instead, I'm fighting my very instinct. The start of my summer will be spent traveling around the tri-state area searching for another old mobster who potentially knows about a murder that happened 27 years ago. In the same breath, however, I guess that is what it means to be a journalist; I guess it's exciting, and my traveling companion isn't exactly the worst.

I question whether I should even have Aiden accompany me, but we're just friends, and his sister will be with us, and it's strictly work. Besides, I think Aiden has his hands full with whatever that girl's name is, and I have mine full with writing. So, I guess I shouldn't be too worried. I jump out of bed and scribble down a list of things.

I think the sun has this remarkable effect on people: internal warmth, a boost of energy that makes you think you can accomplish anything and everything…of course, it's only temporary. I plan on using all this positivity to good use; for the next week, it will be Aiden and I and a couple of mobsters. He told his father that he's taking a two-week internship in Washington to stay close to Amelia in case she needed anything, but I think he's just avoiding the enviable political career his father has chosen for him.

The only thing that's settling my nerves is knowing I'll have someone with me; despite having only known Aiden for a month, it's better than going on my own. My father sat Aiden down to ask him a million questions (to scare him, of course) before even allowing me to go; my father knows the

Mayor and his family really well, and though he was extremely hesitant, knowing the family eased his worries.

I finished packing; I debate which books to take with me; sometimes, I wish someone would create a magical bag that holds all your books and is as light as a feather. So, you have endless of stories and characters with you that you're never left alone.

"Amala!" yells my mother, making me jump out of my skin. I lose my train of thought, pick up the pile of cashmere sweaters sitting on my desk, and return them to my mother. She's also packing, but for Oman, every year is the same: my mother packs, and my father unpacks all her clothes, and then they laugh. He convinces her to stay, and she convinces him to join her. They are still as in love as they were in the 80s, inseparable then and inseparable now.

"Sweetheart, have you finished packing? We really must get going." My mother said, zipping up her bags.
"Yes, Aiden should be here soon," I tell her, checking my phone.

"How sweet of him to drop me off at the airport."
My phone buzzes: it's a message from Amelia letting me know they're here.
"Okay, sweetheart, open questions only and record everything even if you're setting up, you'll never know what

you'll catch. Most importantly, you message me every hour! You got it!" My father says in his intimidating voice. "I spoke to Aiden's father, too; he advised his brother will be in Washington to meet you guys!" He squeezes me tightly and kisses my head before helping me into the car.

My father kisses my mother one last time, affectionately…a little too affectionately. Amelia, Aiden, and I look away, pulling our seat belts over us. The car is full of its passengers; Aiden begins driving away, towards JFK first. I look up at the big city, hoping to return to it, a made woman. I feel small zaps of excitement, but mostly, I'm nervous.

Staring up at me are my books peeking out of my tote bag; I always question, when is the appropriate time to take your book out without looking like the biggest nerd? When everyone's fallen asleep, it seems like the right choice until you feel responsible for keeping the driver awake, and just like that, you've reached your destination, and all your book did was see Venice Beach from your bag. Three Bedrooms in Manhattan by Georges Simenon is itching to be read, and I cave and pick it up. I love it when a book hooks you right from the start, but what you initially anticipate is far from the truth: someone falls in love, someone else is jealous, and someone dies. A completely unpredictable journey.

I look up for a quick break to see we're near the airport; Aiden and my mother are talking about life, mainly about him- he doesn't hesitate to answer her. Probably because my mother has this warmth about her, she knows the virtuosity of decorum. There is a word in Urdu/Persian that we try to live by, '*izzat,*' and it holds no true definition in English, but to attempt to define it, it's to have humility with honor. That is my mother, humility, and honor.

Aiden rushes to help my mother with her bags.

"Okay, honey, stay safe, and be sure to call me every day. I love you and Aiden; drive safe, sweetie." She kisses me goodbye.

I stretch my eyes ahead of me; by now, we've left the Manhattan skyline behind; the tall buildings have swapped for tall trees, the air free from smog, and I have a strong feeling we may even catch a star or two out here. I read the signs as we pass them by; the town we just passed reads, '*Welcome to Ansonia, population 17,814.*' Everyone must know everyone, I think to myself, and my mind runs to the land of imagination. A small-town girl, a troubled boy, and a questionable councilman, a story that begins to sketch in my mind. I ask Aiden if he's okay and if he needs anything, and he dashes a quick smile at me.

"Nah, I'm good. Are you guys good?" he responds, quickly shooting a look behind him to see for himself that we are truly okay. Amelia is blissfully asleep with her head on my lap and Aiden is hitting the three-hour mark. I'm running out of *'would you rather'* scenarios.

The sun sets on the horizon, and its fading light casts a long shadow on the road ahead. With darkness comes trouble. Aiden turns in to stop at a diner. Suddenly, the car begins to vomit; it splutters and shudders until, eventually, the car grounds to a halt. Fortunately, it breaks down outside the diner. Unfortunately, we seem to be stuck in the middle of nowhere. Amelia must have been signaled by the powers above because she wakes up from the sheer smell of greasy fries and vanilla shakes. I try to be of use while Aiden does the guy thing and pops open the hood. I look around to see if there is someone who can actually help; all I can see, for what seems like miles and miles ahead, are trees. I wasn't sure if we were still on the I-95 or if it was the I-91; I'm sure I saw signs for I-91.

"Excuse me, sir, is that" I point to the road, "the I-95 or I-91?"

Aiden walks over with a serious look, a look already predicting the man's response.

"I-91, where are you heading?" he asks, observing our mismatched group, two 'young adults' and a teenager all heading in the wrong direction.

"Washington DC," Aiden steps in. The man takes hold of his wife's hand and walks away laughing, but not before he informs us that we've driven three hours only to end up near Boston. Three hours. Three hours of laughing at *'would you rather'* scenarios, getting lost in brief moments of eye exchanges that we missed the signs screaming, waving, jumping up at us. Now what? We have a broken car, a hungry Amelia, and three, maybe four hours added to our journey. Surprisingly, I feel somewhat calm. I thought I would panic by now, but I'm not sure if it's the company I'm with or the breeze, but it reminds me of a line from a poem Baba reads to me,

'I am the restless wind in love with a rose.' When his words come to me, I feel serenity.

Aiden refuses to call his father to explain the mess we've gotten into. He's adamant about finding a local repair guy who can fix our car for us, magically, in an hour. I find the nearest auto repair shop about 3 miles out, and I call Connie's Carshop,

"So, what they say?" Aiden asks, leaning on the trunk of the car, his leg bouncing up and down.

I lean back on the trunk, leaning my leg next to his to get him to stop, "She said she can have one of her guys come over with a pick-up truck, but it won't be for another hour or so."

"Okay, so that doesn't sound so bad." he pushes himself away from the trunk and stands tall in optimism.

"But," I break it to him slowly, "she said, depending on the repair, it will mostly likely be done tomorrow morning."

"I'm sure they'll get it done by tonight. I don't think it's a big repair."

"Yeah, it's definitely not getting fixed tonight."

"Why?" he looks at me, annoyed.

"Because Connie said her cousin Andrea is getting married tonight."

"Why didn't you just start with that? Okay, so now what?"

"Now we get food!" Amelia jumps out of the car, she grabs our hands, and drags us inside the diner.

I scan through the menu. I want something that won't sit heavy on my stomach like cement, but alas, the only halal options we have are fries. Aiden and Amelia order their famous fries and shakes,

"Oh shit! Amelia, you'll miss your first day of camp?" Aiden bursts out.

She shrugs her shoulders and continues chomping on her fries, smothering them in ketchup.

"Amelia, this is all you could talk about for months, and what now you don't care?"

She stares at her brother a while before rolling her eyes, "Okay, fine, I don't start camp until Wednesday; I knew you would mess something up, so I told you two days early."

I smirk to myself.

"Why would you think I would mess it up?" he asks defensively.

"Hmm, remember the time we had to attend that state dinner for Dad?" She went on about the time of her birthday, the time he was two hours late picking her up from her weekend club, and she had to have dinner with the Robinsons. She had to tell them she was vegetarian because there was no halal food. The time they missed their flight because he wrote the wrong date down and on and on.

"Okay, okay, I get the point; it's not my fault my head is so messy." I glance at Aiden's face quickly, long enough to observe the crack in his mask; it's the first time he's said that aloud, 'My *head is so messy.*' I look up at him again, this time with sympathy-not that he needs it or asked for it.

THE NEXT MORNING

The night passed by in a hurry. The motel, to our surprise, is a cute little bed and breakfast. The owners, an elderly couple, bought the place thirty years ago, and they seemed to have captured every beautiful moment in their own version of happiness. Somewhere between the ungodly hours of three or four a.m., we eventually fell asleep talking for hours, laughing until our cheekbones tapped out. Amelia and I shared the bed, and Aiden took the couch outside. Aiden let us sleep in while he snuck out and retrieved the car from Connie's. The car is back to her nonvomiting self, and with $300 down, we are back on the road. It is a seven-hour journey; God willing, we should arrive in Washington DC by six this evening.

Thinking of Washington, I wonder if they allow food inside the Supreme Court of Justice, the ultimate dinner show. My father tells me stories about reporting on some of the most sensational cases in the country. I wonder when the next Brown vs the Board of Education will occur or the OJ case, something that gets everyone wrapped in the mess. I wonder what my children's versions of the OJ case would be, what will happen during their time that makes the hit list of the most televised trials. Or what is secretly happening right now behind closed veils that are soon to come out? I find it humorous that we have to drive through New York again. Is this a sign telling me I should have taken the summer job at Columbia Review? Am I not meant to return a made woman? Or perhaps it's a sign for a do over-not a compelling sign. I text my father to update him on our unsuccessful start and return my gaze to the outside. Maybe it's the lack of sleep or Aiden's calming 'green noise,' he listens too, but I feel my eyes getting heavy like butter sinking into warm toast.

CHAPTER NINE

AIDEN.

The long, quiet drives stimulate my thoughts like wood to a burning fire; I remember when I first got my license, I took my mother's car out, but as soon as it got dark, so did my thoughts; each headlight became a spotlight for a thought. It grew and tumbled over one another, like dropping a filing cabinet and watching all the papers run away. Until I hit my car into a tree. So, nothing but nature sounds for me, or sometimes just the sound of Manhattan does it. I turn my head quickly over my shoulder to see them both asleep.

I stop for gas somewhere outside Philly, I think. I look at the maps; we're about three hours away, and I'm hungry. Fries and shakes just don't cut it like they used to. Amala ruffles around, and I hope she's awake because I miss her voice, her stupid would you rather questions.

"Hey, Mr. State driver." She says, stretching, and I feel my heart make little summersaults. I question why she has this effect on me, but in a world of chaos, I guess peace is a stranger.

I smile at her, "How was the sleep?"

"How was the drive?" She asks.

"You hungry?"

"Starving!" Amelia groans. Stretching her arms.

We're about forty-five minutes away from the best Philly cheese steaks ever. I tell them to hold on, and I grab a couple of snacks from the gas station for Amelia.

"Wake me up when we're there," Amelia says, snuggling herself back to sleep.

I look over at Amala through the rear-view mirror, wanting to say so much but not wanting to ruin it.

"I called it off with her, by the way," I say, trying to lead into a possible conversation.

She looks over at me subtly, "with whom?" she asks.

"Urm, the girl I've been getting to know."

She stays quiet for a minute, "why?"

I don't know, I tell her; I guess it's because I wasn't feeling it. Our mothers introduced us to each other, which had a certain level of added pressure.

"Did you love her?"

"I... don't think I did. I did like her; she was nice."

"What was it that didn't click?"

"It was..." I stopped to think what the reason was; why didn't it click? "I didn't see a future with her. I guess you just know when you're with your person."

She stayed quiet at my response for a second too long.

"Aiden?"

I look at her.

"How do you know it's the right person?"

"When you have a woman with a phat-!" we both laugh, and she whacks my arm, "All jokes aside..." I pause and contemplate, "God just makes it easy for you; being in the presence of that person only uplifts you. I don't know, but it just feels so right."

I think about how I feel in the presence of Amala, how she makes me feel, how she quietens my thoughts, and how, without knowing me, she allows me to see clearly. I feel her eyes on me, so I turn the spotlight onto her. Clearing my throat before I ask her, "How about you, Amala? Who is your ideal guy?"

She takes a moment to think about it and finally says, "I've never really thought about it. I've never dated." She blushes.

"No, I don't believe that; not one guy has asked you out."

"Oh, I didn't say that." She laughs shyly.

"Like whom? Who has had the honor to ask you out?"

"Okay," she smiles and blushes all in one, "you can't tell anyone!" She demands.

"My lips are sealed," I tell her.

"The ambassador of Oman."

"The old guy?" My jaw dropped.

"No! His son!" She corrects me, "We went on one *'date'; of* course, baba chaperoned us."

"Damn, that guy is a handsome dude. So why aren't there any wedding dates?"

"Because he was a materialistic douche that I'm sure pushed pills. And so, I respectfully declined; I may not have it figured out, but I know what a good person is." She said proudly.

"So, you're a Grace that could have had a Mickey Cohen." I test her Mob trivia.

"Please don't disrespect Mickey Cohen... I could be Kay Corleone... oh wait, no, I wouldn't get an abortion." She laughs.

"Yeah, but she stayed with Michael." I fire back. We both ramble on about the Godfather and how strangely short Al Pacino got over the years. We have the ultimate debate on the best mob movie, about how they don't make mob movies like they used to. We walk into the spot with the best Philly cheese steaks. My sister comes back to life; the minute she takes a bite of her food, she is the main character in everyone's life. Watching Amala and Amelia spark with each other makes me smile.

Father: *Your mother is not doing too well today, Aid; sorry to spring this on you. Maybe give her a call. Love Dad.*

I keep my face as normal as possible while reading the text from my Father. I don't want to ruin our trip, and God, I can't drop everything and let Amala down again; she's counting on me for this paper. I also don't want to worry Amelia; she's worked too hard and too long to get her spot on NASA. I'll call Ma when I get a moment alone.

"Hey, Aiden," Amelia said softly. "Is mom okay?" She asks in worry. I feel myself getting agitated. Why does my father have to dump her on us? My chest puffs out; I feel irritated. Amala, a silent observer, while I explain to Amelia that she's having one of her migraine attacks, which is the truth but not the full story. When we were younger, my aunt, Selene (Uncle Z's wife), used to look after us whenever our mother wasn't feeling good. I tell Amelia she's going to be fine and that she needs to take her migraine medication and sleep it off…I hope. Amelia is wiser than most teenagers her age, and she's mature; it's not that she can't handle it, but why stunt her growth right now?

"Aiden," Amala says, "go, give her a call, we'll stay here…check out the shakes."

Ma answers the call straight away.
"Hey, ma, how you doing?" I ask her

"Oh, Aiden, I'm so sorry, baby. You didn't have to call. You know how your father gets. Especially around this time."

"No, Ma, I wanted to call, have you eaten?"
"Yes, how is the internship going?"

"Just finished eating, took a detour, but on our way."
"Oh, should I ask? Is Amelia there?"

"She's inside with Amala. But we're all good."
"Amala, now who is she?"

"A good friend, you know her mother," I tell her.
"I do? What is her surname?"

"I think Zidane, her father is Ahmed Emami Zidane."

"Aiden, I don't think that's a good idea."

I pause, "Huh, why? You don't even know her, ma."

"I don't need to, but her father's a journalist. I don't need them snooping into our lives."

"Ma, I'm not getting into this; she's not doing any snooping into us."

"All I'm saying is, be careful, Aiden."

"Yes, ma'am, I love you; talk to you soon."

"I love you too, baby."

I don't want to think too much about why my mother wants me to stay away from Amala. I know sometimes she spins the irrational mother's protection. I can't think of why she got worked up as soon as I mentioned Amala's father. Do I ask Amala if our parents know each other outside the formal dinner parties, or do I leave it be? I know they know each other, but are they close? All this thinking is getting me paranoid; I don't need this right now. It's Amala; how could I second guess her? Maybe if my father said something but my mother? No way.

"Aiden," I turn around, and Amala looks at me as if to ask if I'm okay.

I smile and nod. "I told you, she's good. She was missing us." I explain to Amelia. We head back into the car, Amelia chattering on and on about random facts like, 'Did *you know that our universe is ever expanding* and that *one NASA space suit costs around $12 million*,' or my personal favorite, '*The sunset on Mars appears blue.*' A blue sunset, I imagine it to feel cool, just complete calmness once a day: every day.

CHAPTER TEN

AMALA.

My mind attempts to paint images of blue sunsets. The ocean and the sky hug each other after a long shift; serenity meets deep red dunes. I wonder why our sunsets are reddish/orange, a display of warmth? Sometimes purple- when we're lucky. Is it because we (humans) need a reminder of beauty? Red for notice, for warning, for an announcement: I think God has purposely left subtle hints in and around our planets for constant relief in our eyes. Red, also a reminder of love, of passion, and warmth, entirely more than Red's Hyde self.

MY CARAMEL

I put my phone on DND. Dreading every email ping I receive, I feel my stomach cramp up at the thought of rejection emails from interns. I check anyway, picturing myself getting an acceptance email- running to my father screaming with excitement, but intuitively, I read another rejection. I silently tell myself, *'it's going to be okay.'* There's something deeply sad about telling yourself things will be okay when you have no idea, as if you're consoling your inner child and, the older you are, pretending to be an adult.

I squint a look outside and see, *Welcome to New York City*. God, I drop my head in shame. I feel as if I've been riding a rollercoaster for the past hour; I feel nauseous; her eyes (the cities) are on me, judging me in silent disappointment. What am I doing? Traipsing around States with a guy and his little sister. I feel like I have to make it big by the time I graduate. I must if I'm my father's daughter- the great Ahmed Zidane. I don't know if this is for me, but I keep telling myself, *'Keep going until you make it,'* but it's just a minuscule voice at this point, getting quieter with every disappointment.

"Wait, Aiden, I forgot my camp stuff. Oh my God, please, please, please, you have to go home." Amelia screams frantically.

MY CARAMEL

"AH HAHA, look who screwed up now." Aiden teases her.

"Aiden, please, this isn't a joke."

"Relax, we're in New York now; we'll be outside the house in twenty minutes ish."

Aiden parks the car; Amelia runs inside to grab her stuff, meanwhile, I feel on edge. I'm back in New York. What if I'm wasting my time? I think to myself, scrolling through my phone.

Buzz. My phone vibrates.

The last of my applications were returned and rejected. Twenty rejections. I want to go home; I feel icky and disgusting. I need my father, I think to myself; he always knows what to say. His words are constant warmth.

"Amala, did you forget anything?" Aiden asks in high spirits.

"Aiden? Take me home, please."

"Sure, as soon as Amelia's back, what did you forget?"

"No, Aiden, take me home. Please." I reply, my voice breaking.

"Hey, hey, what's wrong?" He turns to face me. Giving me all his attention. We stay quiet for a moment until he speaks again, "You can't back out now; this whole detour was a test of commitment…you gotta see this through." He says gently with certainty. I want to believe him, but I'm way out of my comfort zone. I took a big risk, far too quickly, like running the meter race, having never raced before. What was I thinking? I'm not cut for any of this. "Aiden, I want to go home. I'm sorry I thought I was ready for this, but it was a mistake."

"Why?"

"I don't want to get into it right now." A lump forms at the back of my throat, and my eyes become blurry.

He looks down at my rejection email, "This will come and go, God, Amala, how important is being a writer to you?"

"Aiden, I appreciate what you're doing, but please, I've made my mind up."

"Nah, I'm sorry, that's bullshit. You wanna take the easy way out, after a few rejections, that's fine, but nothing good will come easy."

"Why are you getting angry?"

"Amala, you're so much more than what you give yourself credit for; you're afraid of what?"

"You want to talk about being afraid? You can't even talk about whatever it is that's eating you up!" I raise my voice, equally in anger and passion.

He stares at me as if all his words have been ripped out of his mouth, and all I see is a scared boy hiding in his eyes. He takes a deep breath, "It's hard, but I'm working on it." He manages to get out.

I stare at him; sympathy overtakes me. I see how hard he tries to fight his thoughts, and so the least I could do is fight a little, too. "I'm sorry," I say softly.

He looks up at me, his eyes drawn to mine, "Amala I,"

Amelia barges in, "Sorry I took so long; Mom made buffalo chicken pastries. I got you guys some... you're welcome." She says she is proud of herself. I continue to look at Aiden, wanting him to finish his sentence, his eyes still fixated on mine until he smiles at me and his-self.

NASA Summer Camp.

I lost count, but to guess, twenty-seven hours later, we finally arrived outside the renowned capital space station, NASA. Aiden and Amelia hug each other goodbye. She speaks wise words to him, and he whispers something to her, and she laughs. In typical older brother fashion, he makes fun of her one last time. They tell each other they love each other, and Aiden tells her they'll see each other on the fourth of July. Amelia pulls me to the side, "he likes you, by the way." She smiles at me and walks away, not before yelling,

"I love you too, Amala." I strangely feel proud; watching success working for someone is encouraging. I want to feel as excited and proud as Amelia is feeling at this moment, walking into her future and love. Aiden, in awe of this moment and his baby sister, he calls her name out,

"Hey!" she turns around.

"Here's looking at you, kid." Her face lights up. Her first core memory of joy, every time she recalls her first day, it'll be a little version of herself dancing.

I struggle to find a core memory of joy; I have beautiful memories, but none for me, none purely of joy- of something I've achieved. Aiden and I make our way back to the car. Talking to ourselves in our heads and experiencing this moment with Amelia has fueled me. I remember Amelia telling me just how much work she put in, hours committed to projects for her application, sleepless nights, and I can't even commit to a story. My mind drifts to what Amelia told me before she left; I'm not sure if there's actually something between Aiden and me. He clearly has things to sort out, and as for me, I've never dated. I can't even commit to a story; the idea of us…of Aiden is daunting. How I feel when he's around or when we're around each other is comfort but the kind you get from a friend. He makes me realize my fears and what I'm missing out on; everything seems less frightening when he's around.

"What now?" he sighs with relief.
"We hit the road, Jack," I reply.

CHAPTER ELEVEN

AMALA.
ONE MONTH LATER

"Remember to inspire them, ask them questions, and show you're well-researched!" My father's attempt at a pep talk. I smile and nod at him, "Oh, and most importantly, don't forget to make dua."

Tomorrow morning, I have an interview with Conde Nast; with *the* Conde Nast, I'm in literal disbelief. I hate to admit Aiden was right about the story after all; it was far-fetched but made for an excellent dramatized, non-fiction short story that landed me the interview. After Washington, Aiden and

I drove around from place to place to nail the story; we ate, we laughed, we gazed at each other, and we were both extremely aware we no longer had a third person with us, and the guilt of compromising our deen weighed heavy on our conscious. I've never crossed that line with any boy, so I don't plan on crossing it now or ever. My mother said,

"Love isn't one night. It's sixty, seventy nights of love, falling in love every day, falling in with all their idiosyncrasies." Love is still so foreign to me. I've read about it, I've watched it in movies, I've watched it up close with my parents, I've watched how my mother falls in love every time my father sits and writes, and his mind is focused, but he never fails to step back into our world to hold her, to kiss her and despite saying it for the millionth time that day, he'll tell her he loves her for the millionth and one time.

So, from the little that I understand, I believe love should be lasting, with only one person, not this culture of borrowing your heart to several people on a trial basis. Dating until 'I get it right,' this enigma of having a fling behind veiled doors, handing your honor out like water from a lake, opaque and open. I struggle to see how people fall in love multiple times, and I question whether they understand what love is or how to define love. My father once defined love as what is, from the thousands of books I've read and movies

I've watched, the single truest definition of love. I asked him to define love, and he asked me to define the ocean without water. I said I couldn't; it doesn't exist. He said exactly people are like the ocean, deep and mysterious and filled with monsters. But the water, the clear, sky-blue water, is what makes it beautiful. The water is love. The two are inseparable, which is more the reason we need pure, unequivocal love.

I'm still determining how my mind spiraled here, but I need to go over my notes for tomorrow. Conde Nast has a six-week internship for the summer, and I'm hoping I get it. I'm literally the only one left not doing anything this summer. Aiden's father found out he was in Washington but not at the office. His father didn't get as crazy as we all anticipated; however, he does have him working with him pretty intensely. Meaning we haven't been able to grab food or watch an old movie since Washington.

CHAPTER TWELVE

AIDEN.

My dad is busting my balls. Waking up early and then going straight to work with him has me beat. Although it's actually not all bad, starting my day earlier, waking up for Fajr, and catching the morning air has been somewhat nice. I can't quite explain it, but my mind has become less foggy, I'm sleeping a little better, I'm less frustrated... I'm... less scared. The only downside of working is not getting to see Amala as much, but when she wins them over today in the interview, we're getting celebratory cupcakes. I sent some cupcakes to Amelia last weekend. She was missing home and, so I made her a little box (of course with the help of

MY CARAMEL

Amala) filled it with Mays Cupcakes, a NYC leaf from Central Park, my hoody that she ends up wearing, money from dad's wallet, a book from Amala's collection, a picture of what the sky looks like at night and joe did me a solid and put his famous pizza marinara in a little jar for her; random but sentimentally funny.

Mondays are now filled with morning briefs that I sit in and 'take notes' but secretly practice my doodling, daydreaming about Washington about Amala, and my day flicks by before I know it. Not that I would ever admit it to my father, but this internship isn't all too bad. I've even made a new/old friend (well, she's a family kind of; we've known each other since we were little.). Yasmin Ali, but she doesn't carry the weight of her family name- unlike some of them, the Ali's, in general, are the family you want to always keep on your good side. But Yasmin is more grounded, sweeter, and funnier. Come to think of it, she reminds me of my aunt Selene. I shake my head, not wanting to go down that rabbit hole today; thinking about my aunt brings up some painful memories. I check my phone for the time. It reads *12 p.m.* Amala must be out of her interview. I sneak away from my desk to ring her,

'Ring', 'Ring', 'Ring'. It reaches her machine. I leave her a message to call me back.

MY CARAMEL

"Hey, Sancar, you ready for lunch?" Yasmin asks. Checking my phone to see if Amala replied, "Urm, yes, sure." I say hesitantly.

"Okay, there is a cute café not far from here, Mays Cupcake or something like that, but they do the best coffee." She rambled on.

"Oh, I know, but nah, I'm going there after work, so let's just go somewhere else."

I already made that mistake, taking another girl to May's coffee spot. We grab our stuff and head out for lunch. New York in the sun is nice. Everything feels kind, happier, lively.

"So Sancar, how's Omar?" Yasmin has been asking about Omar for weeks now. I reply with the same response: he's good, and then she stares at me for a while, lifts her eyebrow, and laughs into another conversation. But not today, "Dear lord, I don't need your 'he's good,' how many times does a girl have to ask before you get it?"

I look at her this time and begin to laugh, "Wait a minute, damn, how did I miss that, you tryna get with Omar?"

"Well, duh, you're still plenty stupid Sancar."

"Hey, that was a long time ago!"

She starts laughing, "Remember when we both fell because you lost control of your bike? Ah, that hurt so much. I think

I still have the scar." She lifts her sleeve to show me the tiny scar on her wrist.

I laugh, shaking my head, "No, remember when you were super into Harry Potter?"

"Oh my God and I burnt your blanket after trying to do a spell with the candle!" She laughs, raising her hands to her face. "Okay, you win!" She admits.

My phone pings, and I immediately transport to my phone, waiting to hear from Amala, but it's Amelia sending her tenth selfie of some rock from space.

"Hello?" she snaps her fingers at me.

I apologize and redirect the conversation back to her,

"So, Omar, you and Omar." I smirk.

She tells me they've been talking and wants to know if he's serious or if he's just going to waste her time. "I'm so sick of you guys that I'm thinking of telling Omar if he's serious, he needs to take my daddy's number, and he can tell you how much the mehr is."

"So how much is the mehr?"

She looks at me, smirking, "You know I'm expensive," she laughs and shakes her head quickly, "You know I don't care for that, honestly, Sancar, if he's good to me, he can take care of me, and God is first and foremost in his life then that's all I care for."

"I respect that; some girls are tripping out for the amount they ask."

"It's a whole conversation, but I will say those girls don't care for marriage."

"I feel that." I nod my head.

"So, Omar? Is he serious?"

I tell her she doesn't need to worry. Omar really is a solid guy, the only guy I trust around my family and sister, but more importantly, he's been my constant reminder to deen.

*'Ping,' a*gain, I rushed to my phone, hoping it would be Amala, but it was Amelia again. It's now *1 p.m.* she should be done by now; her interview was at *10 a.m.* It's been three hours. I ring her again, but it forwards to her machine. My thoughts start to seep in. What *if she didn't get it? What if she got too nervous and didn't go? What if something happened?* I shake it off quickly; she'll respond, I tell myself firmly. We walk back to the office; I sit in another meeting. This time, it's about the 4th of July and city budgets. I hope no one thinks to open my notepad, the one I 'take' notes in, but instead spend 45 minutes doodling random things like Fred and the gang or just the mystery machine. My mind slips nicely into a scenario of me breaking out of the meeting, pretending I'm T.J. and my father is principle

Prickly and Johnson Pecker is Ms. Finster (which, oddly enough, he looks a little like, definitely built like her).

"Yep, we'll pick the last two agendas in tomorrow's meeting, John." Said Reid, closing his laptop and my daydreaming.

Two hours have ticked by, and still no word from Amala, radio silence. Now, the worry starts to melt in. I finish the tasks on my list, say bye to my father and Yasmin, and head out. I swung by Mays Cupcake World to grab her favorites but also to see if she was there waiting for me. May's during the summer is insanely busy. They just bought out May's ice cream crumbled with their famous cupcakes. Last week, Amala and I tried an affogato with a chocolate hazelnut cupcake crumbled on top, and a vanilla ice cream with a chocolate praline cupcake crumbled on top; hands down, the best combinations.

I look around the café, but no one resembles her. A bunch of girls looking all too similar; I finally get to the front of the queue and place my order. I grab the takeout bag and head to Amala's, hoping she's at home with some good news.

Her father opens the door, "Aiden, Asalam wa Alikum, what brings you here, son?"

"Wa Alikum Salam, I brought Amala some cupcakes…to congratulate her. Where is she?"

"Oh, she's not home yet, son."

But where is she? I thought, "Urm, okay, well, I'll leave these with you." Not wanting to ask him again.

"I can't promise they'll still be here by the time she gets back." He chuckles. I walk away, questioning where she is. It's now *5 p.m.,* seven hours past her interview.

I hop on the subway to go home before my ma begins to worry. With Amelia gone for the summer, she hates eating dinner by herself; sometimes, my father gets back late, so I try to be home- on time most days. Omar's mom is spending the summer in Pakistan for a big wedding, so he joins us for dinner almost every week, which has been nice. Ma cooked up lamb with rice and her famous Persian salad, including tiny, cubed cucumber, tomatoes, onions, cilantro, and seasoning.

We take our seats at the dining table, just the two of us. Ma starts telling me how we should do something different for the 4th of July; she never really talks about that holiday weekend; for her, the whole month sends her to blues. My aunty, Selene (Uncle Z's wife), passed away in July. My mom doesn't really have much family since her father

MY CARAMEL

passed away three years ago, and her mother died when she was two. She has two half-siblings who are the polar opposite of her. I guess because they were raised in the projects, not to look down at them, but they are very different from my mother. It started when my grandfather left his second wife after he realized she was a gold digger; he just up and left her. He still took care of the kids, but his ex-wife would use the kid's money for her nails, bags, clothes, and just bull. My grandfather just stopped giving her money; he simply set aside some money for them to receive when they came of age. It sucks because they were so accustomed to the projects that they just ended up like their mom; they threw their money on clothes, drugs, and bull. Occasionally, my mother would check in on my uncle Adam, maybe because he was the youngest, but her sister never cared for her. She often just ignored my mother. And then, when my father suddenly became mayor, she started remembering my mother. My father always warned my mother- he couldn't stand Ma's sister, but my mother's different; she's too sweet for this world. She hopelessly tried to cling to the only family she had, but it never lasted. Once my ma gave her some money, she disappeared. This is why when Ma met Aunt Selene, they instantly became each other's best friends, literally inseparable. To the point where Aunt Selene didn't have children of her own, and so when

Ma had me, Aunt Selene would joke around telling people I was her son until my mom had Amelia. Ma told her now we have one each, you can have Aiden, and I have Amelia, and then she would laugh and say, 'And when you feel like you need a girl, you can take Amelia; what's mine is yours.'

"You okay, sweetie? You look like you've gone somewhere." My mother says gently, a feeling all too familiar to her.
I fix my eyes and shake it off, "Yeah, long day at work."
'Ping',
A tingle rushes to my stomach as I rush to my phone,

Amala: *I'm so sorry, Aid; thank you so much for my cupcakes. I love them!*
Aiden: *Don't mention it, so how did it go?* I text back reluctantly.
Amala*: Call me!*
Aiden: *K, give me 5!*

I scoff down the remaining bit of food on my plate; I help Ma clean up the dining table and kiss her forehead before heading upstairs. Plug my phone into charge, click open my Airpods, place them into my ears, jump on my bed, and ring Amala. Two seconds in, she answers,

MY CARAMEL

"I got it, Aid!" She screams down the phone, full of excitement.

"I told you, Amala, you were stressing for nothing." I laugh with her, wishing I was next to her. "What happened? I thought your interview was at 10?"

"It was, but Aid, it was such a good interview that she asked me to join, and oh, you know the, Ali's daughter, the one who got engaged months back, they are doing a whole wedding profile spread on them! And do you want to know the best part?" Excitement is vibrating off her that it's making me smile.

"What's the best part, May?"

"May?"

"Oh, your new name, Amala, is too formal, and Mala sounds like gala, but May, May sounds cute."

"Okay," she laughed, "anyway, the best part, Aid, is that I'm writing a tribute piece. Granted, it's the smallest part, but it's a start, right?"

"That's more than just a start, May; it's huge. Listen, are you hungry? Because I'm thinking Ice cream or pizza, or even both." I ask her, wanting to see her.

"Didn't you just eat?"

"Okay and?"

"Ah, let me ask Baba, and then I'll meet you in about twenty minutes."

"Okay, meet you at our spot."

AMALA: *'Okay, see you in twenty minutes, DO NOT BE LATE!'*

I jump up and throw on a polo until I smell myself; yep, I definitely need a shower. I quickly scrub myself with this fancy shower set Amelia got me from London, spray myself with the scent Amala loves, throw on my fresh white linen shirt and some pants, and head out. I don't feel like walking, so I catch a cab to our spot. Surprisingly, I arrived before Amala. Mays isn't as busy as it was earlier; the sun is fading, and so are the Instagrammers. Ms. Khan sat at her usual spot, tapping away at her laptop, always the most focused.

"Hey, you!" Amala calls out softly.
I turn around, "Hi," I look down at my watch, "It just shocks me how people are late in today's society, with all the ample technology; perhaps it's because society is growing inherently lazier." I mock her whilst attempting to keep a straight face.
She whacks my arm, rolling her eyes at my impression of her,

"It's true, and our social standards and expectations are declining." She adds on.
"Okay, Mrs. Prysselius, let's get some food."
"Why did we meet here?"

"Because you easily get lost, you honestly should lose your rights as a New Yorker." I shake my head at her.

She scoffs at me, "whatever."

We walk out of Mays Cupcake and begin swapping day stories,

"Oh, guess what Yasmin told me?" I ask Amala, who is busy taking pictures of the moon for the hundredth time; she lifts her head up to ask what. "Her and Omar are a thing!"

She looks up at me, her eyes a deep brown. Her smile sinks into her face, the same smile that snatches my heart,

"Everyone knows, where have you been? Amelia was telling me this last week."

We continue to walk, continuing to swap day stories which have now turned to week stories, to future, to present to past, to remember when to I wishes; each change is escorted by laughter until I look up and we finally see…Pizza. She seems extra smiley tonight, so much so that I feel myself smiling, my mind eerily quiet, unnervingly frightening- my thought; even when absent, I feel nauseous. I plead with myself, as in I, Aiden, have a part of me held to ransom, and God, at times, I'm holding on to dear life.

'Come on,'

'Focus!'

'Aiden'

'You're fine'

'Caramel'

Suddenly, I remembered what the Imam advised me (well, everyone at the Friday prayer): "God will never burden a person more than they can handle." I breathe out, remembering Him, and feel my lungs expand. Amala's eyes are glued to the menu even though we can only get three items from the menu. She finally looks up and says, "Yep, let's get the Margareta." She smiles, her smile reaching ear to ear now, most likely because of the food.

"So, May tell me more about your internship? What famous dead person are you writing a tribute for?" I ask.
"Oh, well, my boss believes there is more to the story, and she wants me to investigate! Can you believe it?" She said, beaming with joy and excitement.

"My little undercover reporter, so who is she?" I smile.
"This woman called Selene, Selene Ali." She says without knowing the weight of what she just said. I feel my face turn sour; how do I tell her that writing this tribute will kill my family? How can I do this to her...*again?*

CHAPTER THIRTEEN

AMALA.

In life, more often than not, we all land on this state of perplexity, an island full of catch-22s, home to *'damned if you do, damned if you don't.'* To make a decision that has the least number of consequences, although sometimes, your test isn't the decision but how best you deal with the consequences. Aiden, for some reason, was adamant about tanking the tribute for his aunt, Selene, Selene Ali. There was much more to this than he was even telling me. I never knew she was an Ali, the prominent billionaires. I never knew she was married to Aiden's Uncle Z, nor that she passed away almost two years ago. I couldn't see past the pain in Aiden's eyes. I've never seen him as startled as he was yesterday; what happened to him that's left him scarred? Is this what he was afraid of when I interviewed him? Will this truly break him? Or worse?

My catch-22, resurfacing Aiden's pain or killing my career. I force myself to think back to my father's words, but I cannot; I can't imagine hurting Aiden. I sink further under my pillow, trying to find a way off this dystopian island,

"Sweetie," I hear my father knock on my door.
"Yes, Baba," I sit up on my bed.
"What's wrong?" he asks.
I dive straight into my dilemma, "I have a friend who doesn't want me to research into something because it will break him."

"Break him how?"
"Mentally, physically perhaps."

"Well, what's the secret?" my father's face narrows.
I pause, "I don't know…I know whatever it is, he doesn't want out."

My father pauses and frowns a little, "Find out the secret and then make the judgment. You need all the facts before you turn down a huge opportunity like this." He kisses my head and walks out of my room but leaves behind the load of his advice. Asking Aiden is impossible; he refuses to open up, and whether I like it or agree with it entirely, I have to understand his decision to keep whatever a secret. I'm not even sure where to begin or with whom without it getting back to Aiden or his family; the only person I can trust is Amelia. She'll understand why I'm asking despite being Aid's sister.

Aiden: *[sent a picture] Which one?*

I glance over at my phone, and it unlocks, revealing the picture Aiden sent, a picture of two different bow ties for next weekend. The fundraiser for the Ali-Aziz Heart Foundation. A grand ball mimicking only the great parts of the past, a magnificent ballroom with artworks so foreign to today, a decorated ceiling, and a diamond crystal chandelier the size of a ship hanging from above, laughter and chatter harmonized with the faintest sound of a piano playing in the background. Regency era is the selected theme for the event. An era noted and respected for its elegance and successes in fine arts and architecture. Shopping with Aiden will help clear my head- for now, as for Amelia, she'll be back on the 4th of July weekend. When the time is right, I can ask her and hope she's willing to tell me. If not, I may need to go to the woman who seems to know everyone and everything, Mrs. Mimi Margaux. I pick up my phone to text Aiden and tell him to meet me; I need a new dress for the fundraiser.

New York is a little gloomy today, but I don't mind it: a little sprinkle of rain and a whole lot of humidity. The only reason I love any 19th-century-themed party is because all the dresses are long, the sleeves full. I don't have to fuss around trying to find the perfect modest dress. I already know what I want: an image of Audrey Hepburn in her black dress from the movie War and Peace; although it was made in the 1950s, it's based on Leo Tolstoy's novel- War and Peace. Aiden finally finds me in the store, and I sweep a look around the store to see if anything grabs my eye until one does.

"Hey, I... just want to thank you for understanding the other day with the whole tribute piece," Aiden says, sitting on the opposite side of the curtains.

"Hold on," I adjust the dress, '*okay*' I whisper to myself.

I walk out wearing a replica of the black dress that Audrey Hepburn wore in War and Peace; the dress- is perfect. I twirl around,

"You look... beautiful." He says, smiling, he attempts to repeat his apology,

"It's okay," I stop him, "I get it...kind of." I smile, but he remains saddened. I squat down at his level, my black dress trailing behind me; he sits up a little and leans forward. Looking up at his sad face, our eyes meet each other just as they met in Washington; just as they met that night I wore the emerald dress. Close enough that I can smell every note of his scent, a woody, amber smell with a touch of sweetness, and for the first time, temptation slithers itself into my mind, and I feel this need to kiss him, to run my hands through his hair, to feel the warmth of his hands, to just be held by him. I stare at him a little longer, confused by this new feeling, before telling him, "Smile; life goes on, and we can't afford to get left behind." I say softly, backing away from him and from this new temptation, seeking refuge from God.

He finally returns the smile, not a forced smile but a sincerely grateful smile. I look at him again, this time with the fog of temptation lifted, and I wonder, for a brief moment, what his intentions are, why neither of us have spoken about the elephant in the room. Is any of this real? Perhaps the idea of *us* simply remains in my head, a version of reality clearly too afraid to surface, afraid of the world just like me; even in alternative realities, I'm sitting on the sidelines, far from what I want. I wasn't going to be the one who brought it up. I feel his presence in every moment between us, but until he conjures up the strength to discuss whatever is going on, those moments will only ever secretly be present in our minds.

MY CARAMEL

Days have passed since I began this insipid search for Aiden's secret, and so far, nothing's come up except two old neighbors whose faces turned sour at the mention of Aiden's name, something about a wrecked car. I don't want to go to Amelia just yet as I'm in two minds. What if it's something she doesn't know, and I lay this on her? What if she starts her own insipid search? Feeling hopeless, I sink deep into my bed, throwing my white linen bedsheets over my head, curling up, and scrolling through our pictures in Washington. Aiden, pulling goofy faces throughout all the pictures, a notification pops up from

Mrs. Mimi Margaux: *Good morning, sweetie; don't forget your beautiful presence is required tonight.*

Ah! My savior,, Mrs. Mimi Margaux is in the city this week to announce her new line of coffee beans- *M Margaux velvet*. I have not seen her since the white party in the Hamptons when she tried to play cupid between Aiden and me. God, thinking back to it, I was so mad at him and to think how time has driven us here, to him being my best friend. Despite how busy Mrs. Mimi Margaux is, for me, she'll cancel all her plans. I equally have a soft spot for the one and only Mrs. Mimi Margaux. Her launch party is held this afternoon in the East Village by invitation only; I secretly believe that Mrs. Mimi Margaux could give the

Aliens a run for their money because she is incredibly well-connected.

Trying to ignore the time, I stay curled up under my blanket and hope it's not time to get up. This search for Aiden's story is tiring me, but I have a feeling Mrs. Mimi Margaux will know a thing or two; even if she just points me in the right direction, it will be a huge help.

Admitting defeat, I climb out of my warm bed and step onto my cold rug, dragging myself to the washroom. I feel a magnetic pull from my bed. The urge for comfort attempts to lure me back, but as soon as the water hits my face, I'm awake; it's as if I washed my tiredness off and, with it, drowned out all my temptations. After getting dressed, I wait for the water to finish boiling; my father walks in and asks how I'm doing. He kisses the top of my head. I tell him I'm good, and he smiles, thanking God, quietly- as he does every morning. We catch up on my latest undercover research, and I tell him tonight I may finally get some answers; we play the whole James Bond thing before I have to leave for my internship.

Checking the time, I run for the subway, making it just as the doors start to shut. Emma, by Jane Austen, is my new read. I reach into my bag only to realize I forgot my new book at home. Instead, I'm hypnotized by the whoosh, the velocity and might of the subway sinking deep into my daydreams. I'm sitting signing book covers for the release of my new book, and Don Corleone is sitting in the front row with his cat on his lap; Aiden sat next to him, smiling at me. The subway halts to a stop, and you can spot the tourists from the New Yorkers; New Yorkers have become experts at holding their stance, swaying with the carriage rather than falling down.

I stop at the kart outside to grab my boss her coffee. The office is busy preparing for the wedding spread for Ali's daughter, New York's very own royalty. I sat at my desk reading the thin file they handed me for Selene; her death was noted down as a car accident. A drunk driver who got away. However, the doctor who signed the death certificate was Dr. Khalil Ali. Suspicion arose, and so many questions coup my mind, but the prevalent question was, what did Mayor Sancar's family have to do with her death?

The hope of Mrs. Mimi Margaux knowing the truth is what is keeping me sane. The thought of Aiden himself being involved in something as sinister as a cover-up frightened me; who was I spending my time with? A thought quickly swept in: God would have never brought him to me without a reason. I took a breath of reassurance and continued to read her file. She was insanely beautiful; she had that 90's barebone makeup look, a touch of blush, a tint of red for the lips, her eyes brown, and her cheekbones held her whole face gracefully. Her eyelashes were thick and full, her skin olive with a few freckles faintly spread across her cheeks, but her eyes were the kindest.

My boss allowed me to leave early; luckily, I missed the rush to go home. I caught up with Momma over the phone; she's soaking up all the sand and sun for the three of us. New York is getting hotter as we make our way deep into the summer; I rummage through my closet, finding a dress to wear. I'm thinking of a cute linen summer dress for Mrs. Mimi Margaux's launch party or a silk dress with a cute cardigan over it. Feeling indecisive, I called Aiden to help me.

"Okay, did you get the pics now?"

"Urm, let me check."

"Okay, yeah, the dress." He confirms.

"Yes, but which one?"

"The white one, May."

"Thank you. I gotta go get dressed now."

"Why, where are you going?" he asks, wondering why I made plans without him.

"Oh, to a thing I was invited to." I try to make it sound boring, "just a bunch of old people tasting coffee." I need time with Mrs. Mimi Margaux without him there. I can't have him come along and ruin it.

"Need company?" He said, and my heart smiled.
"No, I'll give you the day off." I hear him smile through the phone, and it makes me smile like a little girl. We say bye and hang up; I get dressed and apply a light beat of makeup consisting of soft pinks, soft blush, my favorite lip gloss, and one last check in the mirror to see if my father would approve of my outfit. I smile to myself and head out.

I arrive outside, and Mrs. Mimi Margaux rushes to greet me, and everyone drifts their eyes on us. I feel like royalty; she sweeps me up in a big hug and takes me straight to her new blend, instructs the server to make me a cup of her new coffee, of course. After the picture taking and all the questions, we're finally at the stage of the party where I can speak to Mrs. Mimi Margaux without getting interrupted. People were too into their conversations to be aware of their surroundings, forgetting why they even came. I walk towards Mrs. Mimi Margaux, seeing that she is free, and as I walk toward her, I make eye contact, telling her not to move.

"Don't you look wonderful, dear?" She says, twirling me around. "You look just like a young Yasmeen Ghauri."

"Who?" I ask.

She rolls her eyes, "The Pakistani Canadian model; she was all the talk in the 90s and absolutely gorgeous."

I smile at her, making a mental note to google her later, "The coffee is to die for Mimi; it's so creamy." Only I was allowed to call her by her first name, but to everyone else, it is Mrs. Mimi Margaux, or if she really doesn't like you, it's simply Mrs. Margaux.

"Mimi, I have to ask you something privately. It's rather important if you have the time."

Her face was concerned but still kind, "oh, shall I shut the party down?"

"Haha, no, no, just a few questions about someone."

"Let's go somewhere private then," she says, taking hold of my hand and leading me in the opposite direction towards a door.

"Oh, but your party," I say, trying to stop her.

"They'll be fine," she shrugs the party off. We walk into the office, and she pours us both a glass of water.

"Now, how can I help you, child?" she asks, handing me my glass.

I take a deep breath, "I'm writing a tribute for Conde Nast about a woman who was killed in a car accident, but a few things on the report didn't add up; more importantly, I was asked not to write it. I was wondering if you knew what really happened." I've never seen her frown or be this focused on something.

"What was the young woman's name?"

"Selene Ali," I replied.

She took a deep breath and a long sip of her water. I knew what she was about to tell me was intense, "Oh dear," She sighed heavily. "What happened to her was tragic. Apparently, she was not very well; she suffered a great deal from mental health and often went through periods of depression, not being able to get herself up. One day, unfortunately, she felt that she had enough; her life, she felt, had no purpose, and she decided to take her own life."

I felt my heart clench and break for their family.

"The worst of it all was that" She continued, "oh, poor Aiden was the one who found his aunt lying on the ground." My hands shot up to my mouth, covering the shock of what I had just heard. To find someone you love lifeless, your loved one not able to respond to you despite how much you scream or shout, they're no longer there. A dark cloud of melancholy hovers over my head, and I start to think back to all the times Aiden's felt suffocated, times he's pulled on his tie, his leg tapping uncontrollably, and the reason he let me down because of questions about his personal life drowned him with painful memories.

"But Mimi, why did they rule it as an accident?" She rolls her eyes, "Because she was an Ali, and they didn't like that kind of image of them, shows people they're weak, dear. So, they simply covered it up." Mimi looks up at me, "Amala, sweetheart, there is more to the story."
I gaze at her, confused, "like what?"

"I can't tell you, but just know you aren't the only person interested in finding out the truth."

I take a deep breath; now I have this information or part of the story. I don't want it; I can only imagine it gets worse. I don't want to know the pain behind his eyes; I don't want to tell him I know and have it all come flooding back with images of his aunt lying on the floor, still warm but unresponsive. As I lay back on my bed, I try to think of what to do with this information; this is exactly the information my boss wanted me to find: my golden ticket. I find myself floating back to the land of perplexities, but I feel that I owe Aiden at least a conversation to give him a heads-up on what I have to do. Shaking my head at the thought of, *'What I 'have' to do,'* I sighed; life is full of options, some harder than others. Even when you feel like your back is against a wall, it's just a stud wall. If I decide to write this and lose Aiden, then that'll be a choice I made, and I have to be okay with it, but it's peculiar because the thought of losing Aiden saddens me more than losing my internship.

CHAPTER FOURTEEN

AIDEN.

"Close game, but I'm always the better player, remember that." I boast to Omar. Wiping the sweat off my face. Omar laughs, throwing the ball at me. Since Amelia is at camp and Amala is busy at her internship, Omar and I have been playing a lot more ball.

I can't wait to see Amala finally; the road trip feels like forever ago, but tonight, I get to see her again in her black dress and watch everyone admire her. Omar drives me to the tailors to collect my suit for tonight,

"So, what happened to that girl?" He asks.

"It didn't feel right. I didn't want to waste her time," I tell him.

"Are you going to tell me about this girl everyone has seen you with?" he asks, smirking.

"It's not like that, she's it's different, there is something there. Besides, when were you going to tell me about Yasmin?" I brush the conversation onto him. I feel strange talking about how I feel.

"Now." He grins. "I really like her; you know I called her father."

"For real? How did that go?"

"I was shitting myself, oh, my, God." We laugh. "But, we met, and surprisingly, he's a nice dude."

"That's huge!"

"Yeah, we're getting married in the fall." He said, glimmering.

"WHAT! Ah, congrats, brother." I hug him.

I finish pressing my shirt; I'm wearing a black jacket, a white buttoned-up vest, and black pants. This whole Regency Era is kind of strange, cool, but strange. I still say the 90s is the best for everything. Last night, Amala finally got some free time and called me. We watched The Age of Innocence over the phone. I felt the need to apologize to her again for being incredibly understanding and respecting my wishes not to dig into Aunt Selene. She never made me feel awkward about it or questioned why, nor did she get mad at me, which made me feel worse because something about her made so much sense, and I feel myself jeopardizing it.

"Aiden, you ready, kiddo?" my father shouts.
"Coming," I shout back. I quickly take a look in the mirror, adjust my jacket, spray the scent Amala likes, and head down the stairs.
Standing in front of me, waiting for me with a smile wider than anyone I know, holding a slice of Joe's pizza in one hand, my heart smiles back at my sister. I sweep her up in my arms,

"Oh, my God, what are you doing home?" I shout in excitement.
"It's 4th of July soon, so they gave us the week off, and I'm like super ahead, and I think they were running out of things to give me." She said, not so humbly. I smile at her again, my smile reaching ear to ear; my mother comes down in a beautiful golden gown, and we gasp, "Ma, you look too beautiful." She blushes.

"Lord, is that my wife?" My father takes her hand and twirls her around, and there are smiles everywhere. He pulls her in and kisses her. I take a million pictures in my head and swamp my mind with them like a disinfectant.

"Okay, family, let's go show them how the Sancars do things around here, but first, a family picture." He places his phone on a timer, and we all stand back, hugging each other, wishing this joy was forever.

We arrive at the grand ball, the Ali-Aziz Heart Foundation, and everyone is looking at the part; of course, the Ali's even arrive in classic 19th century Rolls Royce; they were all lined up at the entrance. The Khans arrive next wearing traditional classic Pakistani attire, a long jacket with slimmer trousers and a pocket square; their attire looks much flier than ours. They came looking for a million dollars. After several security checks, my father and our family are escorted into the building.

I immediately scan the room to see if I can find Amala sitting in the corner reading her book.

"Hello, dear." I recognize that voice, Mrs. Mimi Margaux.
"Aren't you a sight for sore eyes?" I smile at her.
"You, young man, are dangerous; that smile is going to get me in trouble."
"Careful now, people might think we're flirting." I laugh, teasing her.

Something or someone snatches the corner of her eye, "Now she is truly remarkable."

There she is, walking down the stairs in her black dress, her long silk gloves, and a diamond bracelet dangling off her wrist. I watch her walk down, I look around to watch the room and everyone in it admire her. Her beauty takes over my rationale, and I think to myself how I have not asked her to be mine. She is all I think about; she is the only one who soothes my thoughts and brings me comfort. She is the caramel; without her, there is no sweetness. I magnetically walk towards her, and everyone in our way melts away; my heart races with passion until her eyes find mine, and she graciously smiles at me; that is when my heart completely fills with serenity.

"Aiden."

"Amala."

We both smile at each other.

"You look... beautiful,"

She blushed but held herself gracefully.

God, I really want to hold her; all I want is to hold her, to have her in my arms, nothing crazy, just to hug her and to hug her for a really long time.

"Guess who has joined us?" I smirk.

Amelia runs up to her and throws her arms around her.

"Oh, my goodness," Amala's face brightens, and she laughs. "What are you doing here? You are not allowed to leave again, young lady; I've had to babysit your brother in your absence." I roll my eyes at the last comment.

Amelia giggles, "You're right; it takes the two of us to deal with him." They both begin to tease me and make jokes, which I really don't mind; I find it cute.

"Amala, I want to introduce you to someone." I take her to meet my parents. I didn't want to waste any more time. "Ma, I would like you to meet the lovely Amala Emami Zidane." My mother never immediately likes anyone, but she smiles and says, "Ah salaam, sweetheart, I've heard so much about you." Ma hugs her.

"And this is my father, Mayor Sancar."

"Oh, you can call me Hakeem," He said; she smiled and greeted him back. "You must be Ahmed's little girl," My father asked.

"Yes, you know my father?"

"Who doesn't? He's a great man, a solid writer. I hear you're following his footsteps."

"I'm trying." she shyly smiles, looking at me.

"Oh, Hakeem, leave the girl alone with all your questions," My mother yelled at him; she took Amala's hands, "you look absolutely beautiful. Where did you get this from?"

"This little boutique I can show you sometime."

"I would love that." Ma smiled.

"It was lovely meeting you guys, but I must get back to my father."

"I'll walk you back to your table."

We notice the elaborate show the Ali's have prepared for the evening. I find the courage to bring Washington up and tell her how I've felt over the past couple of months, "Amala."

"Yes, Aiden?" She looks up at me with her brown eyes.

"I've been meaning to ask you something."

"Me to Aiden." She chimes in.

We both face each other in the middle of the ballroom, looking picture-perfect together. I ask her to go first; her eyes meet the floor, "What's wrong, May?"

"Aiden, please try and understand everything before you get upset or angry."

What on earth is she about to tell me? I stand up straight-stiff, preparing for what she has to say. I stare at her before telling her to continue; she takes a deep breath, "You know how I was asked to find out the truth about Selene, your aunt Selene." I tried to hold a straight face, but I felt my eyebrows frown. "Well," I ask her to continue.

"I did."

It frightens me how quickly my heart is able to switch to anger; what did she find out? Why? Why did she have to find anything out?

"Aiden," she says softly. "Say something, please."
"I need air." I panic, trying to loosen my tie and unbutton my jacket. I don't like how I feel; I don't like how I'm losing control of the man she likes. I rush outside. I hear her footsteps follow me behind, *'why'* is what circulates my mind; why *did she have to find out? Why didn't she just trust me? Why did my father leave me that night?* I feel the caviar making its way back up.

"Aiden, I'm so sorry; believe me, I wish I didn't find out."
"Amala…I can't…" I try gasping for air, but it's as if the air is punishing me for what I did.
She tried to distract me; she pointed to the cars and the funny top hats, but I still couldn't breathe. Until she said, "Talk about it, Aiden, please talk to me, tell me how you feel. I know it's crushing you. Finding your aunt after she killed herself couldn't have been easy."
My face full of confusion, I look at her, "What did you just say?"
She repeats what she said, "Finding your aunt after she killed herself couldn't have been easy." This wasn't my

story. I felt guilty for feeling relief, relief that she still doesn't know.

"Amala, who told you this?"

"Mimi did."

I take a deep breath, "That's not what happened, Amala."

"God," she sighed, "Then what happened that night that you're so afraid of?" she sounded frustrated.

"Amala, not right now."

We fell into silence; I could tell she was disappointed, and I hate that I'm the cause of her feeling this way. "You wanted to tell me something before I ruined the evening." She said with sadness. I almost forgot about that; my heart slowly starts to come back to normality. I feel the heat drain from my head, but after what happened, the moment seems too far in the distance to grab.

"That you look remarkable, and Amala, you could never ruin the evening. I'm sorry for my reaction." I smile at her, my heart feeling a little lighter.

She half smiles at me. There's another moment of silence, and then she calls my name, "Aiden," she looks up at the moon, "I'm sorry I snooped when I told you wouldn't."

I smile at her and apologize for all this mess.

She continues to stare at the moon, and I continue to stare at her; my heart returns to calmness, and we both stand in the silence of comfort, not awkwardness.

"Aiden?" she finally says again. "When do you know you love someone?"

I pause for a moment until I realize, "When you want to skip all the time-wasting stuff and go straight to marrying that person."

CHAPTER FIFTEEN

AMALA.

I spoke to Mrs. Mimi Margaux to make certain her story isn't just another cover-up, but she swears by the story. She informed me that a very close person in the family told her directly and that there was more to the story. She further advised that perchance, *'the boy has made another story up in his mind, a version of the story where he saves his aunt or one where he doesn't find her dead on the floor.'* She went on saying, *'The mind, dear, is a powerful thing. It will consume whatever you feed it and, from it, will grow a mirror reflection of what it ate.'* And the more I thought about it, the more it started to make sense. Aiden is having a hard time accepting what he witnessed; of course he is. I would be a mess, too- anyone would.

I thought long and hard about writing what Mrs. Mimi Margaux told me for my Conde Nast paper, and I think I should write it. I thought there was something special between Aiden and me, and I keep waiting for him to bring it up to address how we both clearly feel, but nothing. Nothing ever happens. I keep thinking that perhaps it's me because I keep pushing him to speak about painful parts of his life, but then I'm conflicted with the fact that he signed up for this. I never asked him to be a part of me. What if he waltzed into my life for an entirely different reason than the one I currently crave? I sigh to myself in disappointment, a world without Aiden. I thought back to three months ago when there was a world without Aiden, weekends I spent watching Gilmore Girls and reading my volumes of books, my only adventures were through Anna Karenina or Layla, Miss Bennet, even the fabulous Mr. Corleone, my life was just comfortable. It was small snippets of black and white highlights, but then came Aiden, a burst of color. As if Christopher Nolan directed the plot line, each scene vibrant and loud with life, depicting and capturing emotions of joy, curiosity, love, confusion, love, happiness, shock, and joy in all of its essence and glory that it leaves you not wanting to leave for a second because if you do, the color may dim until eventually returning back to small snippets of black and white highlights.

Above all the what ifs with Aiden and me, I know he's my best friend- this much I know, and he should support me, which is why I still believe in writing the piece for Conde Nast. I'll tell Aiden this weekend in the Hamptons before the 4th of July weekend. I really hope he's okay with it; I don't want to ruin our weekend.

I walk into the office to update my boss on what I found; although there isn't much proof yet, I have a feeling she'll want to hear what I have to say.

"Hey, Charlotte." I knock on her office door, but she's on the phone. I wait outside and watch the office, and it's always the same: a circulation of people running around with files in one hand and coffee in the other. Iced, steamed, hot, most likely lukewarm by the time they remember to drink it.

"Yes, Amala, how can I help?"
"Hey, I have an update on the Selene Ali file," I say in a sort of whisper.
Her eyes beam wide open, "I'm all ears; shut the door behind you." She says, sitting up in her seat.

I tell her all I have, the full story of how Aiden found his Aunt Selene dead on the floor, how the Ali's covered the entire story. She looks at me, unimpressed and unphased at what I told her.

"We already know that my boss wanted to know if Aiden had told you anything." She asks coldly.

"Aiden? I'm sorry, I'm a little confused."

She clears her throat, "Well, you see, Amala, we just wanted you to dig as much as you could. You've been seen with the mayor's son at multiple events, and it worked out perfectly for my boss when your resume landed on my desk."

I stay quiet for a moment, a horrible feeling of- I can't even explain it. Insecurity married with anger. She reads my face, "Look, don't be disheartened, Amala, it's just journalism, and the price, if you deliver, will be very promising for your career."

"Who is paying for this information?" I asked.

"I can't say, but unfortunately, if you're unable to deliver in a week, you'll have to let you go." She said without hesitation. I remain professional and smile, placing my feelings aside until I'm excused.

My gut deepens in disappointment; all this self-doubt is only just amplified. I walk over to my booth. I mostly keep myself to myself; I haven't made any friends in the office. I open up the file again, looking at Selene and her kind eyes. I think to myself, I don't really know much about who she was, what she liked or disliked, what made her, her. I tried googling her, but only a few pictures of her are on the internet, some of her in the background of other pictures but mostly of her in family pictures with the Ali's. I thought if I was ever going to find out the truth, I needed to know who she really was—starting off with Amelia or Aiden, as they were the closest.

I type up a series of questions to appear as if I'm doing work; today seems fairly quiet. I think everyone's already clocking out and getting ready for the 4th of July weekend. I type in *'Emma by Jane Austen PDF'* in Google, scroll down to the chapter I'm on, and continue reading. Of course, I have Selene's file open in case anyone walks by, but until I know who she is, I won't be able to know her story or be able to write the tribute. Writing can never be a task for me; I have to feel something that's hard to explain, but it's like this: when we watch a movie, it's not just the scene that's magnificent. It's the speech, it's the people, it's the music in the background, it's the lighting, it's all those things orchestrated together to make the perfect scene, but with words, there aren't any special effects, it's just words and if I can't feel them then how can I expect my readers too?

Two chapters later, lost in the world that belongs to Jane Austen, it's time for me to go home and eat. I walk through my door to see my father napping on the couch. Placing a throw over him and picks up the book that's resting on his chest. The house eerily silent; I wish my mother were here. We would be sat with our teas, and she would be spilling the tea about the funniest stuff about people or family drama. I have such different relationships with my parents; come to think of it, with my father, our relationship is fueled with literature poetry, writing, old mob movies, and food, but with my mother, it's the opposite. She shares her problems with me; she loves fashion or going out and just shopping. Thank God, he gave me enough personality for both because I can't imagine a world without knowing who my parents are and not being able to connect with them. I really miss my mother's cooking too; normally, I would have come home to a spread for dinner, the full work, and she would have everything ready whilst looking beautiful.

I fish through our mail to see if she's written to us yet, and there was nothing. So, I decided to write to her instead. I quickly whip up some ramen noodles (by whip, I mean boiling the water and following the instructions) and load Gilmore Girls; Rory has to decide between Dean and Jess. I take a sheet of paper from my father's collection and an envelope and begin to put pen to paper.

Dear Mama,

Let me set the scene for you: Baba is asleep downstairs on the couch; I've just come back from work. I made myself Ramen (yes, the one you add boiling water too), and I'm really missing you. I'm watching Gilmore Girls, and Rory starts to like Jess back. I don't know why you hate on Jess; Dean is so annoying this season- such a moaner. I wish you were here, though I have my own Dean/Jess drama, well, just boy drama. I'm just not sure, mama, what you and Dad have is so special; how did you get it so right? I'm scared I'll get it wrong. In the long run, Dean is the obvious choice, but she chose Jess and got it wrong even though it made sense at the time. What if the boy I like only makes sense right now? What if he's not my guy? What if I think it's him because he's the only one I've ever gotten to know? See why you're not meant to leave; what if you come back and I've chosen Jess? Instead of waiting for Logan! Forget Dean; I meant Logan. Logan is clearly the better guy, and how do I know that my guy is Jess Dean or Logan? But I also don't want to see a better 'offer' oh Mama. See, this is all so confusing. I need you home.

Anyway, I hope you're having the best time. I can't wait to see you soon. Stay happy and sun-kissed.

Lots of Love
Your Amala

I seal my rambling letter and place a stamp on it, ready for it to be sent. It's only 8 pm. I sigh to myself and pick up my phone to see zero notifications. Feeling jaded after today's meeting about potentially getting fired, I do what I do best, and I pick Emma up but quickly place my book back down as I feel a headache creep in. Everything seems too quiet, slowly surpassing comfort and moving towards unnerving. Aiden pops into my quiet thoughts, making me smile and frown, a conflicting feeling; if I get fired, it'll be because of him. I shake my thoughts and proceed to call him.

"Hey." He quickly answers, as if I too were occupying his thoughts, his voice deep and rugged-handsomely rugged that it fills up my silent room, rescuing it from its eeriness.

"Hey, back." I sit on my bed, getting comfortable.
"How was work?" He asks.
"Story for another day, Aid." I didn't want to get into that.

"When are you leaving for the fourth?"
"Tomorrow, you?"

"Same, first thing in the morning." He says, letting out a heavy breath.

"Are you looking forward to it?" I hesitantly ask.

"Yeah...No...kinda a little both."

"Yep, because that makes sense."

"Ah, you know what I mean. So much has happened there, but I'm just focusing on the good memories...you know it was my favorite place because of Aunt Selene."

That's the first time he's mentioned her or acknowledged her existence.

"Aiden?"

"Yes, Amala"

"What was she like?" I ask him.

I hear a deep sigh followed by a weak chuckle.

"She was like... warm cookies on a snowy day, like no matter how bad the situation, she would instantly put you in a good mood. She just had to look at me and smile, and I would smile, and then she would laugh, and as much as I would try to fight it, I would end up laughing."

"She sounds beautiful."

"Yeh...she really was, May." He says quietly to himself.

"Hey Aid?"

"Yes, Amala?"

"If you had to choose between a chocolate cake or a Levain's chocolate chip cookie. Which would you pick?"

"Oh, damn, that's hard...cake, no cookie...wait...nope, definitely a cookie."

"Cookies every day, it's not even up for debate."

"Hey, Amala?"

"Yes Aid?"

"I think you might just be my best friend." He says, and I smile all over.

"You're welcome." We resume talking about random subjects: food, books, movies- mostly mob movies until I feel my eyes getting heavy.

CHAPTER SIXTEEN

AMALA.

Next Morning

I wake up to see Aiden still on the phone. I carefully listened and heard him breathing deeply; we must have both fallen asleep on the phone. My father is up; I hear him rummage around. I get up and walk into the hallway, "What are you trying to find?"
My father sounded frustrated, "My suit, the vintage linen suit."

"I'll find it. Let me just finish packing up my bag." I had a few things left to pack, namely my books. Our drive down to the Hamptons is what I'm most excited about; we'll arrive there before the sunset and head straight to our favorite Italian restaurant on the beach. It's our little tradition.

"Have you found it yet?" My father asks, not even looking properly, for it himself.

"Yes, it magically turned up in your wardrobe, exactly where Mom said it was." I'm not sure how, but mothers have this magical ability to say something is somewhere despite you searching high and low until they have to come; it's right there staring you in the face.

"See, this is why I don't go looking for stuff your mother has put away."

I roll my eyes at him, "Please, even if it was staring at you in the face, you'll pretend you didn't see it so that we pack for you."

My father chuckles, "Oh, and you're any better- Miss I-can't-find-my-jumper-so-I-guess-I'll-miss-school." I start laughing; I remember that day. It was Monday morning, and I had spent the whole weekend watching Dawsons Creek, and I just had to find out about Joey and Pacey's trip.

"We all packed?"

"Yep"

"Let's hit the road"

We lock up, throw the luggage in the trunk, and hit the road. I love traveling with my father because he has endless stories about his very real adventures with hints of hyperbole, but sometimes, most of the time, they beat any story I've ever stepped into. My father truly has a way with words- he feels them. "Did I ever tell you the time your mom and I got stuck in the Everglades?"

I shake my head, and he runs with the story, one hand on the wheel and the other moving around with passion to help capture it.

The smell of fresh pies and the ocean swim into the car, and I know we're nearby; excited, nostalgic memories rush to me of all my favorite summer hits that I forget about my failed internship. I finish my chapter; there's a new girl on the block. It's safe to say Emma isn't a big fan of hers.

My phone buzzes,

Aiden: *You here yet?*

I swipe to reply, '*Yes, are you?*'

Aiden: *Yes, I can't wait to see you!*

My father interrupts my smile, "Whose got you smiling to yourself?"

I roll my eyes, "My friend."

"It better not be that boy!" His tone changes.

"Which boy?"

"Aiden." He says.

"Why?" I say with genuine confusion.

"Sweetie, we're Muslim first and foremost, and so is he; he wants to get to know you. He does that the respectful way and comes to me."

I go quiet with realization, "I don't think he sees me like that; I think we're just really good friends."

"Nonetheless, you make sure neither of you are alone together."

I think back to Washington; though nothing happened, and we were always ten feet away from each other, guilt still fills me up.

"Amala, a man who truly wants you and loves you, thinks about forever, not just today. Believe me."

"I do, Baba, I do. I've never compromised myself or my religion, and Aiden's never tried anything." My cheeks fill with embarrassment; why did I say that to my father? I throw my head into my hands. "Anyway…just…don't worry."

"I know you'll always do the right thing."

I quickly texted Aiden back.

Finally, we arrived outside our little condo. We throw our stuff into the rooms and head back into the car.

MY CARAMEL

The restaurant is busy with hungry locals and tourists; a handsome, tall young man in a loose white shirt, beige loafers, and a groomed beard greets my dad, "Uncle Ahmed, how you doing!" He pulls my dad in for a hug. He sends a wide smile my way, giving me salaam; I stare at him a little funny until I realize who it is, "Oh my goodness, Zak, is that you? When did you grow a beard?" I laugh, and he laughs.

"Zak, where's your father, son?" My father looks around for his best friend.

"He's just in the men's room; you totally should join us?" Zak insists on.

My father, of course, agrees to it; since Uncle Abdallah moved out of the city, my father's been best friendless. Growing up, all my memories had Uncle Abdallah and a little skinny crying Zak in the corner. Uncle Abdallah was the sweetest, but Zak was the epitome of annoying. When we were little, we were always put together because we were both of similar age: summer BBQs, holidays, family Eid, and at every event, he sat crying next to me. Until one summer, I picked a book up at the age of six, and little Zak followed me; we were both falling in love with the world of literature, which is how we became pretty inseparable- bound by our love for reading. My favorite memory of us was in grade 7; school was canceled because of the snow, so Zak and I built a huge fort inside- using up all the pillows.

Zak got my mom to make us hot cocoa. Once the fort was assembled, we climbed in, read our books, and fell asleep. Sadly, after middle school, they moved, and only my father and Uncle Abdallah remained best friends.

"Haha, Ahmed!" chuckled Uncle Abdallah and bear-hugged my father.

We sat down, and immediately, they were in their own bubble of memories and laughter, so I turned to adult Zak with a deep voice. His smile still wide, "Careful, your jaw will hurt in the morning."

"It's Amala Emani Zidane, the first girl I shared a bath with."

I whack him on the arm, "When we were six, easy there, you weirdo." I blush.

He laughs, his eyes still on me, "You haven't changed one bit, Red."

I totally forgot about that nickname; when I was young, I would easily get embarrassed …now, Zak would relentlessly tease me for it because my cheeks turn red.

I roll my eyes, "I'm not red anymore." But as soon as I spoke, I felt my cheeks turn red, "Okay, so I'm bashful…modest. It's better than wet-boy."

His eyebrows instantly frowned, "stop right now," he put his finger in my face, "I mean it."

We both emerge into a fit of laughter; Zak takes a sip of water to calm himself down. He looks so different, good, different. I mean, I didn't really pay attention to him this way, but now I'm sitting across from him, looking at him...he grew up handsome.

"So, Red, what have you been up to?"

"Just finished my 2nd year at Columbia, you?"

"Same, computer science and mathematics at Yale."

"I like how you slid that in, Yale, but wow... tech nerd."

"I'm trying to live that flip-flop Silicon Valley life."

"Hmm, sounds breezy."

"How about you, Red? What kind of life are you trying to live?"

I'm so afraid to say it, to say a writer, "Flip flop on the beach, anyway what brings you here?" I changed the conversation.

"Why not? Plus, I heard you'd be here too."

"And why would that be an incentive?"

He smiled again, bringing his dimples out, "Because..." he hesitates; suddenly, Aiden popped into my head, and I didn't want to hear what he had to say. "Because...I couldn't miss out on the opportunity to tease you, Red." Phew, I thought to myself.

MY CARAMEL

Dinner went by smoothly; my father and Uncle A went to play cards with some old friends, leaving Zak and me behind in the restaurant.

I look down at my text,

Aiden: Meet *you at the ice cream shop, Amelia said to bring your appetite.*

Zak still sat next to me, "Okay, Zak, I have to go."

"Woah, woah, woah, where are you going?"

"To meet some friends for ice cream."

"Okay, I'm coming with you!" He said, already grabbing his jacket. Zak is like that. He is not shy like me. He grew up to have much thicker skin, and not many things phased him; he had all the confidence in the world.

"No, Zak, you're going home."

"No, it's late, and you can't be on your own; your dad, my dad, would kill me…literally."

"Fine, let's go, wet boy before you start crying."

"Oh, real mature Red."

"Okay, stop right now; you can't call me that anymore."

"I can call you whatever I want, Red."

We went back and forth like this the entire way to the ice cream shop. It's fun, not that I would admit it to Zak, but he's just so carefree like anything in the world is possible.

MY CARAMEL

Zak and I walked in together and sat at the table, waiting for Amelia and Aiden. Aiden and I make eye contact from across the shop, and for the first time, he isn't smiling at me; I see his eyes land on Zak, and I follow them up and down. Amelia rushes over and hugs me; we walk over to the table. I read Aiden's body language. He's not his warm self; he seems frustrated.

Zak pulls my chair out for me, and I can feel Aiden's eyes on us. Zak, being Zak, introduces himself, "Hey, I'm Zak," he extends his hand out to Aiden.

Aiden looks at me and then looks at Zak, "Hi, Aiden." Moodily responding whilst shaking his hand.

"And I'm Amelia!" She says, breaking this weird stare off.

"So Red, you still like mint choc chip?" Zak says nonchalantly as he gazes over the menu.

"I've ordered her ice cream; sorry, I didn't know you were coming, but you should probably go up and order," Aiden responds, his tone direct and firm.

Zak looks around and then back at me before getting up to place his order.

"Aiden, what is the matter with you."

"I don't know, you tell me... Red." He says mockingly.

I stared at him, confused; I knew Zak being here was bothering him, but I didn't know why.

"Who is he, May?"

"Zak, Uncle A's son, we grew up together, and we bumped into them at the restaurant."

Zak makes his way back to the table, "What did I miss?"

"We were figuring out who you are?" Amelia says.

"I'm Red's best friend." He says, winking at me.

"How come we've just met you?" Amelia asks. I watch a moody Aiden sit scrolling on his phone.

"Oh, Red has me hidden in a closet."

The ice creams arrive: five ice creams: chocolate, mint choc chip, vanilla, Oreo, and cookie crumble.

"Excuse me, ma'am, you've given us one extra," Aiden says, looking down at the tray, confused.

"Oh, nah, brother, I ordered two; Red always likes a little extra chocolate with her mint choc chip." Zak jumps in, taking the tray of ice creams back.

"Okay, I'll take mine then." Amelia reaches over and grabs the Oreo, "Just for reference, I, too, like a side of extra chocolate with my ice cream."

Aiden didn't even touch his ice cream despite me pushing it towards him.

"The perfect bite, Red." Zak extends his spoon towards me, with parts of cookie crumble and chocolate on his spoon for me to try.

The look on Aiden's face is fired with anger; he stands up, his jaws clenched, "I have to get up early, so let's go, Amelia."

"No, Aiden, wait." I stand up, too.

"It's okay; not all of us can hack it," Zak says, putting a spoonful of cookie crumble in his mouth.

"What!" Aiden says, turning to Zak.

"You heard."

I'm not sure what Zak's problem is. Aiden snickers, but I know he finds absolutely nothing funny, "I'm out, May; see you tomorrow."

"Don't worry, I'll take care of *'May,'*" Zak said mockingly.

"Zak!" I look at him to tell him to stop whatever he's doing.

Everything feels intense and stiff, like one slight movement and something might break.

I can see Aiden trying his very best to ignore him, "What's that supposed to mean?"

Zak turns around to face him, "Exactly what it means."

Aiden smiles, and as quick as his smile fades, he punches Zak in the face. Amelia and I both gasp; in a hurry, Zak rushes up and extends his fist to Aiden's face.

Amelia and I squeeze in between them to stop the fist-throwing, "Go home, now," I tell Aiden, and Aiden pants with blood dripping down from his lip. I turn to Zak, who is somehow still smiling even though his eye has swelled. The waiter brings over ice for his eye, and I turn back, but Aiden is long gone.

We were only a block away from the house; our fathers expected him to walk me home. It's Funny how that turned out. I look up at Zak,

"What was your problem tonight?"

"You!" He grunts, slowly dabbing the ice on his eye.

"Me? What did I do?"

"You bug me."

"You bug me! But that doesn't explain why you were being a jerk."

"Red...I got jealous," he sighs. "I see you after so long, and there is another guy in your life. I just had to make sure he knew I was here first."

I shake my head, all of this because he is feeling jealous,

"Zakariya," I say softly.

"See, even the way you say my name, Red, you're killing me here." He laughs.

I smile at him, "Zak, I'm not sure what is between Aiden and me. To say it's complicated is an understatement, but you can't start a pissing competition with someone because you're feeling jealous."

"You were my Amala before anyone else... I think I'll always have a little crush on you."

I feel my cheeks blush, "I'm sorry, Zak."

"He's got a mean punch on him," he said, touching his eye.

"You're an idiot." I laugh.

"We good?" he says, making his puppy eye face.

"Yes, we're good."

"So, Aiden." He looks at me.

"I told you it's complicated."

"I don't know about you, but I know he's into you."

I pause for a moment, trying not to get too caught up by his words, "How can you tell?"

"Because I'm a guy, and I was trying to get under his skin, and it worked."

We continue walking the night off,

"You should text him; if I were in his shoes, my mind would be running like crazy," Zak said.

"Why did you push his buttons if you don't even want anything to happen between us?"

He looks at me, rolling his eyes too, "Red, I told you; I wanted him to know you were my Amala first…and… I was bored."

I sigh, looking up at him, "I think I might be a little envious of you right now."

He suddenly gets a little quiet, "Amala?" he says softly.

"Yes, Zak?"

"Would you have ever gone for me?" he asks vulnerably.

"I think you got hit too hard."

"Damn, Red, that hurt more than the punch."

"You were my first best friend, Zak…" He interrupts me mid-sentence,

"What do you like about him?"

"Like about who?"

"Aiden." He says in his bluest voice.

"I don't know, he's kind." I laugh; I didn't want to talk about Aiden with him.

"Anyway, I think we're home," I say, looking around in the dark.

"I guess we are; well, thank you for taking me with you. I'll see you tomorrow, Red."

"Keep the ice on your eye, Zak."

"Yes, ma'am, goodnight, Red!" he stood opposite me, smiling in with his dimples.

I roll my eyes at him while smiling.

I walk into the house and head straight into my bedroom, rushing to get into bed so I can call Aiden and check in on him. Zak's voice was stuck in my mind, thinking about Aiden being *'into me.'* I throw my PJs on, brush my teeth, pray, and get into bed.

I dial his number and wait.

It rings forever until it reaches his voicemail.

I try again.

It rushes straight to voicemail.

I tell myself he must be getting ready for bed, too. Watching my phone, I stay a little longer.

CHAPTER SEVENTEEN

AMALA.

'Buzz, buzz, buzz'

It's Aiden calling me back.

"Hey."

"Hey."

Silence of this nature is loud and probably the most uncomfortable kind of silence.

"Aiden." I bravely disrupt the stillness.

"Yes, Amala."

"Are you okay?"

Another blimp of silence; I worry I'm one blimp away from becoming a stranger again.

I hear him sigh deeply, "I'm so sorry for how I behaved tonight. It's this place that puts me in a bad mood."

"No, Aiden, don't apologize, please; Zak had provoked you."

"Yes, but he knew he could get to me, and I foolishly let him."

"Why?"

"You know why, May." I sit up on my bed in anticipation, clinging to every word of his,

"I don't, Aiden."

But alas, nothing; we fall into silence again, silence in the form of hesitation.

"Amala…" He eventually says, "…did you like the ice cream?"

Coward! is what came to my mind, "I'm tired. I'll see you tomorrow." I hang up in annoyance. I arrive at the conclusion that I cannot be the woman he is, in any sense of the word, in love with. I feel crushed by an idea of something that only perhaps took place in my mind, a crumpled idea…none of my dreams I've dreamt of for as long I can remember were meant to come true; whoever said *'follow your dreams'* was a capitalist collecting revenue on broken desires. My love for literature has died, my ambitions for writing wither away, and the man I've come to love isn't for me either. A life where dreams are literally just dreams- distant and blurry.

CHAPTER EIGHTEEN

AIDEN.

I sat up all night wondering why I couldn't tell her how I felt; I prayed long and hard to my lord to ask him if Amala was for me. My mind is on a perpetual loop; why does it feel like there's a barrier between me and my words. I couldn't help but think there was a reason, nor could I sleep last night knowing I annoyed Amala, knowing I kept letting her down. God, I hate being back here; I know it's playing with my mind. This morning, I walked out onto the beach just before sunrise; I took my prayer mat with me and prayed Fajr.

I've been sat watching the sun come up since, accompanied only by my thoughts. The sun delineate from blue to purple to orange until it was bright and brilliant. I lay back into the sand and look up at the wide blue sky, my heart feeling much more at ease after praying. It's been a long time since my father's advice came to me.

At times, I remember important snippets of my father and the life lessons he taught Amelia and me, and though he's so busy now, there was a time when he was my go-to superhero. He knew the answers to every single thing- he's still my superhero, but I guess he's just sat collecting dust on a shelf in my mind. One piece of golden advice that comes to mind is when he told us, *'Any decisions, big or small, cannot be made without the guidance of God. We rely on him and him alone, and once you've asked, sit back in patience. Trust him even if the outcome is not what you hoped because, ultimately, only he knows what is better for us.'*

As I lay in the sand, I think about that reminder. I lay, not wanting to move. Spending too long in the beach house has my mind confined; despite my father's renovations, I'm still haunted by raw flashbacks mixed with my favorite memories, both dancing around with each other in a huge, contorted horror clip. Deep down, I must accept it's something I have to talk about, but I can't, not right now, not whilst it's still so very fresh that I can still feel the warm blood and hear the screams. Being here isn't helping either; I feel suffocated. My train of thinking made my heart race.

    I sit up in panic and feel the grains of sand under the palms of my hands. I'm not okay, I think to myself; I look around at the empty beach and try to calm myself down. Feeling like a little boy in need of his mother, tears making their way down, ignoring my urge to stop them.

> *It's okay,*
>> *It wasn't your fault,*

I try taking deep breaths, but it's like I forgot how to breathe.

> *How were you meant to know?*

You ruined everything.

> *Aiden,*
>> *Stop!*
>
> *You got this.*

My feet sinking into the sand, I make my way towards the water until the cold water hits my face, and I finally exhale.

I submerge my whole body into the water to rinse off my negative thoughts.

Feeling completely exhausted and drenched, I make my way back inside, the sand leaving a trail behind me. I have a warm shower, put on some fresh shorts, and jump into bed, falling into a deep sleep.

CHAPTER NINETEEN

AMALA.

I wake up annoyed.

It's the 4th ^{of} July, and everything the three of us planned: brunch at Sarabeths, followed by a Polo match, Kings for the best lobster rolls, Aiden wanted me to meet his best friend Omar and his fiancé Yasmin, finishing the night off with the three of us watching the fireworks. Now, I don't even want to see him.

Zak's loud voice traveled up to my room, the sounds of my dad and Uncle Abdalla laughing. Pushing my feelings to the side, I slide perfectly into my gorgeous white Jonathan Simkhai maxi dress, a perfect length that means I don't have to bother wearing an undertop or tights in this weather. Before I head downstairs, I apply my clear lip gloss and grab my book.

"There's my girl." My father got up from the breakfast table to hug me.

I hug my father a little tighter this morning. I let him squeeze the negativity out of me. Hearing everyone's laughter and seeing the sunshine so bright made me want to have a good day: my blues can wait until tomorrow, I thought.

"Good morning, Red." Zak smiled at me, and so did his black eye.

"I thought I told you to keep this idiot out of trouble." Uncle Abdalla said.

"Impossible, Uncle Abdalla, you know Zak, if he's not the center of attention,"

They all chuckled, "So, what are you kids up to before the event?" Zak shot a look at me; I wasn't sure where Aiden and I stood, especially as I woke up to no messages from him. Amelia messaged asking if I bought my beige dress, but nothing about last night, and I felt lame bringing it up. Just as I'm ready to rule him off, I receive a text,

Aiden: Meet *me on the beach. I'll send you my location.*

I sigh both out of a little relief and annoyance. I swipe to respond to the text, asking him if it's important.

Aiden: *Yes.*

"I'll be back. I'm going to meet my friend, and then we can all grab lunch, perhaps?"

My father looks at me, and I know exactly what he's thinking; I look right back at him to tell him it's okay and not to worry.

The beach is quiet, only the sounds of the ocean whooshing. I take my sandals off because I hate sand in my shoes. I follow the location Aiden sent and walk along the sandy beach until I see him. Tall Aiden, in the far distance, sat scooping the sand in his hands and watching gravity pull the sand back down.

"Aiden," I call his name.

He looks up at me and smiles; he moves over and gestures for me to sit, and I reluctantly sit down about five feet from him, remaining quiet and waiting for him to speak.

"Amala... I..." he's trying to find the right words. "I'm sorry about yesterday; I know it's not what you wanted to hear. I'm so sorry I keep failing to say the right thing. Every time I try telling you, I get nervous, or my mind takes me elsewhere, and being here is making me feel claustrophobic."

I stay quiet, listening to him, and as he talks, he looks straight out at the ocean.

"You..." his phone interrupts us. He picks it up and sees that his father is calling but turns the phone over. "You Amala..." he attempts to continue, but his phone continues to ring again. It's his uncle Z; he looks surprised, "I'm so sorry, this shouldn't take a second."

I tell him to answer it,

"Hey Uncle Z, what's up."

"Wait, what, where?" Aiden's face changes.

"Okay, I'm coming." He says, already jumping up.

"What's going on?" I get up, too.

"My mother...she's in the hospital." He says slowly.

"Oh, my goodness...go," I tell him.

He runs towards his beach house but jolts to a stop, "Amala," he turns around and shouts.

"I'm so sorry; I promise I'll be back."

I nod at him and tell him to let me know how she is. Slumping back down onto the sand and feeling blue again, praying his mother is okay and processing what he was about to say before he answered his uncle's call.

Finally, I headed back home, after watching the ocean hypnotize me, to have lunch with my father, Uncle Abdalla, and Zak. Zak wanted fresh lobster rolls, so we went to Kings for the best rolls on the island. The sun is beaming hot today,

MY CARAMEL

an uncomfortable hot, the type that drains you of your energy. Kings' restaurant is refreshingly cool, with the AC fighting the heat off; everyone is all smiles and festive for the 4th. My father orders for all of us, and I sit there, but I'm entirely somewhere else. An hour has passed by, and I wonder if his mother is okay. I texted him to check in on his mother. I feel Zak's eyes on me, and he mouths, *'Are you okay?'* I smile and nod. Uncle Abdalla talks about how proud he is of us, how he expects big things from me just like my father, and again I smile and nod; my father jumps in and adds, *'Oh, she'll surpass my talent. You should read her work!'* I sink further back into my seat and simply smile and nod. Zak, however, reads my body language and abruptly stands up,

"I need ice cream now, Amala; you wanna go get some?" he looks at me and nods his head to the right for me to follow him, and so I do.

"Looking a little blue today, Red?"

I smile at hearing Red, "I'm okay; the sun is getting to me."

"Let me guess, Aiden is still mad?"

"Zak, you literally have no filter."

"Well, is it true?"

"No, he was about to tell me something, but his mother was taken to hospital, and I'm just a little worried about her."

Zak stays a little quiet, "She'll be fine...why don't you check in on him?"

I nod in response.

"You really like him, don't you."

"Yeah...I do, Zak." Zak didn't deal with awkward situations well, but in some ways, he did. He isn't the type to talk about feelings, but he knew exactly how to be the perfect distraction. My phone buzzes in my pocket, and I rush to it. It's Aiden.

Aiden: *She's going in for an emergency surgery.*

Me: *We'll be making dua. She'll be fine.*

Aiden: *Thanks Amala.*

Me: *Have you eaten?*

Aiden: *Nah, I'm not hungry.*

Me: *How's Amelia?*

Aiden: *She's not herself, she could do with you here...me too.*

My heart swells up; quickly, I respond, telling him I'm on my way.

I've been fortunate enough to have never stepped into a hospital; I've never really had to, never seen anyone pass away or break an arm or anything. The hospital smells strange, like someone masking the scent of death with stale cafeteria food and pie. The nurses and doctors seem to pace back and forth along with families, either waiting on news or results. Everything looks bright white but really dull, all in the same notion: being in a hospital alone is enough to diagnose you with an illness; if it's not depression, it's sadness. Outside the hospital doors is like the Truman Show, and behind it is reality. I don't like being here. It's extremely unsettling; I look around for Aiden and Amelia.

"Amala." I turn around to find Aiden's voice.
"Hey," I say softly. I handed him a bag with food from King's lobster rolls, as we couldn't even eat them together, for him and his father.

"If you guys get hungry."
His smile grew a little.

"Where is Amelia?"
He points in her direction. I walk towards her with her own care package, but she shakes her head and says she's not hungry. I grew sad to see Amelia not quite like Amelia; she rests her head on my shoulders, and Aiden sits next to us. The three of us together on the 4th, but not how we anticipated.

Two hours have passed by, waiting to hear for an update on his mother. The sun breaks through the windows, and I can tell by the color of the sun that it is Asr. Aiden went to pray, and I wait for him to return so I, too, could go pray; as the multi-faith room is tiny, we take turns. When I returned, I saw Aiden and his father talking to the doctors, and they looked serious. Amelia and I wait patiently for them to return, but he doesn't.

Aiden turns to his father and hugs him, sinking into him, and his father embraces him. It looks like a rare moment that I'm intruding on, something beautiful and painfully private. A child, no matter how old, will always be a child to their parents. I look away, giving them their private moment.

"Sweetheart," Mayor Sancar walks over to Amelia. Amelia rushes up to hug her father, too, "She's…" he sighs heavily. "She's going to be okay, thank God."
I feel instant relief and thank God, too.

"You kids should head back to the house; let your mother rest, and we'll see you tomorrow."
Aiden nods and grabs his stuff.

"Oh, and Amala, thank you for the food. I could do with a lobster roll." He smiles at me.

We all head back to the beach house.

CHAPTER TWENTY

AMALA.

We escape from the hospital and head back to Aiden's family's Beach house; it is gorgeous; the back has a porch that wraps itself around the entire backyard overlooking the ocean. The inside smells of fresh paint (Aiden mentioned something about them renovating this year); it also smells like burnt-scented candles. The kitchen is spacious and white; in the middle of the island, someone had placed beautiful lavender flowers that scented the whole room. We walk straight into the living room; it matches the interior of the rest of the house: oak paired gorgeously next to white, huge off-white and beige rug centered in the middle, comfy white couches and flowers that bring everything together.

We were all pretty beat from the melancholy of the hospital and eating way too many lobster rolls that we were slipping into an ultimate food coma, and so we settled on a movie. Some of their belongings were still in storage, like their collection of movies, but Amelia managed to find three DVDs: Ghost, the Scent of a Woman, and Pretty Women.

We select the Scent of a Woman- obviously for Al Pacino. Grabbing enough chips, candy, and soda to regret in twenty years, we all sit under one blanket with Amelia in the middle of us. Aiden shoots a look my way and smiles before Amelia hits play.

One thing for sure is Amelia will re-enact every scene she knows; feeling completely like herself now, she turns to Aiden and grabs him by the shirt, and in complete sync with Al Pacino, she shouts,

"What life? I got no life. I'm in the dark here, you understand…"

Aiden laughs and shouts with her I'm in the dark, I'm in the dark." Suddenly, his face isn't laughing, nor is his voice; he sits up, holding onto his chest, repeating *I'm in the dark*, his breathing rapidly getting heavier. His eyes have gone to a place of fear, "Amala." he whispers; my heart shifts to panic for him. This urge to hold him and hug him takes over, "I can't breathe." he says, grasping for air.

I'm not sure what to do, but I know I need to do something; he needs me. I tell Amelia to go and grab a cup of water. Meanwhile, I attempt to divert his attention to outside…. the air, the stars, and the whoosh of the ocean, going back and forth, but nothing seems to work. I can see streaks of tears hit his shirt as he tries his best to inhale and exhale. We forget the luxury of breathing until it's been poisoned by trauma.

I tell him the story of how I found Mays cupcake world and why it's my favorite place. His eyes glued down at his clenched chest, his deep amber eyes so full of pain and sorrow, I feel his dark shadow cast the room. I continue to tell him my story until, unexpectedly, a faint smile; he slowly gains control of his breathing, standing a little taller. A few moments pass by without any words. We all just sit together in silence. Amelia eventually throws her arms around him, hugging him and squeezing him. I remain at the edge of my seat, replaying the scene in my head, and sadness overcomes me. This isn't something small; whatever Aiden is guarding is destroying him. A million scenarios run around in my head; what really happened that's left him so scared, so paralyzed? Meanwhile, I think about Condé Nast breathing down my neck; this is the story they want, but all I care about is comforting Aiden.

I glance over at Aiden, and I can see his breathing become slow and heavy as he slips into sleep. I get a blanket and place it over him, Amelia holding onto his hand, her face full of concern, a face rarely worn by her but worn twice in one day. I gesture to Amelia to come and take a walk outside.

The air is still warm, encased by humidity, the sky shimmering with stars, the sand soft and grainy under our feet. I hear the crickets faintly, but the whoosh of the ocean pulling back and forth is what sounds the loudest. It's so close to the beach house. I breathe in fresh air and turn to Amelia,

"Are you okay?" I ask.
"Urm, I don't know…worried."
"He's going to be okay."
"I'm not sure; I haven't seen him like this in so long."
I really felt the need to ask her the real story, but I don't think this is the right moment.

CHAPTER TWENTY-ONE

AIDEN.

I wake up to fireworks sizzling and launching into the sky. The colors of red, pink, and purple flash through the window. I sit up and look around; the credits to The Scent of a Woman roll on the TV. I feel dehydrated and disorientated. I get up from the couch to see no Amelia or Amala. Grabbing my phone to call them and I see messages from Omar asking where I am, but I ignore him. I throw on my trainers and head out to the beach to look for Amala.

The fireworks are much louder outside, with bright colors splattering in the sky and distant sounds of laughter. I walk the long stretch of the beach, my feet sinking in every step I take until I see them both. "Aiden," Amala calls my name as she recognizes me even in the dark.

I walk over closer to them. Amelia immediately reads the situation, "I'm going back to the house to check on Dad and stuff." She hugs me before heading back, and I kiss her on her forehead.

It's just us now. Amala and I, there never is a perfect moment, but while we're here under the warm night sky, I feel the need to tell her.

"Amala."

"Yes, Aiden," she says softly, turning her attention to me.

I look at her, and I see the fireworks reflected in her eyes.

"You know, I sat in this very spot and watched the fireworks with Aunt Selene."

"It's really pretty out here." She said.

"About earlier,"

"Aiden, it's okay. You don't have to tell me." She interrupts me.

"No, I want to. I'm sorry it's taken me so long to tell you this." I feel my heart race, but in a good way, in a way that doesn't scare me. How could it? It's Amala...my Amala. I turn to her, and she looks at me, "Amala, I don't know why I've been so afraid to say this, but you mean the world to me; you did the moment I saw you in the green dress and every other moment after that. Everything around you is calm, and I tried challenging it because I believed that I was just a disappointment to you, but I want to do right by you."

She looks up at me, and though it's dark out, I can see her cheeks blush until she finally smiles at me, a smile that consumes her face, eventually mirroring my face. We turn to the sound of fireworks and look up to see a million sparkles of colored gunpowder spread in the sky.

CHAPTER TWENTY-TWO

AMALA.
The scintillating night sky reflects how I feel, sparks of pure magic in the air and sounds of people cheering- just for us, for *Aiden and Amala*. We sat on the beach absorbing the wonder of fireworks, adoring each other's stillness. I was taken aback by what he said; I wasn't sure what to reply with. I've spent a long time thinking about what he had to say to me, but I never really stopped to think about what I wanted to say to him, how he made me feel, or what he brought to my life.

"Aiden?"
"Yes, Amala?"
"Thank you."

He smiled at me and understood my thank you.

The fireworks faded into the night sky, and we both decided to head back to the beach house; we didn't want to be alone for too long, nor did we want to leave Amelia.

"How are you feeling now?" I ask him as we get closer to the house; I can see much more of his face from the lights,

"A little better now I've taken a little off my chest." We walk inside, and Amelia is on the phone with her father. I circle back to our conversation, "What else is sitting on your chest?"

He takes a deep breath in, "So much that you won't look at me the same."

I look confused, "Aiden, that's impossible." We move towards the living room, away from Amelia. "Aiden, I know it's something related to your aunt."

I see that I've struck a nerve with him as his face changes, "God, Amala, why didn't you just come to me instead of asking around and hearing lies."

My face changes, too. I feel my brows arch down, "I did, Aiden, I DID. I tried so many times, but you don't trust me!"

His face is hit with shock, "What! Of course, I trust you…It's not about trust. I tried, believe me, but it's not easy."

"Aiden, I understand whatever it is is difficult, but you can't want me and not trust me. That's not something I want!"

He looks at me, his eyes wide with sadness. "Stop, that's not fair."

"Aiden," I sigh, "Maybe you're right, but this can't be healthy."

CHAPTER TWENTY-THREE

AIDEN.

"No, you're just afraid, Amala. You have been since I met you." I snapped back.

"Don't turn this on me being afraid; you are allowing something that happened to you to haunt you; it's ruining you, Aiden. Look at you; you can't even sleep most nights. You can't even get through a movie and what was yesterday about? When were you the type to start fights?" Her words felt so loud that something of bravery and realization clicked for me. Perhaps this has turned me into a coward. I haven't been able to move past it or see past it, and the worry of turning like my mother scares me more than what had actually happened.

I pause, gathering my thoughts. I take a seat because this isn't going to be easy.

I begin my story from the very beginning, how Aunt Selene was my favorite human in the whole world.

"Growing up, my mother suffered from episodes of severe depression. We weren't able to get her out of bed despite how much she loved God despite how much she prayed; it was her test, just like what I'm about to tell you is my test. Some people might believe that God failed her, but in the end, we're all responsible for our own actions. My mother never reached out for help. Even though we tried to offer it, she continued to turn it down. When her father passed away, things went from worse to impossible; she would spend her days crying for hours, not wanting to leave, not wanting to see people. If she wasn't crying, she was arguing with everyone and then crying about how ungrateful she was, that God has given her everything, a loving husband, a house, two beautiful children, but she couldn't see past her pain." I take another deep breath,

"My Aunt Selene was always there, every meltdown, every argument, and every scary moment. She was always there to comfort us. On that night Aunt Selene died, my mother was particularly bad…I begged my father not to leave us alone. Only he could comfort her, but he ignored me and told me he wouldn't be long. Amelia and I were watching Goodwill Hunting that night, and halfway through, my Aunt Selene came over to join us... after I had begged her. My mother was upstairs the entire time napping…so we thought. I don't know. The entire day, I had felt his unnerving feeling in the pit of my stomach, and in that instant, my stomach was in knots, and I couldn't shake it off. I quietly went to check on my mother, and there she stood,"

I felt my face get hot as I was so deep into my memories,

"She stood there with a gun to her, and panic above rational took over, and I called out to my mother in fear," Time is measured by circumstance because a second can either be too long or you could blink, and someone is lying dead. "I ran over to grab the gun from her, but we ended up in a tug; the harder I pulled, the angrier she pulled. That night I hardly recognized my mother, and it terrified the shit out of me. After that, everything happened so fast, and Aunt Selene wasn't meant to be standing there when my finger pulled the trigger. I see her shudder, and I drop the gun and run over to my Aunt, to the woman, who, in the absence of my mother, taught me what love is and taught me to be the man I am. I grabbed her, not knowing what to do, my hands covered in her blood, and at the time, I had no idea what I had done; there was too much adrenaline and screams that drowned reality out. My aunt kept telling me, *it's okay, it's okay,* and sometimes that's all I could hear her say: it's *okay, Aiden, it's okay honey, I'm okay*...she read her Shahada quietly, and remained smiling at me, I kept shaking her to wake up, but she wasn't responding I..." My eyes start to well up again. My mother wasn't meant to be standing there with a gun, my father wasn't meant to leave us, and I shouldn't have leaped at my mother, who was holding a loaded gun. "I sat holding my aunt's body until I started feeling the warmth leave her, and that's when the consciousness of my actions sunk in, and I looked around, and all I saw was blood splattered on the walls, on the ceiling, on me, on my face, on my hands. I didn't want to leave her. Shortly after, Amelia heard the screams and called our father. He and Uncle Z rushed over; I think they were over within minutes of the call. After that, all I remembered was that I was sat on the floor where my aunt was and watched everything in a trance, there but not there."

I believe shock is the eraser of logic.

"My father dealt with it the way he dealt with everything: politics first and then family. He didn't want to explain to the Ali's that his son had just killed Selene, nor did he want me to get dragged through the court on involuntary manslaughter, so he made it all go away. By telling the Ali's she committed suicide knowing they would cover that up."

I sigh, shaking my head; I finally look up at Amala, her face stunned like a deer in headlights, her deep brown eyes wide open and glazed with sadness. I didn't expect her to say anything, just to listen and understand the rawest part of me… and she did.

Amelia came in and hugged me. I feel as if I'm finally allowed to exhale, and someone has irrevocably lifted the weight off my chest. Nothing can now stand in the way of me, in the way of us. Moments passed, sat in silence; the tension in the room slowly started fading, and after all that, the only thing that is on my mind is food.

"I'm ordering Pizza; you guys want anything else."
"Thank God, I was getting so hungry I thought I would have to go to sleep starving." Amelia cried out. Amala and I look at each other and burst into laughter, forgetting the immensity of tonight: my sweet Amelia, my savior.

"So, when you guys get married, who will you guys have as your best man/maid of honor because you do know there is only one of me?" Amelia asked, and I could see Amala blush, looking away at the idea of us until we both, as if in a race, said, "You'll be mine!"

"The highest bid wins."

"I'll take you anywhere you want," I quickly offer.

"Amelia, sweetie, I will buy you whatever you want to eat."

"Done, sorry Aiden, you lose."

I roll my eyes, "like I had a chance."

The doorbell rings, the pizza arrives, and we all sit on the floor, having bizarre conversations and laughing. I take a mental picture of the three of us and smile.

CHAPTER TWENTY-FOUR

AMALA.

My 4th July weekend, despite heightened emotions and truth revealing itself in all aspects, especially of the heart, will forever be written down as my most remembered. Over the weekend, I got to know all of Aiden, the rawest and sweetest. A mask, once removed, is like oxygen hugging you, liberation breaking through. Over the past few days, having observed this new Aiden is like watching a swimmer finally learning how to relax and float above water instead of drowning, and as I watch him, observing him silently, I notice myself feeling lighter. I, too, have learned to float just by watching him, a beautiful new swimmer.

But yesterday will be my favorite memory to look back on, one filled with the kind of animation that's laced with magic and spark. The stuff I read about and see in all my favorite 80s/90s movies. I don't think people expect me, the quiet, afraid-of-everything Muslim girl from New York, ever to view romance through the lens of great hits like Jamie from A Walk to Remember, Laney from She's All That, or even Jane in A Bronx Tale, the start of a forever that's so wholesome it may be accused of being innocently cliché, and that's okay. Love isn't about grand fireworks and epic gestures; love is simple, and it's forever: like leaning over and unlocking the car door for your person. And yesterday was just that, no grand fireworks or epic gestures; it was simple, but oh my, was it perfect.

I met with Aiden and Amelia at Sarabeth's for brunch. We shared a stack of pancakes, of course, I ordered the halloumi and Hash with a lemon iced tea because the sun was wonderfully bright (as opposed to the day before it). Amelia ordered eggs and avocado, and Aiden got eggs with a side of hashbrowns. After lunch, we strolled around to digest our food; Amelia was already talking about our dinner plans while I quietly watched Aiden. I contemplated the idea of us and smiled secretly to myself, the boy who caught my attention from across the ballroom... Aiden Hakeem Sancar.

MY CARAMEL

After lunch, Aiden mysteriously drove us to an unknown location. The drive didn't take long, but Amelia was adamant we were going to a maze. But yesterday Aiden thought of everything, learning and inspiring himself from all my favorite books. Arriving, outside a cute little ranch, Aiden had called ahead and even pulled in a favor from Ms. Mimi Margaux. The three of us took the horses out but with a little caveat: instead of riding on the open fields, Aiden got them to agree to ride their horses on the beach, and like many things in my *'sheltered'* life, riding horses on the beach was like something I had never experienced before. The sun was cheering us on from behind, and the horses galloping incredibly free-spirited, freckles of water splashing on our legs, and best of all, Aiden smiling…floating freely. Every layer of the day got better, and as the day went on, the heaviness of the day before only seemed further and further. The horse riding had built up our appetite, so we made our way to the restaurant. The food took its time as the restaurant was busy, so we played a game to pass the time, 'try to guess the person's story.' The game is simple: we scan around the restaurant to people watch, people on their first date, the cheating husband, the breakup meal, and the endless versions of stories; Amelia even got one right. There was a married man having dinner with his eighteen-year-old nanny, and the wife came just at the climax when they were kissing. When we asked her how she knew, and she finally confessed, she told us the nanny was in the grade above her and often bragged about dating a married man.

I wanted to ask Aiden so many times throughout the day about how he was doing after offloading such a huge secret, but then I saw him laughing and smiling, so I remained quiet. I didn't want to ruin it by bringing up his aunt. The night led us back to his father's beach house; his mother was finally discharged and returned home. The mayor and his wife were sat outback looking out onto the beach. The sun was making its way down, and everything had turned a beautiful, subtle blue color. It felt like a very private moment, and I insisted on leaving and getting back to my father and uncle Abdalla's five-hour card game…and Zak. Aiden's mother called me over and demanded I stay for ice cream, and so I did. Aiden, Amelia, the Mayor, his wife, and I all sat outback eating ice cream and watching the sky turn from different shades of blue until, eventually, it had reached midnight blue. His mother thanks me for staying and hugs me goodbye; Amelia hugs me goodbye a little longer, knowing she'll be returning to space camp in a few days. The Mayor joked around, thanking me for keeping his kids entertained whilst he was busy with his wife, and then left was Aiden; I felt my stomach flutter thinking about him and his smile; *God,* it made me dance inside. He drove me home and walked me to my door, and he looked at me and said, 'Tomorrow May, we'll see each other tomorrow.' He waited for my father to open the door and gave him salaam; my father had his eyebrow raised until they both started diving in about football and the Giants.

My father asked me about my day, and my face lit up. He handed me a letter, *'from your mother,'* he said, *'it arrived this morning.'* I hugged him with joy and ran upstairs. I wanted to get ready for bed and be comfy before reading the letter. I did my four-step skincare routine, threw on a hoody, and climbed into bed. I opened the letter and read,

Dear my sweet Amala,

Oh, how I miss you too! The weather here is beautiful, you would have loved it here, a dream writing spot. I can imagine your father looking lost without me; make sure he's taking his vitamins whilst I'm not there. My Amala finally likes a boy; I'm sad that I'm not there to advise you in person. We could have gone to Mays Cupcake World and spoken all about this mystery boy.
As I'm not there, ask yourself this Amala,
1. *What's his relationship like with God?*
2. *Is he kind and good?*

3. *How does he make you feel? Safe or unease?*

Sweetie, I'll let you in on a little secret, I never felt electric or felt the sparks when I was getting to know your father. I was as afraid as you probably are, but I decided to focus on the type of man he was, how I felt about him, and where he placed God in his life. I then prayed and asked God if he was good for me and. God had placed this feeling of security in me, and I knew from then on he was it for me. The electric and the sparks came afterward after we were married, and they've been going solid for twenty-eight years now.

It's not about what you solely feel because emotions are determined by moments; it's about placing your trust in God and what he's planned for you. Rely only on God Amala, ask him, and the rest will unfold just how it's meant to. Just trust it, sweetheart, even if the outcome isn't what you hoped. I hope this helps you in your decision, but I do hope it's the tall, handsome Aiden.

Write back to me and tell me all about your 4th of July weekend. I hope it was filled with love and joy.

With love always
Momma

MY CARAMEL

I held the letter close to me and smiled, running through the checklist in my head,

1. *What's his relationship like with God?*

    He adores Islam and understands that God is always a prayer away. He never misses a prayer despite where we are; he'll find a place to pray.

2. *Is he kind and good?*

    He is the absolute kindest; his relationship with his sister is what I love most.

3. *How does he make you feel? Safe or unease?*

    He makes me feel brave. Brave to do all the things I secretly want, but I'm too afraid of.

Quickly, I decided to throw on my abaya and hijab and pray to my lord for clarity and guidance and to keep me away from harm. If Aiden is for me, then allow us to make it halal, and if not, then … my heart flickered a little at the next sentence, *'If he's not meant for me, keep him away'* as if my ears couldn't bear to hear those words but as my mother said, *'Rely only on God Amala ask him and the rest will unfold just how it's meant to. Trust it even if the outcome isn't what you hoped,'* Which is what I will do. Aiden and I have never crossed a line with each other, and just because he told me how he feels, it doesn't give me or us a license to act any other way. My father told me a long time ago that even a fiancé doesn't mean anything; nothing will ever be as permanent as marriage; everything else is just words.

I'm nothing but Aiden's friend until I'm something permanent…something forever. Until then, I place my trust in God and focus on my writing. As for Condé Nast, I guess I'm fired because I can't imagine sharing that story with the world and have it break him.

CHAPTER TWENTY-FIVE

AIDEN.

Today, Amala's tribute piece on Aunt Selene is coming out, and I'm crowded with anxiousness and excitement to read about my aunty through the words of a beautiful writer... my beautiful writer. We arrived back in Manhattan not long ago. I kinda missed the city, but I think I'll miss the beach more, especially after the weekend I've had. My father gave me today off. On the drive home, we spoke about many things, even briefly about that night, the night Aunt Selene died. He apologized in his own 'dad' way, but that was enough for me; it wasn't his fault she died, and I couldn't hold him responsible for my mother's actions either. At some point, we have to learn to stop playing the what-if game. Amelia decided to have the Monday off, too, and came back to Manhattan with us before heading back to camp in a few days; I'm glad she has.

The worst part of the trip is unpacking; I finally unload the car and throw everyone's bags into their rooms. I help my mother into bed as she's still recovering. My mother and I still need more time before I can ever speak to her about the past; she's much more fragile than I am. I'm okay waiting for her to come to terms with what happened that night and how it was all her fault, but if I told her the truth now, it may just push her over the edge again.

AMALA: *tonight at 6 pm, meet me by Pier 35...bring Amelia.*

I unlock my phone and reply to her. I grab my dirty clothes, and as I make my way to the laundry room, I pass by Amelia's room and see she has just tossed her bag to the corner of her room next to a pile of clothes.

"Amelia, you hungry?" I ask her.

Her eyes widen, "always Aiden, I worry I'm pregnant!"

I frown at her, and she quickly snaps back, "Relax, I'm obviously not. I just have a high metabolism, don't get jealous."

"Anyway, you wanna watch a movie and order pizza?"

She looks at me suspiciously, "What did you do?"

"What do you mean?" I ask, confused.

"Well, normally, I have to beg you to watch a movie with me."

"Yeah, well, you haven't been here so…"

"Alright, don't get emotional on me…no pineapples, and I'm picking the movie but nothing Al Pacino…because, well, you've ruined that for me."

I look at her in shock, trying to keep a straight face but failing to, and end up laughing, "Oh, you deserve what I'm about to do." I sprint over and suffocate her with my dirty laundry. She coughs and kicks me out of the way, "You are so disgusting, Aiden, and for that, we're watching Sixteen Candles." She throws my dirty socks back at me.

I stand laughing, regaining my breath; I miss having her in the house; I can't wait for camp to end, to have her lighten the house up again. I wonder how Amala doesn't get bored on her own, but then it explains why she's constantly got her head in a book; she creates a world for herself.

Amelia and I agree to put our shit away before we sit to watch Sixteen Candles and eat a whole box of Joe's pizza; I throw everything in the laundry room and change my bed sheets. I can hear Amelia dancing to *Snow on the Beach* by Taylor Swift, and I roll my eyes, "Amelia," I yell, "take that shit off."

"I know you're a closet Taylor fan, Aiden." She yells back.

"Hurry, or I'm not getting that pizza."

"Fine!"

I laugh to myself; I throw my pillow on my bed and step back. My bed looks kind of okay. I mean nothing as close as what it looks like when my mother does it or when she pays someone to. I shrug my shoulders and grab my phone. I order the pizza and check in on Amala.

I ask her how her writing is getting on, and she replies back immediately,

Amala: *OK, I feel good about it, so that's something.*

Me: *I can't wait to read it…no pressure.*

Amala: *You're not making this easy.*

Me: *I'm sorry, I'll leave you to work your magic, May.*

I tell Amelia to load the movie, and I grab the pizza and soda; we sit back, watching Samantha Baker lose her shit because everyone forgot her birthday. Every time the scene comes up when Jake Ryan kisses Samantha, Amelia covers both of our eyes, one hand across my eyes and another on hers.

"Aiden, are you to Amala what Jake Ryan is to Samantha?" She asked.

I'm pretty sure she's asking if Amala is my *'girlfriend,'* I take a minute before answering the question, "One day I hope to, but not as my girlfriend as my…wife."

She looks at me awhile before responding, "Good, and I was just checking; you can't do that to Amala, not like what you did to… you know who."

"It's not like that with Amala, she's…"

"Different." Amelia cuts me off.

"Yeah."

"Be original, Aid."

I sigh because I know the point Amelia is trying to make, but what she doesn't understand is that "She's all I think about Amelia; it's not the same, believe me."

"It better not be; I love Amala."

I smile at her response; Amelia isn't an overly emotional person. To her, punching me in the gut is only her way of telling me she loves me. I also know she cares a whole lot for Amala. I'm not sure what I'm supposed to do next, but whatever it is, I want Amala there with me.

"Anyway, you ready to leave?" I ask, looking at the time.

She nods her head, and we pray Asr before leaving to meet Amala at Pier 35.

I see Amala swinging slowly back and forth, watching the Manhattan skyline as it starts to light up. I wish I could go to the same places she goes to and see life through her and with her. Amelia runs up to her and sits next to her on the swing.

"May."

She turns to look at me.

"Aiden."

A smile takes over her face and mine.

"Why have we been summoned?"

"I wanted you to be the first to read this."

She hands over an article titled, '*My love and my soul mate.*'

I look up at her to ask what it is.

"I thought as I'm getting fired-"

"Wait, what! You're getting fired?" I abruptly interrupt her.

"Not important right now, I decided to submit the tribute in anyway, and I didn't want the world to read about your aunty before you do…before the both of you." She says.

I take a deep breath in.

"Read it to us," I ask her. I see her cheeks turn a soft pink.

"Oh, I would rather you." She says softly.

I hand her the article back. "I want to hear your words from you…please?" I ask gently.

She smiles and clears her throat, "My love and my soulmate, a tribute to Selene Ali by Amala Zidane."

My Love and My Soul Mate, A Tribute to Selene Ali
By Amala Zidane

Love is the first language a child recognizes; the warmth of a hug, the smell of his mother, the softness of kisses, and the comfort of slow back rubs when they cry are all dialects of love, the only intrinsic language a child needs to learn. Love, not words, is what everyone experienced with Selene, specifically her family. She was the epitome of comfort and compassion to her family, and though she never birthed children of her own, her niece and nephew were only an extension of her; she coated their lives with the highest saturations of color and luxury, the luxury of laugher and play.

Throughout Mrs. Ali's life, she managed three prosperous charities to aid young children and families in war-torn countries such as Palestine, Afghanistan, and Syria; she lived her life to help others. She was a horrible cook but a wonderful baker; she became well known for her perfect oatmeal chocolate chip cookies; it came as no surprise her cookies were served at the State dinner. She hand-made three hundred cookies at the request of the First Lady. She later told her husband the reason she stayed back and handmade them, instead of getting the Whitehouse staff to help, was because there was a trust placed upon her to deliver three hundred handmade cookies, and she had to see that each one was perfect. Not because she was a perfectionist but simply because it was within her character to ensure the trust placed in her was bestowed and delivered.

To define Selene Ali is to say she was an emblem worthy of emulation; she knew the secret to pure characteristics and thus experienced every form of love, romantic love, friendship, sisterly, parents, and love from a child.
Her husband quoted in his interview, "When asked if I was her soulmate, she laughed and replied you're my one and only love, but Aiden is my soulmate. He has my whole heart; he just sees right through me."

Selene taught her family in both life and death that it'll be okay, life will be okay, maybe not today or tomorrow, but it'll be okay. Mrs. Selene Ali, though no longer here, leaves behind a wealth of knowledge, and she will be remembered for her love, if nothing else.

Amala finishes reading. She folds the article up and looks up at me, my eyes glazed, and there is a gleam of silence…of appreciation for her words. I couldn't describe how much it means to me to hear my Aunt honored; I begin to think back to the time Amala first told me about having to write this, and panic overwhelmed me, and now we're standing here, and I think God why didn't I believe in her, in her talent, I mean I did but why did I jump to the worst conclusion. I feel dumb having not trusted her to do the right thing; how could I have questioned Amala, my Amala?

"So?" She's staring at me with her big brown eyes, how I adore her eyes. Moments like this, I forget Amelia is with us, or anyone for that matter. "Amala, you are truly and utter beautiful…your writing…I mean." I see a smile creep up on her face, "Seriously, May you really outdone yourself."

Amelia chimes in, "Amala, you really captured my aunt; thank you so much for writing this because up until now, I feel as if all anyone knew was that she was some socialite who died in an accident."

She smiles at our compliments, but I can see the joy in her eyes; I know damn well she's dancing inside and that tonight she'll most like not be able to sleep as her first written piece is published, despite its significance to the rest of the world, to me it means the world and so does the writer.

CHAPTER TWENTY-SIX

AMALA.

Last night, I scarcely slept. Excitement engulfed me, and I know it's not a front page or a story in the New Yorker or The Times, and though it'll be in the corner somewhere, towards the back, it's still my work published, and I can't help but feel the excitement. I feel a natural inclination to do better and push myself. I want to write something new or even set up my own blog until I hear back from other jobs, particularly because I got fired from the internship. Though I have three glorious weeks of summer left, I want to get ahead and complete all my reading for my first semester back of my final year.

Tonight, another extravagant charity dinner awaits us in Manhattan; the city lights, the clothes, the way money makes everything glisten, even our sight. I'm in high spirits today, and the idea of dressing up and having the boy you like watch you from across the room, ignoring everyone except you, melts me like never before. To stand in the middle of the ballroom and dream the night away, lost in a reverie of Aiden taking my hand and gently placing the other around my waist, and we slow dance, envy running amuck around the room of women wishing they could stand and dance with the most handsome man in the entire ballroom. With Aiden Hakeem Sancar, the man they wish they had the privilege to know, I can't wait for God's permission to allow me to experience him up close in the comfort of his arms.

Every event gives Aiden an excuse to shop for a new suit or tie or Loro Pianas, but I don't mind entertaining his excuses because I'm in need of a new dress, too. I slide my feet into my New Balances and head out to meet them both at May's Cupcake World. I get off the subway a little earlier because I want to pass by the newsstands and see my name printed in the magazine; I walk up to the one outside the subway and rummage through the rack, ignoring the New Yorker for the first time, I find mine and flick through the pages until eventually I see it, *'by Amala Zidane'* I smile to myself and walk to Mays as if floating on air.

"Amala!" Amelia screams.

We embrace each other in a hug.

"For you." Aiden hands me a gift. It's wrapped in brown paper. It looks too big and too thin to be a book. I tore it open, and to my surprise, he framed my written piece for me.

He smiles, and I capture his smile...his perfect, wholesome smile: "I love it, thank you!"

He clears his throat, "shall we, ladies?"

"Cupcake and coffee first," Amelia called out.

"Oh, I'm with her," I respond, already knowing what I want.

Coffee in hand, the three of us take 5th Avenue and shop around for dresses for Amelia and me and a tie for Aiden. Luckily, there are no restrictions or themes of such for tonight's party because though I had become lucky for the Regency Era charity, the restriction places a psychological block on you, and all you find are dresses that aren't suitable for the set theme.

I glance over at Aiden discreetly; I can't help but wonder when I will know when I will get God's permission. My mother told me it's a feeling to just go about life as normal, and things will fall into place, but then, what happens after I get the feeling? Aiden and I already know each other, and I'm not one to date around either; what if he finds that boring or his expectations of me are different from what I hope? What if he expects me to be his girlfriend? I close my eyes briefly and shake my head. This is exhausting. How do other girls do this?

We arrive outside our first shop. Amelia sees a dress she likes, and we walk into a cute little boutique with dresses that are beautiful, not old lady dresses but classic one-of-a-kind pieces.

"This for sure," Amelia called out, grabbing a gorgeous powder blue dress. "I'm going to try this on, guys."

"Okay, we'll be out here," Aiden replies to her.
While we wait for Amelia to try her dress on, I gaze at all the other dresses to see if anything catches my eye. They are all stunning, but my flawed theory is that if it doesn't grab my attention, then I don't really want it. I know it's flawed, but I hate too many options; it hurts my head. Amelia comes out to show us the dress; she twirls for us and pretends to be a runway model. That is what I love about Amelia. She is so full of life that being around her, you're infected with joy; she keeps the people around her alive, especially Aiden.

Amelia has Aiden's smile, too, but not his jokes... luckily. I sincerely love that despite being a teenager, she is incredibly mature.

"I love it."

Aiden nods, "May we leave now."

"Aiden, don't rush me now."

"Mils, please, you know I hate shopping."

She rolls her eyes at him, "You're literally finding any excuse to go buy something new,"

Aiden darts his attention at me briefly, "I have shit to get; anyway, are you done yet?"

Amelia ignores her brother's remarks entirely, "Did you find a dress, Amala?"

I shake my head.

"You should try the lavender right over there," she pointed to the distance.

"I'll check it out."

"You won't like it," Aiden says, completely sure of himself.

"How do you know?" I ask him.

"I know you, it's too bold for you."

"What makes you so sure you know me?"

"I do..."

"Okay, I'm done," Amelia says, holding her new purchase.

"Well, that was easy," I say.

We continue walking around in the sweaty, humid heat and jump from store to store to get relief from the cool air conditioning inside. Aiden locates a gentlemen's store with multiple suits and hundreds of shades of ties; I see one that instantaneously clasps my line of vision: light navy tie with tiny detailing, nothing flamboyant yet, against a beige suit that will make heads turn.

"This one, Aiden!" I picked the tie-up.

He observes the tie as I hold it up to him, and we turn to face the mirror. I can't help but notice us side by side. I've never seen myself side by side with any boy before. I feel as if I'm in a Nicholas Sparks' novel.

"I think I'll take it, thanks May."

The woman in the store wraps his tie up for him. We leave the cool store to return to the hot streets, and it is only me left on the list: a dress for tonight's charity dinner. We've walked up and down Millionaires' Row, and I can feel my stomach rumble, my body burning all the calories from this morning. The dress is far from my mind now; my mind is filled with billboards of food. My appetite has taken over, and all I see are food trucks, even coffee shops, anything with food. I try to convince myself that once I find a dress, I'll be rewarded with food. I can sit and relish my food. The need to buy a dress slowly disappears; sushi, noodles, and fries all take over. Images of clothes made out of fries pop into my mind; I wonder if this is what it's like to be Amelia, but just as I'm about to give up, Aiden yells, "Hold up," He stops dead in his tracks. "I think I've got it."

I look at what he's looking at from outside the boutique. I see the prettiest midnight blue dress, and I follow Aiden inside. He has already asked one of the staff members to take a new one out in my size. He insists that I try it on, and I don't argue with him; I just let it be and appreciate the moment. The woman places the dress in the changing room; I run my hand down the dress, feeling the organza. I slip into the dress, smiling to myself. I step out to show them, and he smiles immediately. Wasting no time, I head back into the changing room to purchase my new dress. The woman who assisted us earlier,

"The dress looked beautiful on you." She says, handing me my dress, already packed and wrapped.

"Thank you, but I'm yet to pay for it."

"It's already been taken care of."

I turn to look at Aiden, "can we eat now?" he asks.

"Yes, please." I smile.

Charity Dinner

My father and I head in, but as soon as he sees his friends, he kisses me on the cheek, rushing straight to them, and I'm left witnessing the ball by myself...once again. I adjust my dress before trying to find my only two friends; I hear from the crowd behind ostentatiously call out *'Mayor Sancar.'* My head immediately turns to the sound of his surname, and I look up to see him first. Standing tall from across the room, smiling, just as I envisioned, as I hoped, and his smile encapsulated my feelings. He wore the tie I picked out for him, a handsome shade that matches my dress; I stay standing watching him from across the room and feel myself falling in love with him, or perhaps I'm high on the prosperity of my article.

"Miss Zidane." An older man approaches me.

"Yes," I responded curiously.

"Ah, wonderful; I wanted to thank you in person for the wonderful article you wrote on Selene."

"Oh, my pleasure, I'm glad you liked it." I continue to stare at him discreetly, wondering who he is.

"Well, I have an opportunity for you if you're interested."

"Yes, of course." I try not to sound too eager.

"Wonderful. Come by my office tomorrow so we can discuss this further; my assistant," he points to the woman on his right, "will give you the details of the meeting."

I smile and nod desperately, trying to conceal my excitement and curiosity.

"It was lovely meeting you, Miss Zidane."

"Please, Amala and likewise Mr...." as he didn't introduce himself.

"Oh, forgive me, dear, Mr. Emir Hassan Al-Kurd Ali." Internally, my jaw dropped the father of Selene, the billionaire himself. I pass over my details to his assistant, and they both walk off; I wait for them to be out of my line of vision to completely let myself go, releasing the reigns of my smile, visions only bestowed upon dreamer's rush to my head thoughts and ideas thrill my mind of new and exciting possibility. I look around me to share this news with someone, but I'm left standing by myself. The thought of Aiden makes its way past the excitement and thrill. I look across the ballroom to discover him again, but I cannot seem to find him until I feel his essence behind me.

"I believe you're looking for me, ma'am." I turn around to face him.

"Might I ask what has taken you so long?" I get into character, trying to keep a straight face.

"My apologies, ma'am. I've been rather foolish, you see."

"Foolish?"

"Yes, it's taken me a while to realize I care deeply and fondly for this woman I have the pleasure to accompany."

"Oh, who is this woman?"

"She," he lets out a little smile, "is a sight for sore eyes."

"Pray to tell who this magnificent woman is?"

"I'm staring right at her."

"Is it me?" Amelia says at the perfect timing.

Aiden and I break from whatever moment we were caught up in. I know he feels the tension between us, but for the first time, I feel perhaps what he's feeling, and I'm not sure what I should do. He invites me to his table to meet his father again. His father is looking tired, and his mother is still recovering at home. Aiden's Uncle Z is here, too. He walks towards me with a kind face, "Amala, your piece," he places his hand on his chest, "is wonderfully written. I know my wife would have loved it…thank you."

"Thank you, Mr. Sancar…I'm glad you liked it."

"Loved it."

He looks over at Aiden and then at the two of us together and back at Aiden and smirks,

"Look after this one, Kiddo." He says, patting Aiden on his back, and walks away.

An older woman taps on her glass to grab everyone's attention. We all turn to face the front of the ballroom. My father makes eye contact with me, and I excuse myself and walk towards my father's table. Uncle Z, the Mayor, and a few others take the stage to address or make a speech about something related to the charity, to which I wholly feel oblivious. I find myself looking at Aiden from across the room,

"Feels magical, doesn't it?" A girl approaches me from behind.

I turn to face her. She looks familiar, but I can't quite place my finger on it, "Hi." I reply, looking at her confused.

"Hi." She sits in the empty chair next to me. "He makes you feel so special, right?"

"Who?" I ask.

"Aiden." She says.

I look at her again and realize she's Aiden's *'girl friend.'* "Leave while you can, believe me when I tell you, he'll get bored. Even a pretty girl like you isn't enough."

I look at her in denial. She can see it on my face, too.

"Let me guess, you think you're different; he's even brought you gifts." She says, and I look down at my dress. "He's invited you to meet his parents."

I remain quiet.

"Next, he'll ask you to take it a step further, and when you turn him down, he'll move on."

I clear my throat before responding to her, "Be that as it may, we are nothing but good friends." My mother always warned me against women with salacious tongues, and if she had my best interest, I sincerely believe her approach would have been more earnest rather than sneering. Moreover, how I feel is a private matter between my heart and me, secrets only my heart can withhold or understand. She threw me a half smile, which fell on the floor along with the rest of the dust. I look back over at Aiden, and he's waving his phone up in the air, wiggling it about, gesturing me to check my phone.

Aiden: *Was that who I thought it was?*
Me: *Yes.*
Aiden: *What did she want?*
Me: *Want to go for a walk and talk about it?*
Aiden: *Coming over now.*

Watching him walk over, his body language is serious. I notice how he stands a little taller when he's stressed or frustrated. I stand up just before he approaches my table; I don't believe a word his former lady friend said because jealousy is a friend of anger; anger alone clenches the ability to annihilate the sanest of person, let alone an individual scorned by love.

"So, what did she want?" he cut straight to the chase.

"In a nutshell, she warned me against you."

To my surprise, he laughs, "What, what about me?

"Implying that you get bored easily and have a tendency to move on."

His face crunches up to my statement he did not like what I said or that she said that.

"Amala, that is not me; please tell me you don't believe her."

"I don't, Aiden," I say without blinking.

Relief occupies his face, "what did you say to her?"

"I told her it doesn't matter because we're just…friends." I immediately regret my words. I should have known he would misconstrued what I said; I can see it all over his face.

"Just friends?" he asks with a tone of high disappointment. "Jeez, thanks, Amala."

Before I could intervene to plead my case, he walked away, "Aiden, wait." I try and call out.

I'm compelled to explain why I said what I did, and it's not what he thinks. I make my way towards him, but by the time I reach him, I'm flooded with the voice of his former friend; doubts flickered in my mind; he *is a guy after all; he was talking to me while he was with her,* I hesitate to approach him the more her voice floats in my mind, *Is this God's sign?* I pause. This *is crazy,* I think to myself. The mention of God starts to erase all the fog, her voice lost in the crowd, and logic makes its way to me as if a relief package; I begin to think to myself, *has he ever tried anything?* No, *is he good? Yes, do you feel safe?* Yes, then that is all that matters.

"Aiden, stop…please."

He turns around, his face serious like a sky before heavy rain with no trace that it was ever a beautiful blue; he remains quiet. "I'm sorry; I know what I said upset you, but I didn't feel that I owed her an explanation of us."

"And what is that, Amala? What is us?"

Again, I pause. I know he's clinging on to every word; I try searching for the right words.

"You can't say it, can you." "Why can't you say it? You think it was easy for me?"

"If you shush for a second, then perhaps I could tell you." he loosens up a little, dismissing the tension, "You know I care for you, Aiden. I don't need to say anymore."

"Sometimes you do."

"It took you time, and this is all new to me."
I hear him sigh, I look up at him; the cloud has cleared from his face, and nothing but the beautiful sky is in sight.
"Aiden?"
    "Yes Amala?"
I smile graciously.
"What?"
    "Nothing."
I continue to smile.

CHAPTER TWENTY-SEVEN

AMALA.

After the dinner, the three of us make a stealth getaway while the rest of the ball mundanely reels around the same tedious boardroom conversations. Ingenuine laughter crowds the room. I take one last look before leaving with Aiden and Amelia; I wonder the reason why I view them as boring; perchance, I have no interest in their conversations. I see no magic here as I do under the judiciously adorned night sky; the truth is there is no denying the starry night; if you stare at it intrinsically, you bear witness to all the layers of billions of years of perplexing wisdom and ethereal beauty. The night sky was decorated with sparkling soldiers spread and scattered across the firmaments, pitching their tents and watching over us through the dark night sky like a lighthouse guarding the obscure sea. Did you ever wonder that the sky, too, bears witness to us, to all it sees, but it never fails to follow its command to guard us despite how much we fail? The night sky, in one breath, eviscerates the discomfort out of us because it's something that profoundly belongs solely to God.

We take the subway in our dressy attire; though the sun had long set, it refused to take the heat with her. Instead, she left with water from the Hudson River, leaving us with humidity. I didn't mind it. I love long, hot summer nights; to me, it feels like living in all my favorite movies. We have no set direction of where we want to go; we figured everything makes sense from May's Cupcake World. However, suddenly, Aiden is struck with an idea, and a mischievous smile crosses his face.

"Okay, trust me on this one." He says, throwing his hands up and down, emphasizing the trust. Both Amelia and I look at him intently to continue telling us his brilliant plan.

"Yasmin and Omar are at Coney Island with Omar's younger brother."

"Ew, Coney Island," Amelia shouts out.

MY CARAMEL

"Come on, it's your last night before you head back!"
I look at Amelia and raise my eyebrows, "I mean, it'll be fun, plus it's dark out, so it'll be empty." Aiden and I both attempt our puppy eyes to convince Amelia.

"Urgh, fine! But I want a bagel first because today's food was so whack."
"Amelia, it was a charity dinner!" Aiden says, laughing.

"Okay, so dinner is implied. Why do they always have to serve oysters? It's so damn salty."
"Chill, sis, we'll get you some food," Aiden smirks. He leans back, and his eyes land on me, his face still smiling, damn it's infectious. My smile creeps in, and I shake my head at him.

The subway at this time is still full of characters. The scent of mother nature's best-known herb surfs itself through the train. Amelia talks to me about stars some more, and I love it; I love her passion just as mine is for writing, or Aiden's is for healing surrounding himself in safer environments. She taught me science's reason behind why stars twinkle, but I have an entirely different theory: they twinkle because they're beautiful- we don't always require complex answers to God's creation.

Coney Island is a slice of unforgotten dreams for many: their first kiss, their first date, the first taste of sugary candy floss, arcade games lights that make some travel back to the 80s, nostalgic feels roam the vicinity, the smell of buttery popcorn and rust. The Ferris wheel is hypnotizing you to let loose, all of which I've never experienced; for me, these memories will be a first. I stand outside, taking it all in. Tingles of excitement circulate through my stomach, thoughts of creating my first unforgotten dream, to get to live and experience it all today. Omar and Yasmin meet us out front; Omar and Aiden embrace in a hug, both feeling elated.

"Ah, Amala, my brother," he points at Aiden, "has told me so much about you...like you're all he talks about these days." I feel myself blush while Aiden punches him to stop. Omar is a smidge shorter than Aiden; he's got the whole streetwear thing going for him, baggy cargos that sit nicely on a pair of Jordans and a white tee; he has a babyish face but seems mature. Yasmin, on the other hand, is tall and slim. In some ways, she resembles her aunt Selene; with the same eyes and facial structure, they are both extremely pretty.

"Amala, it's nice to put a name to the face finally." She reaches in for a hug. I try to play it off cool, "likewise, Yasmin."

"I hear you're a book girl."

"Somewhat," I laugh.

"Well, hook a girl up; I need a summer read."

I smile, "I'll have a list ready." She turns to the youngish teenager behind her who looks reluctant to be here. Aiden picks him up in a bear hug, "You grew Khalid!" Khalid laughs and pushes Aiden away. He shoots a look at Amelia, the first look of many to come, the very first that makes your heart tingle; that's all I can see in his eyes; nothing in the world matters other than her now. Amelia looks his way but breaks it off and turns to Aiden, "You promised a fun last night."

Aiden claps his hands together, "You're right, let's go."

I'm not sure whether right now is the appropriate time to mention I'm afraid of rides; in fact, I hate them. The idea of flying off because my seat belt malfunctions or I get stuck on top and my only way down is to climb down, no thanks. They all rush and race to their first roller-coaster like junkies running to a free fix; I remain walking slow-paced. I decide to video call my mother to have a reason to skip the first roller-coaster, but of course, Aiden notices that I'm not near and turns around to find me. He throws his arms around to communicate why I'm not running; I point to my phone and pretend I'm on a call, but he sees right through me, and part of me…all of me loves it.

"May, what's up." He asks, panting, having just run back to me.

"Nothing, I got a call for my mom." I avoid moving, trying hard to remain still; I remember reading a book about body language and nonverbal communication, but my nose gives in and twitches. He looks at me suspiciously, "You little chicken, May," I laugh, letting my deep dislike for rollercoasters slide out. "Okay, now you know, please don't make me go on one."

"Nope, sorry, that's lame let's go."

"Aiden, please, anything but that."

"Come hurry... either you come quietly, or we're all grab you against your will."

"Aiden! Please don't make a scene." I plead.

"Guys," he turns to grab their attention. "Amala-"

"Wait...okay...God, I hate you."

"Nah, you don't."

I reluctantly walk towards the ride. I look it up and down, almost breaking my neck to see how high up it goes. I hate him; I hate how he can convince me. I frown at him, and he smiles at me. "You got this, May, just don't take your eyes off me." He whispers. I take my seat, telling myself I still have time to run off and not fold to peer pressure, but alas, I cave, my eyes glued to Aiden's, who is sitting a seat away from me; Amelia sat next to me. Yasmin, Omar, and Khalid are sat behind. I take a deep breath. The guy operating the ride comes around to check our seat belts, and I think to myself, I still have time, "You got this; you can't back out now!" Aiden motivates me. The guy tugs hard on my seat belt, but it's not budging. I feel some relief, but it is fleeting because as soon as I hear mechanics run and the ride gently starting to move, I think to myself, this has to be the complete antithesis of what will happen in thirty seconds. The ride moves out of the inside tunnel and hangs off the edge as if contemplating death until it drops with sheer force, speed, and velocity. I feel my skin jolt back. Amelia grabs my hand, and we hold each other tightly. I turn to look at Aiden to yell at him; I don't '*got*' this that if there was an eject button, I need it. "May!" he screams. "you okay!" I manage to shake my head no.

The ride goes through a loop forwards and backwards until a sharp break of suspense, a moment of pause where we can catch our breath, and Aiden's kind eyes on me, "May I-" The force of the ride cuts him off as we ride through the loops again. The ride makes its way back to the tunnel, and I gladly rush off the ride to return my feet on solid ground.

"No more rides for me; I'm out."
"Boo!" Omar shouts.

"Oh, my goodness, that was so much fun. I forgot how good rides are." Yasmin shouts.

"Tell me about it!" Aiden agrees with her.

"I'm sorry, but I hate rides, and I'm in a dress."

Khalid chimes in, "Are Amelia and I allowed to go ride the blue one?"

"Yes, but meet us back here," Aiden says protectively.

"Omar, you promised me a bear," Yasmin states, pointing to the one she wants.

"Me vs you in hoops, Aid?"

"Hell yeah!"

We walk over to the basketball shootout. I know Aiden can win, but he'll choose to lose the last shoot so Omar looks cool in front of his girl.

"Ah, better luck next time, my brother."

Yasmin squeals at Omar winning and picks the biggest obnoxious-looking bear from all of the cushioned prizes. I stare at all the prizes, thinking which one I would get if I won or if Aiden won for me. There's a big yellow banana, a huge pink marshmallow, teddies, the entire cast of Winnie the Pooh, and a cute little rabbit. The little rabbit reminds me of the Velveteen Rabbit, and I remember my father reading it to me- I think that's what I would get- the little rabbit.

Amelia and Khalid return with huge candy flosses the size of their heads, laughing the entire way…is love roaming the air? I watch the merry-go-round, the center of every fairground, the horse traipsing up and down, the rest of the animals and the carriages evermore smiling, "wanna go on it?" Aiden asks.

"I think so," I reply slowly, lost in my daydream of Pinterest pictures of us. Sometimes, I wish someone would follow us secretly with a hidden camera to capture pure candid pictures; though words capture my heart, it is movies that capture my dreams. The six of us take over the merry-go-round everyone running to pick their seat. Aiden and I grab the two horses side by side. Omar and Yazmin grab a carriage. Khalid jumps on the camel, and Amelia climbs the Zebra. As the night comes around, the heat fades and hides with the sun, the merry-go feels calm, a cool breeze surrounds us, and though we're all together, we're all in our own bubbles for this ride.

"Amala?"
"Yes Aiden."

"You ready for one more rollercoaster?"
I roll my eyes at him. "absolutely."

"Aiden?"
"Yes?"

"Earlier at the ball, why did you get so annoyed."

He gently sighs, "Because May, there is so much I want to tell you, but sometimes I don't know if you're there with me or it's never the right moment."

"Hmm, have you ever thought that life is full of unexpected moments?"

"True."

"Sometimes," I hesitate. "I don't know if it's all in my head or if any of this is real. How do you know."

"You know it's real. It's something you can feel, something that just feels right with that person."

I think about his response, but I'm not sure why I even have to think; I knew deep within me he was right for me, and though certain of his response, I'm still afraid of his response because once it becomes real, there is a real possibility of life without Aiden and that saddens me more than I can explain.

"You can't always be afraid, May. Earlier, you said you care for me, but care for me the same way you care for a friend."

"Aiden, of course not; Aiden, in the past five or six months, you've brought me out of my comfort
helped me see new things and experience life in ways I thought were out of reach, and in the process, I think...I think I've fallen for you and not in a way you do for a friend but in a way that terrifies you, the all-consuming, fireworks

in the sky type of fall, and I'm sorry it's taken me time to tell you."

He looks at me as if, for the very first time, the first look one that makes your heart tingle, that nothing in the world matters. "You have no idea how long I've waited to hear this."

The first of many looks.

CHAPTER TWENTY-EIGHT

AIDEN.

I constantly slept through Mr. O'Conner's English class, but tonight, I'm reminded of Shakespeare. Sat next to Amala on the merry-go-round, and I think, *'I would not wish any companion in the world but her.'* I try to etch this memory deep in my mind: her beautiful brown eyes. I can't help but pour my mind with thoughts of wanting to hold her, but I can't, and so I suppress them. She means more to me than ten minutes of guilty pleasure; I have to do right by her and respect her, but more apparent, I thank God for bringing her to me when I needed it the most when the world started to feel cold, she brought it warmth, and when my mind was fueled with cancerous thoughts, she came and extinguished them. How, then, can I jeopardize her, be ungrateful to God, and ruin it all to be incarcerated by my thoughts?

I look down at my old, worn-out watch; it was a gift from my aunt Selene when I turned 16; it's almost midnight; I wish I could stay here like this, a rerun of summer's favorite day. "Aight, guys, we got to go soon," I say hesitantly, not wanting to end the night.

"I know there's a party happening three blocks from here," Omar states with obvious intentions to keep the night going.
"Nah, I have to take the girls home. It's late," I say, trying to be responsible.

"Boo, Deen," Khalid shouts; Deen is Khalid's nickname for me because growing up, he couldn't say my name. I look out at the rest of the guys to see if there are any votes for going home, but everyone is still pretty much looking alive.

"You said it's my last day, Aiden; you promised fun." I pull my tie off and place it in my pocket; this night stopped being formal a long time ago; the minute I heard Amala tell me how she felt, I felt comforted after so long.
I want to do something to match the thrill I feel inside, "I know exactly what we should do."

"What?" they all asked.

"Just follow me."

I walk towards the go-karts, and they follow me behind; a young teen is working his first shift, his demeanor nonchalant and unphased; I'm feeling extremely confident. I walk tall and straight up to him, "I need six go-karts, and I need you to go take a break," and hand him a crisp hundred-dollar bill. The young teen looks at me straight-faced and then at the hundred-dollar bill, "I need another hundred."

I hand him another bill, "done."

I collect the keys from him and push the gates wide open; I throw everyone a key and instruct them to follow me. I jump into a blue-colored go-kart, push the key in the ignition, and the motor fires up roaring; the smell of petrol takes over my nose, and the rest of them follow my lead. I push my foot down, racing and rushing to match my internal thrill. Omar tries to overtake me on the left, but I cut him off, leaving the track race, making Coney Island my racecourse. I hear someone come up on my right; I push my foot down further, adrenaline engulfing me with excitement for a change. I turn my head slightly to the right to look over my shoulders to see who is creeping up on me, matching my speed; I catch a glimpse of her smile, and my heart races, too. I speed up and watch her maneuver to the left. The path ahead is narrowing,

MY CARAMEL

but she isn't backing down. I put my foot down to try and squeeze ahead, but I feel her kart tap the side of my kart, and for a split second we're side by side, wrapped in our own time warp. A new world with just the two of us in it, and life is in slow motion; her smile, even here in this new world, is the best I've ever seen. She pushes her foot down, pedestrians run out of the way, and just as quickly as we entered, our world is as quick as we leave it; I let go before we both crash, allowing Amala to zoom past. I watch her throw her hands in the air to rejoice her win, I follow her down the narrow path with her at the end of the narrow road.

We're now in the center of Coney Island with our go-karts; ahead of us are Omar and Yasmin. I can see security with angry looks on their face and this, *'shit, my dad is going to lose his shit.'* Thought, but I couldn't help but enjoy the moment; we all race back recklessly, Omar knocking over a stand, and the sky above us is covered with teddies, soon falling on us. We all swerve to dodge the pour of teddies; one falls onto my lap, a small rabbit. I look down, smiling at myself. I slam on the brakes when I arrive back on the actual racecourse, switch the motor off, and push myself up to get out. I see the security running towards us, adrenaline running the course of my body I run over to help Amelia out, and then Amala, I look at Omar, yelling for him to hurry, and we run as fast as we can out of the Coney Island.

I think we've reached safety after five minutes of running for what seemed like for our lives, I feel alive and present, and though panting, I'm able to gain control of my breathing. I'm surrounded by laughter of the people I love and care for.

"Holy!" Omar shouts, panting and laughing.
"That was close. Can you imagine if we got caught!"
"My father will kill me."
"Father will kill us."
We all say simultaneously.
I look back at Coney Island in surprise at what has been the best night in a very long time.
Amelia runs up to me, throwing her arms around my neck, and thanks me for, and I quote, *'the best night of her life.'* It sucks that she'll be gone for the rest of the summer, but at least we have tonight. Something we can both look back at as a pretty good last day. My phone buzzes, and I pull my phone out of my pocket to see a text from my father.

Father: *When are you coming home, kiddo?*
Me: *Sorry, Dad, I'll be home soon.*
Father: *within the next 15 minutes?*
Me: *everything okay?*

Father: *Yes. I'll see you home soon.*

I rarely get weird feelings in my gut like a sixth sense; I had it the day Aunt Selene died like something awful awaits around the corner. A predator lurking behind the bush, watching its innocent prey sinisterly, waiting for the right moment to strike, tearing into its prey with no mercy, with no empathy of what it'll do to the lives around it or what state it'll leave it in, dead or severely injured. I don't know why this feeling has suddenly set in, as if God is warning me to go home. A flashback of that night hits me, a blurred dream playing on the projector in my mind, me persisting for Aunt Selene to come over that day. For that reason, I can't ignore my gut, "Let's just go home."

"What?" Yasmin shouts in shock, "Why?"

"I feel like we should go home, and it's late."

"Why do you always do this? Ruin a good day." she continues to object.

"What do you mean I ruin a good day?"

"You know what I mean."

"No, I clearly don't Yasmin."

"What happened on the 4th of July?"

I scrunch my face at her, "What happened?"

"You were meant to meet with us."

"Oh, I got caught up," I tell her.

"Doing what?" she stares at Amala.

Amelia, Amala, and I all glance at each other suspiciously.

"Nothing, we watched a movie, why?"

Omar chimes in, laughing, "Nothing let's just head to my car." Yasmin seems unlike herself, but I'm not sure what could be bothering her.

"That is all?" She asks again.

"Is there something you want to ask?" I ask bluntly.

Omar interrupts again, which is pissing me off, "Everyone is tired. I think it's best if we go home."

"No, clearly she has something to get off her chest."

"More like you; you have something that you need to get off your chest." She bursts out.

The three of us gaze at each other again, paranoid.

"Nope, nothing I need to get off my chest."

"Bet." She sneered sarcastically.

Amelia's eyes widen, "what's gotten into her?"

"Seriously, guys, let's go," Omar says for the third time.

"Omar, let her say her damn piece!" I say, getting angry.

"Aiden, let's just drop it. Okay!" Omar insists.

"No, clearly she needs to get something off your chest, so speak."

"Nothing, let's just go," Yasmin yells.

"No, you started this, and now you want to drop it," I ask her.

She looks around at us and takes a deep breath, "I'm sorry, you guys, I'm just hungry, and we were all having a good time, and I didn't want it to end." She says, laughing. Switching around her mood entirely, none of us buy it, but for the sake of moving on with the night, we all just accept it.

In life, I'm learning that the stuff that bothers us the most have a way of coming out whether we want it to or not; the longer we try to keep them hidden, the longer they sizzle and burn, overspilling into things we don't want them too. I tried hard to conceal my story, I found myself detached from reality, until my heart found comfort in Amala. We need people, to confine in, to heal with because, without it, we're scared children lost, looking for our parents to comfort us.

We all walk to Omar's car and squeeze in, making our way back to Manhattan; the atmosphere is back to laughter and in-the-moment jokes, there is this one late-night pizza spot Omar and I love that I'm craving, so we make a pitstop. The pizza shop is empty, but we still take a booth in the corner;

MY CARAMEL

Amala speaks to me from across the booth in silence, and I tell her I'm okay with a smile.

My phone buzzes again, and the sting of dread returns.

CHAPTER TWENTY-NINE

AMALA.

I'm the last one to be dropped off home; Aiden stayed in the car with me; the entire ride, we enjoyed each other's silence, gazing at the same star that rushed to shine for us in our night sky. Omar pulls up outside my house. I thank him for the lift, and as I get out of his car, Aiden gets out seconds after me, telling me to wait, "Here, for you." He reaches into his pocket and hands me a cute little, soft, chocolate-colored rabbit, and gosh, in that instant, my heart decided that Aiden Hakeem Sancar knows me deeper than I knew. I hold the rabbit close to me, and it smells just like Aiden; I look up at him, his face brilliant and happy, a happy that is synonymous with liberating. Watching him let go bit by bit and enjoy life made me feel internally happy, "Thank you, Aid and not just for the teddy."

"Your entire life is about to change. I hope you're ready for it, May." His smile grew handsomely.

"I know... I really meant what I said...earlier on the merry-go-round."

"I know."

"So, what now?" I ask with the hope of him understanding how I feel; I'm a woman who adores my faith and God, and if Jane Austen can create a world of swoon-felt romance without ever compromising the woman, not even so much as a kiss, and still getting the happy ending than I can adhere to my faith and get my happy ending.

"Just trust me, it'll all happen in perfect timing...in God's timing." A perfect response from the perfect guy.

Still fueled by yesterday's rush of emotions, I lay in bed watching all the clips of yesterday in my mind like an old nostalgic movie you love, and despite having watched it a hundred times, you still laugh and gush at all the same parts. Aiden Hakeem Sancar, the boy who now lives amongst my world of literature and old mob movies, once a blurred face of my own versions of Mr. Darcy, Mr. Maxim DE Winter, Augustus, and even Landon but I now have a face to dream about at night, I have my very own Landon all now replaced with Aiden, someone I don't have to alter or change. I hold on tight to my new little Velveteen. I hear my father's feet making their way to my room, "good morning sweetheart." He walks in, kissing my forehead. "Do I have to start setting curfews?" he raises his eyebrow.

I smile, "Hmm, it depends; let's see if I'm out late again today."

"Someone is feeling brave; wait till your mother comes back; she'll whack it right out of you."

We both laugh, "I'm sorry, baba, we were having fun."

"Well, I'm glad, but remember we-" I cut him off, knowing exactly what he was going to say, "Yes, I know. Don't worry, I'll never forget who I am, and I'll never compromise my faith."

"That's my girl."

I smile at him, and his face lights up, and all of a sudden, I'm a little girl taking comfort in my father's smile. "oh, I almost forgot this came for you." He hands me an Amazon parcel.

"Always start with the parcel, it's the most important thing, especially when it's a book." He shakes his head and throws the parcel at me. I rip open the package, and there it is my new book; I hold it, I flick through the pages, I smell it, and it's like smelling a newborn baby's head. I can't wait to start reading my new book. I open the first page just for a quick teaser, but I immediately shut it because I know I'll not want to move, mainly as there are so many things on my to-do list. One of them is arranging a meeting with Mr. Ali's assistant to hear about whatever proposal he has to offer. The other is to meticulously sweep the house, cleaning it to my mother's standards, which is, of course, showroom perfection; even though my father hires someone every summer to clean it, I know it's not what my mother considered *'spotless clean'* (as she puts it). I drop an email over to Mr. Ali's assistant; I swipe off my emails and check my messages from Amelia; she sends over a sad selfie. I hate that she's leaving for camp today, I've had one of the best summers this year with the both of them: our road trip, shopping in the city, nights on the beach in the Hamptons, and last night at Coney Island, it made me forget all about my insecurities and fears of failing as a writer. Letting loose for a blip, I guess really is good for the soul, I respond to her with a sad emoji but also a little optimism as she'll only be there for two weeks. I click on Aiden's message,

Aiden: *Good morning, May, how did you sleep?*

I tap the keyboard to respond b*eautifully. Aid, you?* Two seconds later, my phone pings.

Aiden: *Same, do you want to come with me?*

Me: *where are we going?*

Aiden: *To Manderley!*

I love it when he listens to me and quotes me lines from my favorite books.

Me: *May we go to Monte Carlo instead?*

Aiden: *Anywhere you want!*

I feel myself blush.

Me: *where are you actually going?*

Aiden: *back to Washington.*

My heart rushes with memories of its first beat when I first looked at Aiden as more than just a friend, and though nothing transcended between us, we both felt the shift. I hesitate in my response because I vowed not to compromise myself or my faith, and last time, I was merely on a trip for research, but this time, it'll be different., I don't know if I can hold back or if the whispers of the devil will finally get me, and I do the one thing I'll regret…to kiss a boy and not my husband. My phone pings again, dragging me out of my thoughts.

Aiden: *I know what you're thinking, but don't worry, Omar and Yasmin will be there.*

Me: *hmm, I'll ask my dad.*

Aiden: *Okay, let me know; we're leaving at 1 p.m.*

My eyes shot a look at the clock; it's *8:50 a.m.* I have four hours before they leave, which does give me plenty of time

to clean. I contemplate going back to Washington; I guess we won't be alone whilst my mind goes back and forth; my phone pings again; it's an email from
Mr. Ali's assistant,

Dear Miss Zidane,
Mr. Ali would be delighted to meet you today at 12 p.m.

I run to my father to show him the email, "Look, he's serious; what do you think it could be."
My father squints to read the email, "I've heard there are talks of him writing a memoir, a dedicated chapter-by-chapter release in the New Yorker about his Gatsby ways. He might want your assistance on the team."
My eyes pop open with excitement, surprise, and fascination, and then I immediately doubt why he would ask a second-year college student with nothing promising under her belt to be a part of something huge like that, "it can't be that he's probably already got a team for that."
"Hm, you're probably right; whatever the position- take it, the man is very well connected and this business is all about having the right connections."
I nod somberly, "you're right."

A few hours pass by, and my father and I have the house looking perfect for my mother's return tomorrow; I head upstairs to shower off all the cleaning products and get dressed for my interview. I wasn't sure what to wear, but I thought a black dress with a cardigan was always safe. I spray my favorite perfume, grab my new book, and head out to my meeting/interview.

I arrive outside the building, which is staring down at me, wholly intimidating me. The top of the building is what I envy; it has the privilege to be comforted by fluffy clouds, be it rain or shine. The windows are remarkably clean; the entire building is assembled by glass. I wonder how they keep it so clean inside. Hung on the wall like the royal family of Saudi were portraits of him and his sons. I nervously approach the reception and show her my appointment confirmation; she looks at me with shock, rushes to hand me a badge, and directs me to the lifts. Eight polished lifts, four on each side. I take the closest one to me and walk inside. Press the very top button to the highest floor; the doors shut, and my legs begin to weigh into the realization that I'll be at the top of a 72-story glass building. The elevator doors ping open to the highest of luxury; I walk towards his assistant, whom I recognize from the party. I smile at the familiar face, feeling relieved. "Miss Zidane, good afternoon."

"Good afternoon." I smile, holding my book tighter, trying to calm my nerves.

"Mr. Ali is ready for you."

Nerves work their way up from the pit of my stomach; nerves are peculiar, just like an illness, and they, too, have symptoms. I walk into his office and see a 360 view of New York. It is an incredible view. If this were my office, I would never leave. I would be forever inspired by the clouds my neighboring friends. I look around in awe. Mr. Ali stands up, stepping away from his large brown desk, and directs me to his sitting area.

"Miss Zidane, thank you for taking the time to meet me." He spoke with care; he had a gentle voice but one packed with authority, never needing to raise his voice.

"No, thank you for wanting to meet me."

"Well, you're probably wondering what the meeting is about, and I'll cut straight to it." I nod attentively, leaning forward. I have my notebook and pen ready.

"I'm not sure if you've heard, but I'm writing a memoir." Internally I feel myself jump with excitement, but outwardly I remain poker-faced. "The New Yorker wants it as a chapter by chapter, but I think it's best to write the entire book and publish it."

"I agree, sir."

I sit on the edge of my seat.

"I would love for you to join us, but first, it seems you know something I need."

I'm taken aback; what could I possibly have that this billionaire needs, "I'm sorry, sir, but what exactly do I know?" I shake my head.

"You know what happened to my daughter."

My skin started to feel hot, and suddenly oxygen withheld itself from me. "I only know what I've heard, what I presume you already know."

"Amala, do note your career will either bloom or die, and how that turns out is entirely within your power...but I know you're close with that boy, and you will find out what happened to my daughter."

I felt the entire room shift, I remain poker-faced not wanting to allude to that fact that I know exactly what happened, the curse of not remaining ignorant. Mr. Ali's words even, in the simplest of sentences feel powerful, his voice is deep and important with minimal effort. I felt excitement but now I feel dread. He knows I know what happened, he knows his daughter didn't commit suicide. He also knows that Aiden's family were involved, I cannot take this job, it's too messy. I pluck up the courage, "I'm sorry sir, thank you for the opportunity but with my final year coming I don't think I'll have the time."

He lets out a chuckle, which feel sinister and unnervingly uncomfortable; all I want to do it run out of here, "Amala, unlike Conde Nast, you can't quit on me,"

I stare at him and suddenly it makes sense, it was him. He had Charlotte hire me after page 6 released picture of Aiden and I together.

"You will find out what happened, otherwise I will have the police put that whole family behind bars."

I waited for him to stop talking so I could run out of there. I think frustratedly to myself why me? Why did my eyes land on Aiden that night? Why have I fallen for the boy who complicates my life and now I'm stuck with this opportunity yet again because of him.

I check the time after running out of the building and breath in all the air my lungs can handle. Aiden left five missed calls and a few messages on my phone. I tap to call him back but it goes straight to voicemail. I call my father because only he has the ability to drown out my fears and remind me that every situation has a back door.

"Sweetheart, how did it go?" He answers immediately

I sigh heavily, "he wants me to be on the team." I lie; I need time to think.

"What, that is amazing, Amals." He can hear my silence through the phone. "Sweetheart, you can do it."

"It's not what I thought it was." I can't lie to my father; he always sees right through me.

"It's big, sure, but you can do this; you have me every step of the way; you have his editors; trust me, you're the right woman for this job."

"No, you're not listening. He's using my friendship to dig dirt on Aiden's family."

"What? Why? You can't allow powerful people to bully you, Amala."

"Dad, I'll fill you in later, but I can't do this…it's bad."

"Okay, sweetheart, don't worry, you have me; I won't let anything happen!"

I take a deep breath in and feel somewhat better. Exhaling with my father's words, they'll forever be hugs for me; if my comfort were a real place, it would have my father in it. I think deeply about Mr. Ali's threat; if Aiden is arrested, so would the Ali's for covering up it. Surely, it's an empty threat, but he's not the type of man to throw around empty threats. My mind springs with new ideas to minimize the danger; if I joined his writing team, I could control the narrative. It's not like he'll have me killed if I don't deliver; there must be more to this. I try to settle my nerves and tell myself to find the back door to this problem without Aiden or his family getting arrested.

My phone vibrates, notifying me there is a call, "Hey, I just got out of my meeting." I answer.

"Ah, I just wanted to check in and see how it went." He says calmly.

"So, you called me a hundred times."

"More like three."

"More like five."

"Forgive me for caring." He says.

"You're forgiven, how's Amelia?" I ask.

"She's doing good, but-"

"But what" I ask, concerned.

"I don't know, you free?"

"Yeah, I'm all yours."

I feel his smile through the phone.

"It's my mom May, she's not feeling too good, and she's been adamant about Amelia staying home rather than going back to camp." He said in a complete sentence without stuttering or turning the conversation into a joke. It's refreshing; he's confiding in me, I think to myself. "We drove almost halfway, and my father told us to come back."

"What's wrong with your mom?" I ask him.

"I don't know, it feels different this time. It's not like last time something else is wrong." He explains.

"How does Amelia feel about not going back to camp? I know that's all she could talk about."

"It sucks, but she would rather be near us if-" he cuts himself off from saying anything. "You know." He finishes his sentence.

"I know...Aiden?"

"Yeah?"

"How are you feeling?"

He takes a long pause, "I don't have it in me, Amala, to deal with any more headache." I hear the tiredness in his voice, in his spirit. Raw emotions erode the soul, little by little, tear by tear, dangerously carving into the soul, turning it into something unrecognizable. "I'm just starting to feel lighter, I'm kinda looking forward to my final year too. I don't know if that's selfish of me." He sighs again. "I love my mom, but I also need to...learn to get out of my head."

"You can do both Aid. You can feel tired or angry it's okay, you're allowed to feel those things and whilst you try figure it out, I'm here."

I hear him exhale with relief, "Thank you, May... you never told me how the meeting or interview whatever it was went?" He asks.

"It went well, he offered me a position" I don't want to burden him with the whole truth, not today.

"Get out of here, everyone step aside we have a new writer in town, that is awesome." He put aside his troubles and cheered me on in his loudest and proudest voice. "Wait a minute, how did you go all the way up there by yourself?"

"Oh, my goodness, Aid, my heart was in my mouth the entire time."

I hear him laugh, and it makes me smile.

"So, are you excited?" He asks.

"I guess."

"You've got this May."

"Hmm, well, anyway, I'm excited to have Amelia back." I changed the topic.

"Don't tell her this because her head will explode, but she might just be my favorite person." I love how he adores his sister.

"She's going to do exceptional."

"She really is. Oh isn't, your mother is back today, right?"

"Tomorrow night, I can't wait, which reminds me I'm going to go buy her favorite candles and pick up some of her favorite snacks. We have this tradition of always watching a movie the night she's back, all three of us cuddled under one blanket."

"Well, try not to get lost."

"Haha, so funny," I say sarcastically and end the call.

I feel a little lightheaded, the meeting took forever, and I can't remember the last thing I ate. My mind will always take me to fries, thin and crispy dipped in ketchup- my safe-haven. I look around 42nd street for French fries but all my eyes are able to see are food carts and a misplaced Mrs. Mimi Margaux, "Mimi?" I call out, surprised.

"Oh, Amala, child, thank goodness!"

"What are you doing here?" I embrace her with a hug.

"Well, I came here to see you."

"Me?"

"Yes, I heard you got the job."

"How? I just left the meeting."

"Child, you know nothing gets done around here without my say-so."

I look at her suspiciously, "Mrs. Mimi Margaux, did you do what I think?"

"I have no idea what you mean." She says with a grin, I stare at her with suspicion. Was it her idea to get him to hire me? Or was it my connection with Aiden? "Don't scrunch your pretty face; where does one eat around here? Because I'm hungry."

"Well, then let's get some fries."

I decide to take her to a place she's never stepped foot in and will most likely pull a face at. We walk in, and I see her hesitation, making me giggle, "is this the place?" Eying it up and down.

"Come on Mimi." I giggle to myself.

We take a seat after I order us two fries and a shake, "Relax, Mimi, you'll like it."

"Goodness, if my mother saw me in a place like this."

"If my mother saw me in this place." We both laugh and agree.

"How's things with that boy?" She asks, which is what I love about her. She's always direct: *'She's not in the business of wasting time,'* she likes to say.

I feel my face light up at the thought of Aiden, "You were right about him."

She smiles widely, "he is a wonderful boy."

"He sure is, but-" I hesitate.

"There should be no buts."

"Sometimes I feel like… when I progress in one aspect of my life, another part of me drops… what I'm trying to articulate is that life is not all good or all bad at the same time; it's a bit of both."

"Life is exactly that, honey. It's not designed to be a smooth sail because then we would never learn anything, we wouldn't know if we truly wanted something without tribulation, and we wouldn't know it's worth; after all the tests, you find out whether 'they' or 'that' thing is still important to me." I stare at her in awe of her wisdom. Since I was a little girl, my mother would make her yearly summer trips back home, but Mrs. Mimi Margaux has always been there, a mother figure I never asked for but very much needed. The waiter interrupted my reflection on life with fries and shakes, "This is most peculiar." Mrs. Mimi Margaux said, looking at it strangely.

"Okay, now take a fry…like this," I hold a fry up, "and dip it into the shake." I hold up a wet fry, "and enjoy." I throw it into my mouth. I see her frown at me, "Would you just trust me." I laugh. I take a fry, dip it for her, and hand it to her,

"Try it." She looks around as if the world of the upper class were staring at her, but she's Mrs. Mimi Margaux. She reminds herself to sit up high and to not care. I watch her face go through the emotions of curiosity, strangeness, acceptance, and enjoyment. "That was surprisingly…brilliant." She rejoices.

We both laugh, returning the conversation to Aiden.

"Mimi?" I want to know if she was aware of Mr. Ali wanting me to investigate Aiden and his family. "Mr. Ali asked me something strange today."

"Oh?" She raised her eyebrows.

"He said he wants the truth about Selene."

"Hmm, do you know something different from what I told you?" She asks.

I remain quiet. I have too much respect for her to lie to her.

"I see. Are you sure you were alone on the 4th of July in the Hamptons?"

I frown out of mere shock; how does she know about the Hamptons the night Aiden told me what happened? I think back to who was in the house that night, but it was just Amelia, and she wouldn't have said anything. Who else could have been there, lurking in the area?

CHAPTER THIRTY

AIDEN.

It kind of sucks that summer is over; I have my first class of the semester, corporate law, but at least I have Yasmin in the same class, someone to copy notes from. I'm looking forward to my other classes, just not this one. The world has enough pretentious Harvey Spector *'wannabes'*. My father believes it's a good idea to experience different fields of law; so far, criminal, like many, is my favorite, or divorce; it's amusing listening to some of the stories. Not that divorce is amusing, just people. After my first class, I'm meeting Amala to show her a new coffee spot near campus that is not as nice as Mays World, but their coffee is incredible; they also do this seasonal salted caramel hot chocolate. Amala finds it funny that I pick hot chocolate over coffee. I take a seat in the middle of the lecture hall, not too high up but not close enough that the professor monitors me. "Wow, you're early," Yasmin says, taking her seat next to me.

"New semester, new Aiden."

"I have some questions for the old Aiden." She says in an ambiguous tone.

The professor walked in before I could say anything, "Good morning, my name is Mr. Conan, and today we'll be looking at men's rea."

"Men's Rea? I thought this was corporate law." I turn, whispering to Yasmin.

"Me too. Let's see how long it takes until he realizes he's in the wrong class." She says, sniggering.

"Men's rea is Latin for the guilty mind, and the plural of it is mentees reae. Now men's rea, simply put, is the state of mind statutorily required in order to convict a defendant of a crime."

Yasmin looks at me deviously, raising her hand, "Sir, does involuntary manslaughter come under men's rea?" and looks back at me. Her actions since her breakout at Coney Island have been sporadically strange at best, as if she wants to get something else off her chest.

"Ah, excellent question." He went on to explain the answer to her question.

MY CARAMEL

The professor didn't realize until the end that he was in the wrong class. When a staff member walked in apologizing for the very delayed message that our lesson was canceled today, it wasn't all bad. The lesson turned out to be pretty interesting, and Yasmin returned to her normal self after a while. Maybe she was stressed about her wedding or girl hormones, but she didn't seem to herself. I walk to the campus library to find Amala; I walk into hushed voices and white noise rather than complete silence, but quiet enough to hear someone chewing. I laugh to myself, seeing students already burying their heads in books; the semester just started. What can they possibly be reading? I scan the room until I see the prettiest head buried in the highest pile of books, almost as if she built a fort around her, fighting off the opportunity of strangers making small talk with her. I walk towards her fort, smiling to myself. I clear my throat to see if she would look up, but of course, she doesn't, "May." I whisper. She immediately looks up, "Aiden." She says loudly, and two seconds later, an older woman comes out of nowhere, frowning and shushing both of us; of course, I find it funny, but Amala's entire face blushes. "Come, let's go get hot chocolates; I mean coffee, let's go get coffee," I say, helping her disassemble her fort. God, her books weigh a ton under her cream jumper; there must be some serious muscles. "How far is this place.?"

"Just straight down and to your right."

"Will Amelia be joining us?"

"Yes, she's on her way."

I order three salted caramel hot chocolates and their famous biscotti.

"Hey guys!" Amelia arrives and goes straight to Amala to hug her first and then whacks me on the arm.

I collect our drinks and take a seat. Amelia jumps right in with the biscotti, but I nervously watch Amala waiting for her approval. I watch her from the side of my eye. She's taking her time. I know it's to antagonize me.

"I hate to admit it, but that is the perfect winter drink." She says finally.

"I have something to tell you," we all blurt out and, in an instant, looking stunned at each other.

I turn to Amala, "What?" I ask her.

"No, you tell me." she insists.

"Okay, it's about Yasmin; something is really off with her, and today, in class, she was going on about involuntary manslaughter, which isn't strange, but it's the way she kept looking at me," I explain to them in a low tone, and Amelia gasps.

"She knows Aiden! Yasmin knows." The feeling in the pit of my stomach returns, a familiar feeling of dread and hot flushes.

"What do you mean she knows?" I ask Amelia.

"Khalid's been messaging me since Coney Island, and lately, he's been asking a lot about Aunt Selene and about who found her and what happened and where I was, and before you go all big brother on me, let's focus on the bigger picture first."

"What, why all these questions now they've had a year."

"Aiden," Amala says, "please don't panic about what I'm about to tell you," She looks around the campus. "I left this out the day Mr. Ali hired me, but I think he knows your family is lying about Selene, and lately, I've seen Yasmin visit her grandfather in the office; she's been turning up to our weekly meetings, too. She's been overly sweet towards me, and at the last meeting, she even asked about us, how close we were."

Abruptly, like unexpected rain on a clear sky, I realized how Yasmin knows the truth, how her outburst on that night at Coney Island wasn't about hunger or how I ruined the night, but it had more to do with her anger towards me. She wanted a reaction from me that night; she knows I killed out aunt. I close my eyes in regret and explain to them how she found out.

"On the 4th, we were meant to meet with Omar and Yasmin at the annual firework party, but my mother was rushed into hospital, and I forgot to tell them we wouldn't make it; I think they came looking for us and might have come to the house, they must have been outside when I told you Amala." I shake my head in frustration, frustration with myself.

"What do we do now, Aiden," Amelia asks.

"I'm not sure." My mind begins to slip into a place it created two years ago, a place where hope dies and self-loathing is undeniable. Where anger towards my mother lives strongly, and guilt and regret bounce back and forth as if trapped.

"NO!" Amelia snaps. "You're not doing this to me again. We need a plan, I can't have this explode on us. Do you know who was there for me all those nights I quietly and secretly cried myself to sleep? No one, definitely not Mom, not Dad, and not you. I would wake up, force myself to smile, drag you out of bed, and pretend I'm hungry so that you would have a distraction, and I still use food as a distraction because that is all my 15-year-old self could think of. So don't sit there and tell me you don't know because I'm not cleaning this mess up again, I'm exhausted, too, Aiden." I look at her, lost for words.

"What can I do, Amelia?" I reply softly because my options seem limited.

Amala interrupts us, "We can speak to my father. He knows both families really well, and he'll know what to do."

"I don't think bringing more people into this is a good idea," I explain to her.

"Why don't we just speak with Yasmin?" Amelia suggests.

"And say what?"

"What does she want?"

"Who is to say she wants anything?"

"There is only one way of finding out," Amelia says.

I look at them, knowing this is an awful idea, but I also don't have many options left. "Okay, I'll call her to meet us…but where?"

"At mine, the house is empty. My parents are in Vermont," Amala said.

I pull my phone out and text her despite knowing this can only end disastrously but come to think of it, a horrible start will only end with a horrible end, my mother in her glimpses of her good days would say, Honey, *don't expect good to come out of a rotting plant.* How can any good come from this entire situation when it was rotten from the start? My mother was rotting, and now I'm infected, and Amelia, Amala, Yasmin.

CHAPTER THIRTY-ONE

AMALA.

Worry seeps herself into the air around us, increasing our temperatures, increasing our heart rates swimming around our veins, spinning our guts around and around to the point of nausea; she instructs our blood to rush towards our head, piling the pressure on and causing our heads to squeeze, her wickedness tramples and stomps on our appetite emptying us all out until all we feel is her, all we feel is worry.

Yasmin arrives with Omar, and her facial expression reads serious. Omar weakly acknowledges Aiden by nodding his head up. We were all laughing a month ago in Coney Island,

and now the sight of each other makes us uneasy; strange how life constantly keeps us apprehensive.

"Okay, so is someone going to talk?" Yasmin asks.

"Okay," Aiden takes a deep breath, "Yas, I know something is bothering you; you've not been yourself lately."

"If you know something is up, then you should know why I'm this way."

Amelia puffs in irritation, "what do you want so we can wrap this shit up."

Yasmin's face scrunches up, "excuse you?"

"Yas, you're obviously after something, so what is it," Aiden says gently.

"The truth, I want the truth; I know something happened that night, and it wasn't suicide." She says, frustrated, but we look at each other confused.

"I thought you knew," Aiden says.

"No, I caught the ending when you were telling her," she points at me, "that your father was protecting you from involuntary manslaughter. So, what happened? Did you kill her?" her voice louder and more frantic, leaving the room to fall into silence once she finished.

"If you don't know anything, then we're not telling you anything. Let's go, Aiden," Amelia says.

"It's too late for that now. I told my grandfather, and he knows it's not suicide."

"What's wrong with you? Why can't you just drop it? Opening all this up again won't bring her back," Amelia yells.

"NO! But it'll bring my father back to me!" Yasmin yells, and we are all bemused at her outburst. "The night she died, she had something important to tell my father, but me being me, I was adamant. I begged him to take me to this show my friends were all at, it was about forty-five minutes out, but by the time we got there he had received a call to tell him that his sister died... he turned to me and looked at me with so much hate. That was the last time he looked at me, since then it's been cold shoulders or formal conversations." She held back her tears, "But now I know it wasn't me that took his sister from him. I want my father back, and if that means he hates you over me, I'll take it."

"Are you insane? She's dead; she's gone, Yasmin; we can't go around in circles with if statements; if you didn't drag your father to some show, he would have met his sister, and she would have still been here, or if Aiden didn't beg her to come over that day, then she wouldn't have been at the house. It was written you can't argue with that." Amelia fires back.

"Amelia, with all due respect, you're a child, so you need to stay out of it. This concerns your brother and I."

"I think you're the only child here, throwing tantrums because your father doesn't love you; your father is an A-hole anyway."

"Watch your tongue because I could go there with yours." Yasmin fires back, anger wrapped around their necks, tightening further and further with every word.

"Okay, that's enough!" Aiden yells, his voice echoing with dominance. "Amelia, do not say another word, and Yasmin, I can't tell you what happened, but your father doesn't hate you. He's broken at the fact that he lost his sister."

"Aiden, when are you going to understand that I'm not leaving until I know the truth? I will not give up." She says with a mad look in her eye.

"Then we'll leave because I'm not telling you," Aiden says firmly.

She looks at me, intent on unleashing her anger, "I will destroy every good thing that comes your way, Aiden, starting off by telling her father the type of man you really are."

"Yasmin, listen to yourself. This can't be you." I attempted to talk sense in her, but the devil wrapped himself around her, caressing her anger like petting a soft toy.

"We'll see how you react when your father rejects Aiden; we'll see what type of woman you'll turn into." She spits out.

"I have faith, Yasmin."

"Well, isn't that cute?" She turns to Aiden, "It's your choice."

Aiden looks around at us, at this pointless argument, at this angry person who is hurting, and I see sympathy take over him; he takes a seat in my armchair and again, for the second time, relives the darkest part of him but this time with more control of his emotions. Yasmin gasps at all the ugly parts, the parts that left that family-wide awake for several months, left them feeling like they had to tread water, exhausted and drowned by tears and sounds of muffled screams. "which is why I couldn't come to the funeral." Aiden finished his story; I feel a slight sense of proudness for he told it with much more courage this time.

"It...was... your mother's fault... your mother should have died that night instead of Aunt Selene." Yasmin says in heights of emotions. Aiden remained quiet.

"Yasmin, please, you can't tell anyone." Amelia pleads.

"I'm sorry I can't keep this to myself; my father needs to know." She says in a mundane voice as if lost in her thoughts; she grabs her bag from the floor and walks away leaving Omar standing by himself, "Omar!" Amelia pleads. "You have to tell her please."

"I'll try." He turns to Aiden. "I'm sorry man I had no idea."

Omar runs after Yasmin in hopes to convince her to not say anything to her father, "what do we do now?" I ask.

"We wait," Aiden said calmly, a little too calmly.

CHAPTER THIRTY-TWO

AMALA.

Chaos sometimes forces rational thoughts, to a test of sensibility and focus, questioning how agile one can be amidst chaos's sandstorms. Yesterday awoke a realization in Aiden that he has control of certain aspects of his life and why wait around in fear of the worst; he sat his father down and explained to him what may happen to prepare him. He sat his mother down and told her that she can't be living in the past, and she needs to accept that help had always been there, but the longer she chooses to not accept it, she'll be sat in the same seat in forty years wondering where her children have gone. Most importantly, he sat Amelia down and apologized to her for leaning on her without asking if she too was okay, he blossomed into the man I believed he could be-brave.

My parents returned from their little getaway in Vermont and they were glowing, and more in love than ever, my father's color had returned in the presence of my mother. I look at them and I pray that in thirty-five years I too will be glowing in love. I join them for a full spread of breakfast, already forgetting the dismay of yesterday. My mother's special eggs and my father's pancakes, a selection of topping from strawberries, banana, chocolate, blueberries and my mother's favorite whipped cream with a little cinnamon. My father visits memory lane and all his favorite things about my mother, I throw a towel at my father when he starts his very public display of affection. The autumn sun bounces in, joining in on the laughter and smiles, my phone pings.
"Sweetheart I think you should go get dressed, put something beautiful on." My father insists smiling wide.
"Why?" I ask.
"We have guests coming over." My mother says with joy.
I look at them suspiciously but make my way upstairs. I shower, washing the scent of breakfast off; I put on my new white dress my mother brought from Oman, put on the lightest bit of makeup and gloss, and spray myself with my scent. I hear the doorbell ring and my father rushes to open

the door, and as he does, my stomach fills with butterflies. Not with worry but with anticipation perhaps, I hear voices, familiar voices, until I hear his voice: Aiden's voice, and my heart warms.

I make my way down the stairs; my eyes find Aiden first through the cracks of the door, the sun shining on this newfound man. I hear his parents and Amelia. I move a smidge over, hoping my mother is there; thank God she is. I make eye contact with her and gesture her towards me. We tiptoe into my father's study away from prying ears,

"Momma, what's going on?" I still feel the need to whisper, though we are in an entirely different room. My mother bounces up and down with excitement as if today were about her, "I promised I wouldn't say anything, but oh," she grabs ahold of my hands, shaking them up and down with animation, "Aiden called your father yesterday and went on and on about you and how he wants to marry you." My world stopped; reality, unlike anything I've ever imagined, now merges with a world I created with all my favorite authors. My very own Mr. Darcy has stepped out into reality and awaits me. My Mr. Darcy, one I can relate to, one that respects our religion, respects me, honors me by never having laid a hand on me, one that I can now call mine, my Aiden. My mother takes my hand, her eyes teary, her face proud, and whispers, *'This is your moment, baby girl.'* I think to myself, it is my moment, finally a memory I won't need reminding of because it'll live in my imagination. Nothing can ruin today.

There are seven billion of us all experiencing today; differently, yesterday existed of angst, but today of joy by the amazement and peculiar ways of God, maybe to show us that no sad day is forever nor a happy day. I walk into the room, and all conversations fall silent. I feel heat radiate from my cheeks; Aiden stands up; he's in a linen suit wearing the tie I picked out this summer. All eyes are on us; Amelia throws her hands around me and squeezes me,

"Finally, I have a sister, and now both of us can bully him." I smile, wanting to tell her how I've always secretly wanted a sister, too, but my nerves avert me from being able to talk. I hug Aiden's mother she looks nervous but greets me with warmth; the handful of times I've met her, she's been nothing but warm.

"Thank you for bringing bliss into my son's life when he needed it the most." She whispers, gently kissing my cheek. I take a seat as close as I could next to my father, my comfort. My mother lays out the finest of confectionary, baklava from the Turkish boutique from midtown, cake from Magnolia, cupcakes from Mays, Levain's cookies,

Jordan almonds, karak chai, the entire works. I'm hoping my mother had a box of cookies hidden for me separately, and his mother compliments the spread. The room hasn't sunk into awkwardness thus far, the mayor and my father discuss politics, and our mothers talk about upcoming balls, but the three of us, Aiden, Amelia, and I, are merely silent observers of it, smiling away silently.

The mayor gathers everyone's attention, "My son very rarely comes to me about anything, and for the past two years, I've been trying to get him to take his studies seriously; Lord knows it's been a battle," Everyone chuckles, "but lately he's not only been taking his studies seriously, but he seems lighter, more docile, and relaxed. I've seen him smile more in the last eight/nine months than in the past two years, and I don't believe in coincidences, Ahmed. I think your daughter is responsible for bringing light into his life and, by extension, my daughters and ours." He points to his wife. "I would love nothing more than to ask for her hand for Aiden."

My father looks over at me, and we have one of our silent telepathic conversations; I smile and tell him it's okay, and he raises his eyebrow to ask if I'm certain, and my smile increases. "We accept, but" I dart my head back at my father,

"I want them to have a simple Nikah at the masjid-" Aiden's mother interrupts my father.

"I agree; I want their start to be beautiful to be protected against rot." She says, and I look over at Aiden, smiling to himself. My father cleared his throat and began reciting some prayers for us to be protected by God, for us to have blessings in our marriage, in our lives, in our love, for us to grow together, to remain respectful, and to love each other every day.

'Ameen,' everyone says once my father finishes his prayer.

"Well, now we have that settled, you can leave the ladies to discuss the fine details, but how about we go out to celebrate?"

"Oh yes, I'm thinking Momofuku Ko?" Amelia suggests, "Or the Oak Room or that Italian place momma likes."

"I think the Italian place sounds perfect." My mother placed her hand over Aiden's mother's hand; her nerves are slowly subsiding, and watching my mother's kindness towards him made my heart warm.

"It's settled then, the Italian place." My father announces, getting up from his seat, and everyone follows.

New York feels calm once again like the night I met Aiden. I wore the emerald dress, and he wore his black suit with a matching emerald pocket square. Our families seem to fit together; they're fries and ketchup. I keep waiting for a moment of awkwardness to show, but thus far, it's afraid to step out. The family walks into the restaurant, but I nudge Amelia to stay behind with me. I want to tell her the feelings are mutual, "Big day, huh?"

"The best day for sure is." She says, smiling.
"How you feeling after yesterday?"

"You know, at first, I was so angry because I felt after a long time, we start feeling like a normal family, and she came and threatened it all. However," She emphasizes, "after Aiden spoke to me, I realized that God has a plan, so whatever happens, no matter how awful or scary, there's a plan I trust, and things will be okay after that super-intelligent thought," I let out a small smirk at her ability to turn everything into a joke, "my fears start to fizzle away especially when he starts telling me about his plans to ask for your hand, ah I couldn't sleep I was so excited."

"I want you to know that you'll always have someone to check in on you and, of course, to annoy your brother, but I feel incredibly lucky to have you as my sister." I hug her tightly, and we head inside to join the rest of the party. I feel my phone vibrate, but I ignore it because I'm with the only people that matter, but it vibrates again and again.

CHAPTER THIRTY-THREE

AIDEN.

I try to capture a flash of my mother smiling, in fact laughing; she's laughing infectious laughter from the gut; tears are rolling off Ahmed's face from laughter, which only triggers my father and, like dominions, the rest of us. My heart beats with warmth and calmness today; not a single insignificant thread of doubt or anxiousness enters my mind. I have everyone I love sitting at one table eating pizza, sitting across from the woman I adore, the woman who made my heart flicker and question everything nine months ago. Despite whatever happens with Yasmin, at least I have this. At least I have Amala.

I look over at Amala and notice her phone pinging constantly. I tell her to check her phone, but she says she doesn't want to ruin the moment. She said whatever it is can wait till tomorrow, and she's completely right. I take her phone, switch it off, and place it in my jacket pocket; whatever it is can wait till tomorrow. We devour the pizza, and our parents seem to be high off nostalgia; they get up giggling and tell us that they're going to the golf club, that we, too, should have fun, and that they'll see us at home, they kiss us goodbye extra tightly something my father hasn't done since I was perhaps ten, he holds Amelia's face and mushes it together kissing her on her forehead.

"I'm proud of you," he says. My mother holds me, Amelia, and I firmly, inhaling and exhaling, "Oh, I don't want to ruin my make-up, but I love you both dearly." She says before leaving.

"Old people get nostalgic over nothing, I swear," Amelia says in her sarcastic voice.

I roll my eyes at her and throw my arm around her neck, "where shall we go?"

"You've got to ask yourself one question: 'Do you feel lucky? Well, do ya punk?" Amala yells, doing a strange impersonation of someone.

"Ah, Aiden, it's from Dirty Harry, Clint Eastwood," Amelia says, whacking me on the arm.

"Frankly, my dear, I don't give a damn," I reply.

"Oh easy, Gone with the Wind," Amelia shouts out.

"I don't want realism; I want magic," Amala said perfectly from my favorite play.

"Ah, A Streetcar Named Desire."

"Well, this is fun. We can just do this," Amelia suggests.

"Let's ask the lady of the hour… Amala?"

"Oh, you know I'm quite okay with anything." She says blushing.

"Boo, not good enough, you're going to be a Sancar soon we can't have shy people in our family." Amelia proclaims.

"Fine," She thinks, her eyes wandering up, and I look away because she's just so beautiful, "I've always wanted to see the city from above."

"Like a rooftop?"

"More like a helicopter."

"Now we're talking!" Amelia yells with excitement.

I haul a cab to take us to downtown Manhattan Heliport. I call ahead to reserve a helicopter. My phone vibrates, and I see it's Omar calling me, I ignore it, but he calls me a second time and now a third, I decline them all; I want today to remain perfect. We arrive outside 6 East River Piers and ask Amala if she wants to back out yet, but she shakes her head, and Amelia skips ahead. Even in her walk, there is happiness. The instructor goes through all the guidelines like a stewardess on a plane going through monotonous instructions, we are finally given the green light to climb in and we do. We adjust the head set on our heads and the pilot gives us a thumbs up before shutting the door, I look at Amala a final time, asking if she's absolutely sure, she gives me a weaker nod. The helicopter hovers straight up, unlike a plane, which needs a runway to guide its force. We pass by Brooklyn Bridge, fly over the Statue of Liberty, over the Chrysler Building (which Amelia confused for the Empire State Building), pass by Ellis Island and the entire Central Park; I glance over at Amala to check if her fears have subsided as we pass Coney Island and I see a smile ascent her face, Amelia pokes me repeated as we fly past the Intrepid Sea, Air, and Space Museum, next is our University, we pass by the New York Harbor and it reminds me of the Mob and Lucky Luciano, finally past the One World Trade center landing safely back on ground.

"So not so bad, right?" I ask Amala.
"No, I liked it, loved it. Thank you, Aid."
Amelia takes a million pictures while I take my phone out; I catch a glance at Omar's message, *'Please, it's urgent.'* I sigh, and I refuse to open the message. *What if it's*

important, I wonder, no, we'll deal with it tomorrow, I haul us a cab.

"Aiden, Omar is calling me," Amelia says, showing me her phone. "Do I answer it?"

"No! We'll deal with it tomorrow." I insist.

"He keeps calling; what if it is important?" She asks. I look over at Amala, "Maybe we should Aid; he wouldn't call this many times if it wasn't serious." Okay, well, let's get into the cab, and we'll call him in the car. I provide the driver with Amala's address, and I take my phone out to call Omar back. It rings, and we wait patiently and increasingly concerned; his line goes straight to voicemail. "I guess it wasn't that urgent, so can we ignore this and go back to planning what to do next?" I say with a smile on my face in a light, humorous tone, but I know something of a serious nature is prowling.

"Hmm, well, let me get changed out of my very formal dress and into something more suitable for lunch."

The cab driver kisses his teeth out of frustration. I turn my attention to him; he's shaking his head, "What is wrong with the car." He yells angrily, huffing and puffing. I divert my attention to behind us, a blacked-out Lincoln SUV dodging cars and swirling lanes as if death is chasing him, adamant to pass us by. My phone rings, it's Omar. I quickly answer, "Omar, what's up?" I place him on speaker.

"Look, man, I tried calling you a bunch of times. I even tried Amelia," he sounds frantic, unlike his calm self, I apologize to him, and he continues,

"Look, Aid, they isn't playing man, Yasmin told her father, and he is angry like I ain't seen before, he went on and on about leveling the playing field. I'm worried, man, you didn't see him Aiden, the dude turned into a villain in zero seconds, Yasmin even tried stopping him. He's not right, just please stay clear of him." Omar rambles on in fear and panic, he isn't the type to talk in hyperbole either. I immediately turn around out of paranoia but the black SUV is long gone, I think back to him mentioning leveling *the playing field,* and I think of my mother,

"Don't worry, Omar, I appreciate you telling me." I end the call. Both Amelia and Amala have worry on their face but I would be lying if I said I wasn't worried either. I grab the driver's shoulder in panic and tell him to take us to the golf course instead, I have to make sure my mother is okay or will be okay, the driver nods his head. I understand Yasmin's father's anger, I can't imagine someone robbing me of my sister, of Amelia, but what does he hope to accomplish? Nothing will bring my aunty back.

The cab driver turns the vehicle around and from the corner of my eye, as quick as light enters a room, I see the black Lincoln SUV charge at us.

CHAPTER THIRTY-FOUR

AMALA.

I didn't see no black Lincoln, I saw the fear in Aiden's eyes, I heard Amelia yell before the car spun, Amelia who always sits in the middle of Aiden and I fell into gravities dominance. It dragged her through the broken glass that shattered into an infinite number of pieces. Though infinite it was the same glass that cut through us all. Once everything briefly stopped moving, as if the catastrophe needed to catch its breath, I saw Amelia laid on the concrete, I only caught glimpses of the accident, I felt panic more than pain in that moment. I needed comfort and I turned to find Aiden, I needed his comfort, I needed him to tell me *'it's okay', 'I've got this', 'keep your eyes on me, May', 'everything will be fine May', 'trust me May'* but I couldn't hear him, he wasn't responsive. I heard civilians do their civic duty and call 911, I heard people gasping and yelling at what they had witnessed. I tried rushing to their aid, but I couldn't get up. I had no strength, I looked down to see that I was covered in blood; an abrupt surf of weakness overcame me, and I closed my eyes. I prayed to God.

Our parents rushed to the hospital once they heard the news, I sat alone, scared, hurt, and panicked until my parents came. The hospital separated Aiden and Amelia from me. I kept asking if I could see them, but no one gave me a straight answer. My nurse came and patched up my cuts, I was physically okay, but I needed something for my heart, something that will rid my fear. Fear of the worst. For, all it took were seconds, seconds for the black SUV to hit us, seconds for us to get hurt, seconds for us to be rushed into hospital. I asked around again and again, but I fell flat, no one would give me an answer until my parents arrived. The moment my heart saw my father, it broke down into his arms, and all the fear purged itself out. I felt that everything would be okay now that he arrived. My father gently explained to me that both Aiden and Amala had to be rushed into surgery, they both suffered internal bleeding. I wondered what they must be feeling or were they completely oblivious, sleeping away, waiting for reality to wake them up. My heart couldn't bear to see either of them lying flat lifeless, with no presences of joy or happiness. A version of them I refused to believe. Amelia my newfound sister who fills the room with joy, who taught me to that emotions spark creativity not rational thoughts and then there is Aiden, my now fiancé, my comfort second only to my father who I truly feel protected by, the only man that allows me to lower my guard because I know he has a fort build around me without even having to come within five feet of me. My pain is dwindled by my worry as we've all been waiting for three hours for news…good news…we await good news.

I feel hopeless and ask my father to assist me to the faith room, where I make ablution, washing off the blood gently. I walk into the empty room, and I rest my head in prostration making sincere pray to my Lord, asking for patience, asking him for health for Amelia and Aiden, asking for him to increase my faith, asking him to place trust in me for his plan, asking desperately for health again. My father touches my shoulder and tells me that the doctors want to talk to us, I get up from the ground slowly, and my father assists me back into the chair, and we make our way back to the waiting room. The four of them standing there, their hearts in sync with worry. The doctor's demeanor is sad, I feel a cry come from my gut as if my body already knows, as if it's already heard this news somewhere, someplace that belongs to a nightmare.

"I'm terribly sorry, but we lost your child during surgery."

MY CARAMEL

CHAPTER THIRTY-FIVE

ONE WEEK LATER

The birds scatter from the sky, making their way to safety as the dark clouds drew closer. He hears the sky roar and let out a cry so loud that it had to ask Gods permission. For all it bears witness to, sometimes the earth too has to release some pain and from the dark clouds pour tears, thick droplets of tears. He stands not so tall today, in a row, his father on his right and Amala's father on his left, the caller calls out the Athan for prayer, when the words, *'God is the greatest'*, *'God is the greatest'*, *'God is the greatest'* hit their ears their hearts tremble recalibrating themselves with life's purpose. Aiden holds himself up embracing his ears for what they were about to hear, he raises his arms up and places them both tightly folded, one over the other, across his chest (under his ribcage), the Imam calls out, *'Amelia Hakeem Sancar.'* and the room fell silent. Aiden unable, unwilling to hold back, unleashes a cry in front of his Lord and his Lord responds to him when the Imam calls *'God is the greatest'*, he is reminded of the sheer might of his Lord and slowly gains control.

The sky continues to cry dropping its tears on them, the sound of rain drowns his hearing of wailing as he lowers his sister, his joy, his peace, his entire happiness into the ground. His heart falls in objection when it's time to pick the shovel up, from that point on all he can hear is his heart shatter, he could feel it crumble in ways he had no idea it could, old band aids falling as if they weren't there in the first place, all his healing unraveling before him, paralyzed of its sheer magnitude that he wonders when will his heart be utterly okay, wound free, scar free but a part of him knew this scar would never heal.

'My sister,' his voice broken but adamant to continue, '*my sister carried joy and happiness everywhere she went, on the darkest days she was my light throughout the tunnel, she loved God and placed her trust in God and in return God placed love around her, it was hard not to be infected by her love or her smile. She defined her character in 17 years far better than any adult I know and though-*' he breaks down, his father grabs ahold of him and Omar. but he hears no comfort in their words, he shrugs Omar off and he walks away trying to gain control, finding it desperately inside of him, he knew deep down that God had given him the power to rise above this too but as of now all he can hear and see and feel is pain, awful deep gut wrenching pain, a

scar that never heals only conceals itself with the prayer of meeting their person again.

"Aiden?" He hears her through all the pain. "Aiden." She says gently and through the softness of her voice she comforts him, he turns to face her looking rugged, his face worn tired, his eyes painfully red, dark circles grew under his eyes for he hasn't slept in days, he spent of every moment in the masjid or in the morgue near his sister. In hopes of a miracle, but there was no miracle, he just buried the last of his hope.

She stands five feet from him, watching the man she adores break in front of her, "It hurts Amala." he falls into her arms, his face on her shoulder, he knew he shouldn't be near her, but his rational had left him today, *'it's okay Aiden', 'it's okay',* she repeats to him, *'you don't have to be tough today.'* she stays with him in silence. There is nothing she can say nor was there anything he wanted to hear. Instead, they stay there for several minutes, comforting each other.

He sees his father walk towards him and he finds it in him to stand straight, he doesn't want to leave her right now, but he stands up to face his father. Tears are still leaking from his face, *'it's time to go home son.'* To that now empty house, he thought to himself, he tells his father he'll meet him at home but he decides he has no intention to go home, now, or ever. All he wants is to see his sister again, to hear her talk about food, or space, or watch a movie together, to run famous movie lines together, to take spontaneous road trips together, he got into his car thinking back to all his favorite memories until all he could think of is seeing her again, to skip life's chapters and go meet his joy. His foot pushing down harder on the gas, a tree in his line of vision is blurred by tears and emotions, he gets closer and faster unclipping his seatbelt, he closes his eyes and allows the sheer speed of the car to take over and crash into the tree taking his life too.

MY CARAMEL

'Amelia?' He asks in shock.

'Aiden?' She runs up to her brother throwing her arms around him.

'Where are we?' he wonders looking around but nothing looks familiar, everything looks peaceful, bright, and rich.

'I don't know, in your dream maybe.' She responds.

'Are you okay?' His eyes well up again.

'I'm perfect, why are you crying?'

'I can't go back and live life without you.' He begins to sob.

'Aiden, you know that life isn't meant to be our forever, just a test. You've got this. Once you're done I'll be here waiting to watch a movie.'

He ponders on her answer but isn't ready to accept it.

'But aren't you scared…alone?' He reflects.

A woman that's familiar to his heart steps forward, *'Of course not; she has me silly.'* Spoke his Aunt Selene.

His tears come out faster when he sees his aunt, *'I'm so sorry.'*

She wraps her arms around him, allowing his head to fall onto her chest as if he were a little boy again, *'Aw my love, would you stop blaming yourself? You can't play God even if you shot me straight in the heart that day, if I was meant to live, I would have.'* She moves him away to look at him straight on, *'Don't you dare get scared now, Aiden, you're strong and brave. You can do this, too.'*

'I don't want to...I can't; this has broken me.' he sobs violently.

'Nothing remains broken forever, Aiden. You have God. Remember that there is goodness in every hardship, but only those willing to find the goodness will see it...don't choose to be blind, Aid.'

He suddenly jolts out of his thoughts, shaking his demons off him. Life, he remembers, is never how we plan or expect it to be; life just is. Either you grapple with the reigns of the beast or allow the beast to eat you alive, leaving you alone in its pit, and without God, we don't stand a chance against the beast. Along this strange battle, faith is what keeps us alive. It's our oxygen in a world that is confused. He pulls the car over and lets out a gush of tears alone, the sky in union lets out a roar once again, warning people of its cry. He remains there for several minutes alone, with his sadness an invisible companion.

CHAPTER THIRTY-SIX

AMALA.

My Momma sat me down the night after the funeral and said,

Grief is a horrible friend.
When in their company
You wallow in sadness
In anger
In sleepless nights
It hovers constantly
It holds a mirror to you, reflecting on what you've lost.
It hooks itself into you
But,
it's still a friend, and you need a friend.

To let it out
Because without it, you're alone.
Denying the memories of the one you've lost
So my sweet girl, please allow your horrible friend your company...
maybe it'll help.

A week has passed since we buried Amelia, it still aches to say Amelia and buried in the same sentence, though we recognize that death has no limitations on age or class or race, it has extraordinary powers to shock us, despite us knowing we cannot live here forever. The nights are the worst, most nights I'm wake worried sick about Aiden, making sure he's okay, making sure his mother's disease hasn't latched itself onto him, grabbling its next victims silently from a room away. I worry about him all the time, every time he takes too long to respond I feel sick to my stomach with ideas that I've only ever had for my parents, thoughts of what ifs intrude my mind unlike ever before, this time I have genuine fear. I can't begin to imagine what losing a sibling feels like, watching them together this past year made me envy not having one. Siblings, from what I've learned are by extension each other's protection, an invaluable relationship more cherished than anything, it is a love that is indescribable they are your first experience to love, friendship, anger, sadness, joy, happiness, mischief and more and to have them absent from your life is to have a part of you amputated- never whole again.

Lately, I just keep him on the phone so long as I can hear him breathe, I know he's okay. The day of the funeral was when he last spoke to me about how he's feeling, since then it's been muffled conversations about his semester and a great deal of silence. Aiden is trying his best to remain afloat but without his presences I feel alone and scared not knowing what to say or how to say it, or what he needs, I keep forcing myself to create a distraction but I don't have it in me and I know he doesn't either. Sometimes all that's needed is a hug, a long silent hug and I can't even give him that. Before Amelia, I wasn't much of a crier, I cried at sappy movies or when love won at the end of a book, but crying out of sadness, I've never really had a reason for it until now. I'm constantly sad, and then I'm reminded of Aiden and his family, and the sadness deepens because how I feel must only be the smallest fraction of their sadness.

Returning back to life after placing it on pause is draining; sometimes, the week given to you isn't enough to wallow. Whether it's whispers of the devil to self-destruct or simply exhaustion from your emotions or sounds, loud obnoxious sounds that rudely wake you from your little bubble. I think I'm just not ready for the noise, for talks about feelings or grief, I want more time to be curled in bed watching old movies and consenting my mind to take me anywhere else, somewhere I don't have to think I just zone out like a static channel: in a limbo of off and on. My bedroom, most days is where I reside, and knowing I have to return to the living world makes me uncomfortable, I have 42 missed calls from Mr. Ali I'm yet to return, I don't want to think about my final year or my semester I chose to retake which means my wicked witch of a professor is back. I have nothing lined up as a prospective job, and the truth is I don't care; all I want is to feel the way I did two weeks ago when Aiden, my love asked me to marry him, when I had a sister and my family of three was extending.

My father gently knocks on my door,

"Sweetheart, I brought you some cupcakes from Mays." He walks in and places the box on my bedside table. I smile at him and ask him to sit with me, I lay my head on his lap and he recites Quran over me, bringing me comfort, washing my heart with God's words pouring water over my dull heart, "Sweetie?"

"Yes?"

"What does Islam teach us about death?" He asks. My love for Islam stems from my father's love for the religion. The way his eyes widen and his ears harken, and his heart sits up at the mention of Islam always inspired me, I thought if a man well-traveled like my father, well versed and has met the best of people yet, has never been rivetted by any of it, the way Islam engrosses him. The way it captivates his soul like a love only seen when the mere utterance of the subject ignites their hearts and makes their eyes glow, is when I knew that something about Islam must sparkle. I began sitting with him when he would read the Quran, when he would study it until I had the honor to read it myself and witnessed the comfort that lies with Gods words. We stubble for purpose in life, be it a great human, the best father, or the greatest in our field but Islam, faith in general gives us a purpose, and direction. It gives us answers for every aspect of our life.

I remain quiet to his question, knowing the answer, but accepting it at a time consumed with sadness is a struggle. Tears push their way up from my core, working their way through the layers, and my father gently wipes my tears, his voice deep yet soft,

"life comes from God and returns to God; it lies solely in his power. When we choose to accept it then that is

Iman, its faith, but when we try and fight against it that's when dark thoughts swoop in, true misery lies in a life without God because, just like a man drowning in the middle of the ocean, and a man in the comfort of his home, they are both in equal need of Gods help. Therefore, make sincere pray that he increases your patience, that he removes ill-feelings from your heart, that he releases Aiden's family from their sorrow."

Tears still streaming from my face, I sit up and wipe them and acknowledge the truth in my father's words, I cannot, in a time like this, abandon my faith and allow anger to win. I hug my father and get up to make ablution.
"God has a plan far better than what we have planned, don't live in anger because you don't know what the plan entails." He said before I left my room.

My head hits the floor in prostration and all my worries fall with it.

CHAPTER THIRTY-SEVEN

AIDEN.

I lay in bed my curtains drawn, my phone somewhere on the floor all the lights off and I lay on my side in the dark. Silence is all I hear, my mind is loud with silence I can't escape it, my normal loud thoughts have escaped me. I just lay here in silence in anticipation of falling asleep, where I can dream because at least she's alive in my dreams. Last night Amelia, Aunt Selene and I watched Ferris Bueller's Day Off and Amelia switched my butter popcorn for her salt one, she found it hilarious when I realized it was salt popcorn, the rest of the movie ended with a popcorn war and Aunt Selene cheated by throwing gobstoppers. Nights like last night feel real and I rush my day just to go sleep again and have them alive in my dreams, where their hugs feel real and their laughter is loud but on other nights, I'm burying her all over again, I call Amala on those nights and she stays on the phone with me all night just to eliminate some silence. At times I've considered taking my mother's sleeping pills for a brief second, I know deep down it's dangerous but it's only temporary. Everything is painfully silent, I use to beg for silence but now I can't think of anything worse, I turn my body around and bury my face into my pillow.

"Aiden," my mother knocks on my door, "Aiden, open the door we're getting late…hurry." She bangs on the door.
"I'm not going," I yell; over the past two weeks, my mother has been taking me out on random errands. I know it's her way of distracting me, but I hate leaving my room.

"Yes, you are, hurry up…don't make me break this door down." My mother says, making her second round of bangs.

Frustrated at her banging, I violently get myself out of bed, pull on the door handle and yell, "I'm not coming, so stop banging on my door!" I know my tone is unacceptable but

I'm not myself and out of everyone, my mother should understand.

"I need you to come with me, you know I'm rubbish at the mechanics."

"I'm not going, why aren't you listening to me!" I try explaining it again.

"Aiden, I don't have time for the back and forth get dressed you're coming with me and that's final."

I clench my jaw, I feel myself getting worked up but I remain calm, she's my mother I remind myself, I throw on whatever I find on the floor and some sneakers and wait for her in the car.

Turns out there is nothing wrong with Ma's car instead, she wanted to get it washed and didn't need me at all. I know this is tough on her too, but I rather do my healing or whatever by myself, I'm surprised Ma's even standing, I was preparing for another episode but my father, not quite, he was preparing for the worst... is still preparing for the worst. She smiled at her newly cleaned car. Per every recent errand we've ran together she insist on, *'grabbing lunch from this new place her friend told her about.'* but I remain quiet today, hoping she forgets and drives towards home. I still can't drive, the doctors advised that I not drive until I'm full recovered. I feel my eyes shutting, the car's temperature feels like a hot summer's day, I look down at the heaters and my mother has them all turned up high, she always likes to keep the car warm as if outside were icy, I roll down the window to let in some fresh air but my eyes feel heavy.

"Aid, my friend showed me this new spot and they serve the pizza crusts as an item." She says eagerly.

I clench my jaw, "I'm not hungry Ma, I'm actually pretty tired."

"Oh, please, I'm hungry."

"I'll just order it for you."

"We're already out son, let's just go, it'll be good."

"I'm tired ma, I don't want to go!" I raise my voice a little.

"I know you are but this will take twenty minutes and then you'll be back home."

"I want to sleep now, whilst I'm tired, if I eat, my tiredness will go."

"Sleeping all day doesn't make it easier Aiden." She snaps.

"I'm not doing this with you, pull over." I demand, "I'll walk home, and you take the car."

She places her hand over mine, "Aiden, let's go get food."

Something of anger takes over me, "stop, stop trying to pretend like nothing happened."

"I'm not, I'm well aware of what happened, but sleeping the pain away doesn't work because when you wake up it's all there again." She yells at me.

"You've been absent from us the past two years; you slept half of our lives and you're telling me after two weeks of losing her that I need to snap out of it?" I snapped.

"I know you are upset, but that doesn't grant you a free pass to speak to me however you want. I lost my father and a sister; Selene was my only sister as far as I'm concerned," Ma responds, calmer than I am, her eyes swell with tears.

"I want to go home, please, ma; I want to sleep." Is all I can conjure up; I didn't want to say anything else I would regret.

"I ruined so much Aiden, I refuse to ruin anymore." She reaches over and kisses my head and holds my face in the palm of her hands, her hands warm, "I can't lose you too." she says. I look at her and find the courage to half smile. My numbness returns on the drive home, I roll my window up wanting to feel sleepy again, my eyes return to heaviness, I walk up the stairs throw my clothes on the floor again and I fall onto my bed, shutting my sore eyes and waiting for my sister to return.

"Nope I'm choosing this time, give it Aiden...I'm telling Dad." Amelia fought to take the remote off me. *"We're*

watching Dead Poets Society…you promised." I cave in and let her put Dead Poets Society on. At the end of the movie, she's adamant to create a secret society, "Oh we can call it AMDEN!" she tugs on my hoodie.

"Amden?" I look at her.

"AM from Amelia and DEN from Ai-den. Come on you know that's pretty good!" Her smile big and bright, I laugh at her and shake my head.

"What would we do at this secret society?" I ask her.

"Oh, first say you're in, and then I'll tell you."

"I can't join blindly."

She clears her throat and does her best Robin Williams expression, "Seize the day, boys. Make your lives extraordinary."

I'm startled by a loud sound and jump out of my dream, it's my mother banging at my door again, "Dinner, Aiden!"

"I'm not hungry!" I yell. I turn over quickly and desperately trying to travel back to a realm my sister is in, but I can't; when I try to close my eyes, she's distant and blurry, a morphed version in between her and Selene. I feel anger build up inside of me, my mother bangs on my door again and again and I storm out of bed and swing my door wide open, I know the devil's whispers are nearer, but I can't think rationally now, I see Ma standing in front of me, "What do you want from me! I'm not hungry I don't want to run stupid errands with you, just please leave me alone!" I yell.

"I can't leave you alone, I'm seeing what it's doing to you and I don't want you to end up like me."

"Well, Ma, you should have thought about that when you picked a loaded gun up, knowing your two children were downstairs."

Shock springs onto my mother's face as she processes what I said, "You're right, Aiden, and it's taken me a long time to realize it, but I want to do better. I can't afford not to be present in your life, Aiden. Please let me help you."

"I don't need help; I'm just tired, so please leave me alone."

"You have one day to get it out of your system, but starting tomorrow, we're getting your life back together." Her face was ferociously serious. I stared at her, wanting to yell at her more, but part of me just wanted to go back into my room, and so I did; I turned around and walk back into my room. I sit on my bed, angry and upset, knowing my tiredness has surpassed me. I'm not sure what to do now; I'm too awake to fall asleep but too tired to do anything else. I lay back on my bed and stared into oblivion. I hear my phone ring, but I'm too tired to search for it. I wait for it to stop ringing. Which it did until it started ringing again; I got up and searched for it, tossing my pile of clothes to the side. I searched my desk, standing still to try and listen to the direction it was coming from…under my bed. I squat down, searching under my bed. God, *there is so much rubbish under here,* I thought to myself. I stretch my arm under my bed, moving it side to side to grab my phone. I feel something hard, and I stretch my fingertips towards it, pushing it closer to me. It's a book, it's Amelia's space book she lent me. I pick the book up and sit up; I wipe the dust off it and open it, *'Read it so we can visit The Smithsonian's National Air and Space Museum soon, Amelia.'* I close my eyes in disappointment. The phone continues to ring, and I reach under the bed to find it. I click to answer the call,

"Hey,"

"Hey," Amala replies.

We fall into silence, each taking comfort in each other's breathing, I want her comfort, her touch, I want to feel like myself again in order to be the man she deserves. I asked God for his forgiveness for not being able to uphold myself on the day I buried Amelia when I fell into Amala's arms.

"What errand did you run today?" she asks softly, her voice soothes my mind.

"Amala?"

"Yes Aiden?"

"Read to me?"

"Read what?"

"Anything happy."

I hear her rummage her bookshelf.

"You ready?" She asks.

"I am." I climb back into my bed.

She begins, "Remember when Joseph said to his father, 'o my dear father! Indeed, I dreamt of eleven stars, and the sun, and the moon- I saw them prostrating to me!" She starts reading surah Yusuf to me and my demons leave me be.

CHAPTER THIRTY-EIGHT

AMALA

"Hi, thank you for getting back to me, I understand it's been an unfortunate couple of weeks. You have my deepest condolences; I pray the family are doing well. I know you have hesitation on your end but before I hear what you have to say, I still want you on this project if you'll have us." Mr. Ali blabs on over the phone.

"Please consider this as my official notice of resignation; you don't have to worry about me going to the press about your son and his involvement in Amelia's death. I will honor your wishes to remain silent on things you've shared with me, but I no longer desire to work with you," I reply in a flat tone.

"Amala, despite what happened, this is a brilliant opportunity for a young writer, don't allow what happened to get in the way; a job is a job."

"Well, that's the difference between you and I, I'm not willing to work with murderers."

"I'll give you a week to decide nonetheless." He says quietly, unlike his powerful voice.

I end the call and throw my phone on my bed, knowing what I'm throwing away is a huge opportunity, but how can I continue now after everything that's happened. I also know Mr. Ali is frantically trying hard to avoid a huge PR nightmare by keeping me employed- if the press got a hold of the real reason for the crash, their entire reputation would suffer. Not to mention dragging them through the media would only put a spotlight on Aiden and it'll end with both Yasmin's father, Aiden, Mr. Ali, and the Mayor behind bars for involuntary manslaughter, manslaughter, accessory before the fact, accessory after the fact, bribery, perjury and about five other serious laws that were broken. Some things are best left covered because of its ability to do more harm than good.

My first day back to class after missing almost two weeks, Sara has been kind enough to send me the work I've missed, but of course I haven't looked them over. My mother insisted on driving me to my first class today, she filled the journey with all sorts of inspirational mom quotes. I wonder if Aiden will show up on campus today, I don't like asking him too much about things his parents are most likely bombarding him with but I do drop him a message to ask what he's up to today. People were walking from class to class some rushing with piles of books, some strolling with their phones in their hands and others walking and talking with a cup of coffee in their hands. The more I observed, the more the nerves in my stomach pushed back instead of forwards towards my class with professor evil.

"It looks like some is dodging class." I hear from a tall voice behind me I turn to peep at this strange voice.
I look up in surprise to see, "Zak! What are you doing here?" I haven't seen him since the Hamptons when he had a black eye that Aiden knocked into him.
He chuckles at the fact that he surprised me, "Well, Yale had enough of me, and so I thought I'd come surprise you." He says all loud accompanied by enthusiasm.
I half smile at him, and I look down at the ground to gather my thoughts and look up at him again, "That was nice of you, Zak." I say in a lesser voice, unable to match his enthusiasm.
He looks at me lifting his one eyebrow, "Urm, everything okay, Red?"

"Of course, I just really hate my professor," I tell him, but I want to tell him how I'm feeling, how nothing seems to be going to plan, and how life is nothing like what I've read about.

Although Zak doesn't buy it, he was always good at looking through me, "come on Red, you can't hide from me. I know it's more than just Amelia dying."

I pause to gather my thoughts, "how's the Silicon Valley dream going?"

He laughs absurdly, "it's about ten years away." he says with a smile on his face.

"You're not stressed?"

"No, why would I be?" He says confused.

"Red, don't let the vultures of life make you run into the ground," he looks at me and scoffs, "you know what your problem is? You want everything to be lined up perfectly, you've got the boy lined up, now you need the job lined up." He looks at me wide eyed and I look away because he is completely to the point- right. "Well, life doesn't work like that you're smart enough to figure that out. Did you plan for Amelia dying." He says but his voice changes from light comedic Zak to a serious Zak, "no you didn't Red, we can't say we trust God's plan but hesitate when the smallest things don't go our way, he led Aiden to you? You trust him on that so the rest will come, you just keep grinding. Stop doubting yourself along the way, things will happen."

"Sometimes I feel like I'm wasting my time, I failed my semester last year because I relied on Aiden to open up, I was only hired at Conde Nast because I knew Aiden and then this book deal because again of my connection to Aiden."

"Okay so what? Did you get exposure?"

"Yes"

"So, what's the problem, Red?"

"I thought it was because of my talent."

"If you had no talent, then they would never ever hire you, they would just hire a PI to get it out of you…perspectives Red, you gottta start seeing things from a different angle."

I look up at him, his face smiley again and his dimple slowly sinking in a beautiful imperfection. I don't have to have it all planned out, is it terrifying? Yes, but I think back to my father telling me his journey on becoming one of the best writers of his time and it was never easy, a man of color building relations with the New York Mob and breaking the story of John Gotti, the guy who got the Mob nicked. My father has been a writer for thirty years and he's had his highs and his lows, come to think of it I don't think anyone who made it was ever handed a golden key to their empire. Not that I thought that or believed it but sometimes you hope things can be easy.

"You're right, Zak," I reply, slowly acknowledging all my thoughts.

"Oh, I know, but now you've stopped your whole panic look come, let's get some food." He says turning me around, "you've missed two weeks, one more day won't make a difference."

I roll my eyes and smile, I smile for the first time in what feels like a long time we walk away from campus, Zak talks my ear off about how he really wants to travel next year and I happily listen to him indulging him in his dreams. I look out ahead of me, the Monday morning rush, the famous New York traffic lined up car after car insufferable beeping and intolerable shouting but to me it sounds like the finest orchestra. One car grabs my attention amidst the New York traffic, a black Lincoln- it's the Mayors car with Aiden in it suddenly, I feel as if I'm caught in a horrible act. I'm aware I'm not doing anything wrong and Zak is simply a family friend, he's a cousin but I felt immediate guilt whether it's because I'm with Zak or simply smiling. When is it okay to feel or be happy again after someone's world is snatched of all its color, when do I start planting flowers in his mind or how long until they are able to grow. We stare at each other from across the street with New York's symphony of traffic playing between us.

Zak still lost in his dreams of travelling East Africa separate from our stare off. The car drove off and that was the first time I saw Aiden after the funeral, he didn't look like his strong self his face skinny, his facial hair ungroomed and his circles under his eyes have deepened. My heart sunk seeing him like that unable to comfort him the way he needs me to. Zak and I walk to a shake house, Harlem's finest, Zak never cared for fine dining he always says it's the easiest way to waste money, *'you're paying to have an expensive poo'* he'd say. Despite his father owning multiple starter companies and is an investor in some of the finest restaurants in Manhattan, Zak is very pretty down to earth. Zak orders for us: fries, shakes, onion rings, burgers, cheese sticks, waffles, and chicken I look up at him mortified, "who on earth is eating all of that?"

"Relax Red, everyone needs comfort food and you aint got nowhere to be right now." He handed our waitress the menus. He looks at my face and sighs, "Amala, what's wrong?" it's strange to hear him call me by my name.

"I feel like I'm losing Aiden because I don't know how to be there for him without constantly worrying something awful is going to happen."

He fell silent, "I..." he clear his throat and sat up again, "I heard you guys got engaged...congrats." He says slowly but insincerely I know Zak well enough to know his tone. "You know my pops was mad when your dad told him...he always called you, his daughter."

I look down at my hands hating the fact that every choice in life leaves someone a little upset, "I've always loved Uncle Abdallah too...I've always loved you too Zak...just not in the way you want me too." I half smile at him, acknowledging his feelings.

"Ah, Red, I think I'll always love you but let's face it we would kill each other after day one. It would never work." He laughs.

"Oh, never! You'd be sick of my old movies and I would get sick of your constant whining." I laugh with him and he throws a fry at me.

"So, Aiden, why do you feel like you're losing him?" he asks. The waiter brings over the food, everything smells glorious. He grabs a hot French fry and throws it in his mouth, chewing quickly as it burns the roof of his mouth.

"I'm scared that I'll end up nagging him rather than helping him, I'm scared of losing him all the time."

"Do you check up on him?"

"Yes, everyday I'm there when he can't sleep or-" I hesitate telling him personal things, I'm not sure Aiden would want me to so I stop myself. "whenever he needs."

"If you're who he's calling then all he needs is that I mean if it was me, I wouldn't want to talk, what's there to say really, my sisters dead and I don't want to leave my bed? I would just want that person near me." I see him hesitate, "and you have no idea how much comfort you bring Amala." He says looking down taking a bite out of his burger.

"I just continue being there for him whenever he needs me?" I ask to confirm.

"Yes but try get him out too like invite him over obviously when your parents are there," he raises his eyebrow in suspicion, "the quicker he's out in the real world the better he'll start feeling." I often forget Zak speaks from experience, he lost his mother a few years back and it took him some time to recover. We spent a lot of time over at his house during that time my father supported Uncle Abdallah and my mom helped him cook, and I would just sit with Zak. Not talking, sometimes we would play video games and I would suck at playing that it would make Zak laugh.

Zak ate most of the food I had some fries and a sip of my shake but Zak ate two burgers, the chicken, all the fries and some of the waffles. He is slowly slipping into a food coma, "come on let's get you home," I realized home isn't New York for him since they moved out of the city many moons ago, "wait where is home?"

"Oh, I'm staying at yours."

"Hmm you failed to mention this when you was giving me all that noble advice on inviting Aiden over."

His mischievous smile creeps in, "Forgive me honestly, my dad and I are staying for the week, your father's famous games night- cigars and cards."

"Great we'll be under the same roof."

"Don't be sneaking into my bed at night."

"Oh please, that happened once when we were five after you spent the whole day scaring me." He lets out this wholesome rich laugh, "Come on, let's get out of here." I say, laughing with him.

Zak wants to walk off the junk he just consumed, and I don't mind the fresh air after hiding in my bedroom for weeks. My phone pings, I look down and it's a message from Aiden's mother.

CHAPTER THIRTY-NINE

AIDEN.

Ma wasn't joking about me having a day because this morning, she marches into my room, draws the curtains back, and throws me a fresh pair of shorts and my running shoes. I check my clock, it's 6 a.m. I was up an hour ago praying.

"Let's go sport!" she says jumping up and down getting ready for our run.
I don't contest her because she'll try harder, I get out of the bed and throw on what she gave me, it smells clean.

I follow her lead into Central Park at first, I lightly jog but I can hear ma yell, "come on you pansy." *'pansy?'* I thought to myself, I speed up to match her, "you have to do better than that!" and she shoots past me. I try again to run, my heart banging against my chest to slow down, *when did I get so unfit?* I think to myself I feel my insides wanting to throw up. I push myself again to catch up with Ma. I feel the burn in my legs, but I keep going, my heart allowing me I feel a boost as I'm etching closer to her and now, we're side by side. She tries hard to get ahead but I run faster and she's laughing and I smile. *'This isn't so bad',* we both slow down, huffing and puffing out of breath we take a seat on the black bench, the bridge to our right and the lake stretched out in front of us. I chug back on my water, sweat dripping from my head I inhale the air, I missed the air I missed feeling something other than sadness for a while.

"When on earth was you going to tell me, you could run the cross-country, Ma?" I say, catching my breath.
She chuckles, proud of herself, "I have many secrets."

"Ameen Sister." I salute her water bottle. "What's next?"
"Home, we need a shower and then breakfast." She says, getting up from the bench.

"What about after breakfast?"
"One step, baby."

She grabs my hand and pulls me up.

She made pancakes, scrambled eggs and a little fruit bowl, which all slid down straight into my starving stomach, all the running had built up an appetite. The past few weeks I haven't cared much for eating I mostly nibble on something Ma made or my father ordered but not a whole meal to myself. I know the next step is to probably to attend class today, two hours ago I would have been completely against the idea of leaving my bed, but now it doesn't seem so daunting. I might actually get to see Amala in person.

"Okay, so your father will take you this morning, and after class I have a surprise for you."
I look at her suspiciously, all this new energy and positivity. I question how long it'll last, before I have to be standing in her shoes, pretending to cheer her on and get her out of bed. I ignore her borrowed time, pick my bag pack up. She kisses the top of my forehead, and I walk out and into my father's black Lincoln. The driver nearing closer to campus is stuck in a snail-speed traffic jam; my father looks at me and looks away, he hasn't been able to say much to me and every time he does, he looks too sad to speak. I make it easy for him and I turn to look out the window, I push the button down to allow some noise from outside to swoop in and rescue the

silence. I look out across the street and see Amala, my Amala, and my shoulders drop with some instant relief at the sight of her. I look over to see Zak with her but don't care. She's my caramel, my sweetness in every kind of way, without her the world seems bitter. I can't lose someone like that. We stare at each other from across the street, it's the first time I've seen her after the funeral and I miss her touch, as guilty as I feel having compromised each other that day, when I fell into her arms, her warmth is like no other, she is comfort in its entirety. My comfort.

How then can I allow jealousy to come and trample its way and destroy us, I continue to lay my eyes on her until the traffic jam clears. The world seems to have a little more color in it when she's nearby.

My class was as expected a snooze fest, Professor Anderson is about a decade past his expiry date and his voice belongs to one of those nature documentaries. During his in-depth lecture on corporate law, I felt my eyes get heavier and I didn't want to fight to stay awake, I rested my head on the desk in front of me and allowed myself to slip into a dream.

"Aiden wake up!" Amelia nudges me. "We're going to get late, our flight leaves in an hour, Aiden." She shakes me. "okay you've left me no choice." She rushes to grab a

bucket of water to dump on my head. "Aiden this is your final warning, get up now or I'm dunking you." She kicks my leg to get me up, "Aiden that's it you left me no choice." And she drowns me with cold, icy water and I jump out of bed drenched and chase her. The guy next to me nudged me until I woke up, the lecture hall was empty as the student had long been dismissed.

I walk out of class waiting for my mother, she texted me my whilst I was asleep to say she'll pick me up after class or something about a class. I sit on the bench and take the space book out Amelia gave me, I begin to read one of her favorite books, "Aiden?" a voice called out.
I turn around to see Yasmin,

"please Aiden I just want to apologize." She pleads. I grab my book and backpack and walk away from her, anything I have planned to say to her results in anger and I'm too tired to bring that monster of emotion up. She grabs ahold of my hoodie, "please hear me out." she begs.
I turn around to face her.

"I never ever meant for Amelia to get hurt or anyone, I thought I would get my father back but I lost him further and I lost Omar. I'm so sorry Aiden I know nothing I say will ever make it okay I just wanted you to know I tried everything to stop my father."

MY CARAMEL

I stare at her wanting to say so much but once she stops talking, I walk away from her, I hear her crying behind me. Unfortunately, just as I live with the pain of Aunt Selene, she'll live with the pain of knowing she played a part in the death of my sister. Neither of us asked for this but it's something we'll live with either learning from it or drowning with it. My phone rings and it's my mother here to collect me.

"You ready?" She ask.

"I don't know what I'm getting ready for."

"You suck the fun out of everything, you know that" she says mocking me.

"That used to be your job," I respond quickly before thinking, but my mother looks at me and laughs; she finds it hilarious, and I smile, too.

"You know you can laugh."

"Maybe if you tell me where we're going, I'll laugh for you."

"I don't take bribes, I'm tougher than I look you know."

I observe this new her and the more I wait for her to crash, the lighter she gets, the more she's joking and laughing, "are you on new drugs Ma?" I ask.

"Aiden," she whacks my arms, "no would you quit this suspicion. We're almost here."

I look around to see what here is, it's an abandoned carpark, I look at her with confusion. "are you lost Ma."

"No, come on we're here." She unclips her seat belt and gets out. I look around again to see if I missed anything, I look for signs or posters I'm sure Ma is in the wrong place, we're at an abandoned car park with no other cars around us. A car speeds down, I get out of the car to rush towards my mother, the car parked up next us and outcomes Amala, in all her beauty and my heart released all its frustration I wanted to hold her in my arms but I hold back and refocus my attention to Ma.

"Life will come and break you in the most unexpected times, and often it will break you more than once," she pops open her trunk, "But that doesn't mean we sit and allow it to break us, learning nothing from it, it'll make you at times wanting to take a bat to someone's head but we can't do that," she takes a box out and flings open the lid, "we can do this." and picks up a mug and throws it with everything she's got at the wall in front. It shatters in front of us, and she sighs with relief, "Here you guys try." She hands Amala and me a couple of plates and mugs; this is all a little strange. I look at Amala and count down with her,

'3'

'2'

'1'

And we both unleash, throwing the mugs and plates with all our force at the wall and watching it shatter and parts of me break, the parts where anger and frustration reside and I feel myself stand slightly taller as if something cleared off my lungs and I can actually breathe. Amala grabs another mug, and launches it at the wall and laughs with surprise, "this is ridiculous but amazing." She laughs, and I watch her, I missed her laugh the way her voice sounds when she's full of life I feel myself smiling, she hands me a plate, "Do the honors Aid." She steps aside. I lean back the plate in my right arm and my weight behind it and spring forward sending the plate flying into the air before crashing on the wall and Amala and my mother rejoice, my mother joins in and we all find a bullseye. We focus on my mother she counts us down and again we throw releasing some tension, my mother screams when she hits her bullseye and does a little celebratory dance which triggers a laugh from Amala making me laugh and within minute's we're all crying with laughter.

"Okay now the part that sucks, we have to sweep this all up." My mother says handing us a broom each. I didn't mind cleaning up the mess, I'm glad my mother did this I'm glad she invited Amala too.

My mother places the empty box back into her trunk and yells that we're going to get food once we clean the rubbish.

"May?"

"Yeah?" She pauses.

"I'm glad you came." I smile at her.

"Me too."

"Got a mean throw on you," I tell her.

She flexes her muscle, "I've been training for this."

"I don't know I think Ma could take you out."

"You're not wrong, I had no idea Mama Sancar's got a swing on her."

"Oh, children you'd be surprised what I'm capable of." My mother says loading the car with garbage bags. "Okay kids let's go get some pizza crust." I open the car door for Amala and let her in before getting into the car.

Ma was right, the spot that do pizza crust was worth it, they have five different flavors imagine eating the best part of the pizza constantly, Ma did good today whatever her reasoning, I'm glad she got me out of bed, I wonder if this is how Ma felt when Aunt Selene died, it had nothing to do with mental health but all to do with a broken heart. All those days she spent sleeping for hours and still feeling tired when she woke up, hours spent breaking down in tears and apologizing for her behavior, guilt of being an absent mother built up inside of her. I spent all this time secretly hating my mother for what she did but not realizing how much pain she was in too, perhaps God took Amelia from me to show me that my mother is as human as the rest of us. My mother only has two people in her life now, my father and I. I begin to feel grateful of the people I still have in my life and though my heart still aches there is nothing I can do to bring her back no matter how many times I dream of her, it's one dream, I have to accept, that's unattainable. My mother drives Amala to her car, where we left it earlier while we destroyed plates and mugs.

"Thank you for a well-needed day, Mrs. Sancar," Amala says politely but means every word.

"Oh, it was my pleasure; we have to take each day as they come together," Ma responds. I get out to walk Amala to her car, although it's only ten feet away.

"Please thank your mom again, I really had a good day." Amala insists before getting into her car. I smile and open her car door for her.

"Of course, I will…oh and May, text me when you get home," I tell her.

"I will…Aiden?"

I turn to lean onto her window peaking my head into her car, "Yes?"

"About earlier…when you saw me with Zak." Her face has worry all over it.

"May, you don't have to explain yourself, I'm glad he's here you need a friend, I'm just sorry it can't be me." She looks at me, "no one competes with you." She makes me smile for the third time today more than I've smiled in three weeks.

"Drive safe May. Call me when you're home."

CHAPTER FORTY

AMALA.

I rush up the stairs after kissing my parents and pushing Zak's bowl of popcorn up to his face; I make ablution and pray to God my head stays in prostration a little long as I thank my lord for all that I still have in my life. Tears drizzle their way down upon the realization that my tiny whispers surpass the seven heavens and are heard by God. I climb into bed, fluff my pillows, tuck my velveteen teddy next to me, and I gather myself before calling Aiden. Not because I'm scared or worried about him but simply because. I snuggle under my blanket and proceed to dial his number with a smile on my face, feeling slightly lighter; at times, it takes only one aspect of your life to align for everything else to be perceived with positivity. A tiny spectrum of excitement grew with every ring,

"May?" He answers quickly.

"Aiden?"

"Did you get home safe?" he asks like the gentlemen he is.

"No, I was kidnapped by ruthless thugs, there is a ransom to be paid."

"Consider it paid."

"You don't want to know how much?"

"For you, there's no limit."

"How did the rest of your evening go?" I ask him.

"Urm okay, my mother continues to surprise me."

"Today was unexpectedly needed."

"Yeah, well it's only day one, let's see how long it lasts." He utters pessimistically.

"Give her a chance, who knows maybe this is it for real."

"Enough about Ma, did you respond to Mr. Ali." He asks.

I pause, I wasn't sure he ever wanted to hear or say their name again, "I did."

"What did he have to say?"

"He gave me a week Aiden…it's only so he can keep me quiet about his son."

"I heard it's a highly anticipated non-fiction."

"Very much so, his marketing team are all ready, he's hoping to announce it at his Man of the Year award in a Month." I sigh.

Aiden falls silent for a few moments, "You should do it." I sit up because I wasn't sure if I heard him correctly, "I'm sorry?"

"Amala I've stood in your way far too many times, first with your grade and then Conde Nast and then this book deal."

"Aiden, I cannot be around that family after what they've done."

"Screw them May, you write his book except with a caveat," he explains compelling me to sit up, "You tell the complete opulent wealth of the story, everything that happened…your very own exposé."

I sit entirely upright grasping Aiden's idea, tingles of interest and devious overcome me, "He'll sue me for defamation or worse and beside what about you?" I must ask.

"Forget me, Amala this is about you, you doing what's right for you, how many opportunities have I robbed from you?"

Ideas begin to plant their seeds in my mind spawning quickly in different directions, he proceeds to convince me, "at least talk it over with your father."

"I don't know it's a huge risk but a huge win too…I'm not saying yes but I'll talk it over with my father."

"That's more like it," He laughs a little.

"Aiden?" a thought that's desperately been with me the entirety of our afternoon/evening, the thought of '*us*' protrudes my mind. I need to know if he still thinks about getting married or even wants to, the day of our engagement isn't one either of us have spoken about. Nor have we entertained the conversation of getting married, I feel as if I were briefly engaged in a dream somewhere when, and now, my Mr. Darcy stolen by vengeances, stuck in someone else's dream. The truth is, up until today, hearing him laugh, brought me back to three weeks ago when we had Amelia in our lives yet, before his laughter the idea of '*us*' has been nonexistent in my mind and I can't imagine it occupying his mind either.

"You still there?" He asks.

"Yeah…I'm still here just thinking about your idea."

"Shall we draft together?"

"Are you sure this is what you want?" I ask him again.

"I'm certain, if it gets you where you need to be then I'm all in."

"Notwithstanding the backlash?"

"I'm all in May." He repeats firmly.

Being cautious comes with the territory, everything in journalism dabbles in a little risk and undeniable backlash but, I'm terrified of what they're capable of and the length they've gone to send a message. I've come to the personal understanding of retribution's work, it truly holds no solace, its disdain bleeds into everything and everyone, diseasing the masses with amnesia, blurred chaos. This will be unlike any assigned essay if I decide to do this, I have to be okay with whatever backlash this will inevitably bring.

"I can't do it alone… if I choose to do it," I tell him. "You've got me."

"Biggest exposé of our time."

We both silently ponder on the idea.

"May," he eventually says, "Read to me." He asks and I gladly oblige.

I read gently, softly until I hear him fall asleep. Comfort from others is to fall back into infinite marshmallows, their comfort cushions yours.

I keep my phone near incase he has one of his dreams and I slid deeper into my bed turning over to dream too but his ideas float around in my mind the possibility of writing everything. I turn over to shake my thoughts off but alas they continue to grow and I get up slip into my baggy hoodie place my notebook and pen into the pocket and make my way downstairs to find my father. My parents are where I left them, cuddled up on the couch watching Once Upon a Time in America, a fitting movie for what I'm about to ask my father can we dismantle the mob?

"Cute Pj's," Zak murmurs under his breath.

I roll my eyes at him.

"Baba, I need to talk to you."

He sits up immediately.

I take a deep breath, "I want to write an exposé on the Ali's…all of them."

"Have you lost your mind Red?" Zak interrupts, "They own Manhattan, it's too risky."

I return my eyes to my father because only his thoughts matter to me, his direction, my father's belief in me gives me the ability to accomplish anything, I watch him carefully as his brilliant mind runs a full diagnostic on all the possibilities.

"Let's go to my study." He says and my entire face smiles.

CHAPTER FORTY-ONE

AMALA.

I step into his oval office, dark oak library that circles around his study from edge to edge every shelf stacked with books, hundreds perhaps thousands. When I was a little girl, I often found myself in here hiding in-between the books, the books seemed infinite and now I'm grown they still seemed infinite. I loved it when my father would place me on his mini ladders and slide me all the way around his oval office. Towards the back of his study is his large oak desk and towards the middle two leather couches and a coffee table to split them apart. The room always smelt the same- cigars and leather. His pieces that made him were discreetly framed around the office and he always prepared it low light, his study is the complete opposite to the rest of our home, my parents came to an agreement she designs everything else and my father has free reign on his study. It's like stepping into an entirely different world here, time travelling back to the 18th century.

My father makes me a hot chocolate and a coffee for himself and hands it to me. We both sit across from each other in the middle of his study, and all his books look down on us, "what's your idea sweetie?" he asks sipping on his coffee, his persona deadly calm yet incredibly intrigued.
"I don't have anything concrete just threads of ideas I just need help with navigating it and to figure all the possible backlashes…someone I care about could end up in trouble."

"Zak's is not wrong they do own Manhattan but so did John Gotti and I'm still here. You need to start by telling me what you have, the whole story this time." My father demanded.

I take a deep breath and tell him everything leaving nothing unturned including what Aiden done, how the family covered it up and then, "once Yasmin overheard us in the Hamptons, she was determined to seek the truth about her aunt, to regain the love of her broken father she wouldn't quit so Aiden told her everything and she ran to her father without a clue of how her father would react. After my engagement, the three of us went out and Omar was desperately trying to get in touch with us, Aiden finally returned the call and he explained how Yasmin's father knows everything and anger was an understatement of how he was feeling. Aiden was sure Yasmin's father would try confronting or do worse to his mother until he saw the SUV charging at us…the rest you know."

My father remained calm, still throughout the story I guess over the years his poker face grew, "How does Emir come into this?"

"When Mr. Ali hired me, he made sure he was after the truth and that my career lies in his hands."

My father dropped his poker face and anger engulfed his face, to which I turn into a little girl afraid of his look, "We'll show him just how much your career lies within his hands…get your notebook and pen ready, we're doing this." He says in his fierce voice.

I grab my notebook and pen as if I'm preparing for battle.

"Firstly, we need proof and a substantial amount, we need a testimony from Omar and Yasmin, you need to convince her," he looks at my doubtful face, "Sweetheart it's time to take the training wheels off now, you know you have to burn sugar before you can enjoy the sweetness of caramel." I nod to reassure myself, "that's my girl."

"What about Aiden, I can't lose him father."
"We'll cross that bridge once we have a plan."

"Are you not afraid of defamation?"
"Did the mob sue me?"

"The mob don't need to; they sue with a bullet to the back of your head but the Ali's they're capable of both."
"Sometimes you have to be willing to take the risk Amala."

"Well, I'm not Baba, I can't gamble on Aiden's family like this. Father this is a classic tale of revenge nothing more. I can't write an exposé painting them as evil when the mayor covered it all up."

"Amala, the exposé would have to expose the Mayor, that is why it's a risk."
"Baba, I can't do it, all his father did was protect his family from an unfortunate incident."

I feel my head go fuzzy dancing between two ideas, we both return to the drawing board, "what do you suggest then?" he asks.

"I'm thinking," I hesitantly tell him.
"Whilst you think, may I remind you that had I been too afraid of the Mob then we wouldn't be sat in this beautiful townhouse on the Upper East Side."

I scrabble through ideas and possibilities, but everything I can think of hurts Aiden's family, I can't have a perfect ending here.

"I can't see a win here father, you've taught me better than to exploit people." I finally say.

"Telling the truth isn't exploiting people, it's merely telling the truth."

"At the expense of trauma and heartache…no I won't do that." I frown at my father's response.

"Who says it has to be a happy ending, Amala?"

I stare at him, questioning how serious he is with his, writing this exposé will inevitably destroy Aiden and I. "This isn't a risk baba and you know it, if there was a chance you would lose mom would you have written that piece?"

My father stares at me with both intensity and sincerity, "no, no I wouldn't."

"Well, I've found my person and I'm not willing to risk it baba."

He looks away, returning his sight to his pile of books and looking up at them for several minutes. I don't want to interrupt his thoughts, so I leave him be and stare at the right side of his library, thinking of a way I can get both my exposure and my happy ending. Throughout all my thinking, all I heard was, *a risk is a risk.' 'Amala, this is about you;*

you are doing what's right for you.' 'Forget about me.' It comes back to what I want; what is it that I want? To step out of my comfort or to hide behind an idea for the rest of my life, continuing to regret not making a choice as time races against me. I run my eyes through all his books, focusing on the titles; I find his classics- Ernst Hemmingway, Fitzgerald, Bukowski until I realize what I love the most. I return my focus back to my father, who, in the same second, I believe has the same thought as I do, "I'm ready to write it, father, but not as an exposé,"

My father attacked by brilliance, "but like Fitzgerald." He says, "you write it as fiction based on true events."

"Yes!" I sit up with excitement.

"A rumor that circulates the media, that tells New York, the book is based on true events to make people talk, of course, we deny any such thing." My father explains. "Oh, I'm going to call my friend at Simon Schuster. This is going to be huge darling…absolutely brilliant."

I sat back and smiled to myself, "yes, it is."

My father stops for a second and looks at me, "are you ready for this?"

With every inch of me I reply with unequivocal confidence for the first time ever I feel nothing but thrill, "let's do this Baba!"

"Sweetheart, I want you to know, this could still hurt the family when people figure it out." My father notes.

"I know, Baba, I know." I know the risks, but they don't seem too scary this time."

"Let's begin then."

My father tells Zak to pick up Joes pizza, "it's going to be a long night." He smiles, my father hasn't had a project all summer and his restless hands have been itching to get back into the world that knows the power and art in words. He pulls out his board and we create a timeline of all the events, a chapter-by-chapter, play by play, plot lines and character names that are closely related to the individuals that represent them. My phone pings, I glance over at it and it's a message from Aiden, I contemplate telling Aiden about the project when a daunting thought hovers over my contemplation, one that secretly lies in my heart and I hate myself for thinking that every opportunity that presents itself crumbles in Aiden's presence. I push the thought to a side as well as my phone. For now, I'm far too captivated on writing this story, a story of heartache, undeniable drama, and sacrifice all wrapped up by love.

Zak walks into the study having already helped himself to a slice, "Oh, they made it fresh." He says with a pizza hanging from his mouth, he places the box down on the coffee table, "so, we really doing this?"

"We?" I question him, I take a slice out handing it to my father first.

"Yeah, we're like the dream team, of course Uncle Ahmed is Shapiro and well I'm obviously Cochran."

"More like a cockroach." I quickly mocked him. Zak clenched his heart, "why must you break my heart?"

"Once you two have stopped, we need to go over how the Ali's gained their wealth." My father said while flicking through old news clips he had written for them in the past.

"I'm guessing just how every bootlegger in the country made their fortune during the Great Depression," Zak responded to my father. My father squints his eyes at Zak's insinuation, I wipe Joe's famous sauce off my hands and get back to helping him, my father instructs Zak to get all the files and research from my room, all the work I had when I was on the project with Mr. Ali. With my father on this project, I have a strong feeling he wants to push and get it published on the same day Mr. Ali's book is due to be released.

My phone vibrates again, it's Aiden I hover over my phone to glance at the message, *'if you're asleep, sweet dreams but if you're writing, keep going you got this.'* I turn my phone over and turn my attention to my father.

I peep over at the clock, it feels as if moments have only passed by, but the clock reads three in the morning; hours have passed by since my father agreed to pursue this peril idea. My father and I have been typing non-stop. Zak is asleep on the couch, with paperwork on top of him.

"Have you written chapter five, sweetie?" My father asked.

"Almost done."

"Excellent." He smiles.

CHAPTER FORTY-TWO

AIDEN.

I stretch my legs as far as I can, relaxing my limbs, I'm up before my alarm today I don't need to trick myself today or feed myself empty motivational lies, nor does my mother have to drag me out kicking and screaming, I'm ready. My body is up before my alarm, I lay in bed for a moment staring at the ceiling lost in its blank canvas, thinking how much has happened and I'm still here by the will of God. I hesitant to give myself credit but I know I should and that's something for today, I'm not tired as much and though I still dream about my sister or aunt, it's not as frequent. Time, I guess does do its part, even if at a snails speed.

I throw my sheets off me, climb out and make my bed, I look around for my clean running clothes and lay them out on my bed. While the shower runs, I quickly tidy my room, place my books on my desk, dust off the shelf and put my clothes in my walk-in. The cold water wakes me up completely pumping energy into my body ready for my morning run with Ma.

Fajr athan goes off, waking my parents up and whilst I wait for them to make wudu, I accidentally glance at Amelia's room, I divert my attention back to my room trying hard to forgot that her room is simply a vacant room filled with sad memories. After salah Ma gets dressed, ties her laces, and jumps up ready for our jog, our water bottles in hand and we both head out slowly jogging until we eventually pick up the pace.

Ma and I have been running the same route since we began but every week we go a mile further, I feel the difference in being consistent, I feel my heart pumping blood easier, I feel my mind calmer, I feel my appetite coming back and best of all I feel endorphins run free in my body permitting me to feel lighter.

It's been almost four weeks since Ma and I have been running, we've spent every morning together having breakfast, trying our hardest to perfect our pancake recipe. Yesterday she suggested a hint of cinnamon in the recipe but accidentally knocked a teaspoon into the mixture- it did not taste good unless you're into Hot Tamales pancakes.

Running through Central Park in the middle of fall is a luxury only experienced in once a year. The entire park covered with brown and orange crunchy leaves laid out like confetti and I know it's silly but I still love running through it… so did Amelia (not that she would ever run but when the leaves were at their crispiest, she'd make the most noise). I love the air this time of year-bitterly cool, as if its only purpose is to cool us down. My legs slow down for Ma, she catches up to me and together, we slowly walk back to the house. Ma chugs her water back hydrated herself, she turns to ask, "how's Amala?"

I hesitate in my response because I feel as if she's slipping away from me. Since she started her project four weeks ago every moment is spent writing with her father and whenever I ask her about it, she responds with a vague answer but I don't want to worry my mother over my paranoia,

"She's…good." I tell her.

"I haven't seen her much, are you sure everything is okay between you guys?"

"Yes of course... she's just busy."

We exit the park and I watch the food cart guys set up for the morning rush of bagels or breakfast wraps, coffees, juices, fruit bowls whatever the people want.

"Are you sleeping better these days," Ma asks casually, but I don't mind; we've been having more of this conversation that I believe the both of us are letting our guard down.

"I am; I think the running is helping," I tell her; spending time with her has helped me more than I imagined my mother, a comfort that I never knew I needed.

"Good, I'm glad, honey." She smiles, she's been smiling more these days even her face seems brighter. A thought has been lingering my mind for some time now- where has this version of her been all these years. Lord knows I keep waiting for her to crash and burn, but she keeps getting braver.

"Ma?"

"Yes Aid." She says looking up at the tall trees that guard over Manhattan.

I look at her one more time to make sure before asking,

"Where have you been all this time."

Ma signed heavily, "Oh, well honey," Her voice almost a whisper and her eyes teary, "I guess I realized that I can't lose another child."

I lean my head on her shoulder Ma and we both take in the moment. Emotions are powerful but we can control them, we can find a healthy way for them to escape.

Ma laughs, wiping her reflection tears; she stretches her arm on my back, rubbing it,

"I love you Aids."

"I love you Ma…thank you for coming to me when I needed you the most."

She rubs my back a little more, "So Amala, what is going on their son?"

"I feel like I'm losing her Ma?"

"Why do you think that is?" She rhetorically asked.

"I know I've been absent, Ma, but-"

Ma cuts me off, "Honey, she is your fiancée, period. Look I know I've made some heartbreaking mistakes, horrible mistakes but throughout it all your father has never been absent."

I ask her vulnerably, "What am I supposed to do?"

"You know what you have to do Aid."

I ponder on Ma's words, I vowed to being healthy, I wanted to fix myself before giving her my all, being enslaved by my thoughts terrifies me and it's already caused countless of problems between us. I want to take control as much as I humanly can but I'm learning maybe I don't have to be 100%, there is no such thing as 100% because nothing lasts, our bad days or horrible days, our good days never last, we just have to learn to be present and know time will do its thing and it'll be okay. Nothing is ever completely scary or sad.

Ma pushes me and yells, "Race you back?" Sprinting ahead of me.

"That's okay. I'll give you a head start, old lady!" I yell. But she seriously took off.

I run after her, the wind helping me pushing me further towards her direction and I edge right behind I'm a leap away from her, I can see her push herself to get to our home. Sympathy overtakes me and I find myself slow down to let her win, a sense of small proudness showers over me-three weeks ago I threw up and now I feel invincible.

"You pansy!" Ma laughs while panting for breath.

I take a million pictures in my mind; her smile and laughter was borrowed to Amelia and it is as if Amelia returned it to my mother when she left. I stand silently feeling overwhelmed but in soft admiration rather than sadness.

Our morning tradition, Ma flips pancakes and I scramble the eggs and we sit and talk about the past, Amelia, work, the present though the first few weeks we sat in silent, Ma tried dragging conversations out of me but I didn't have it me.

I check in on Amala, but there's no answer; she's most likely busy, I presume. I throw on my sweater and jacket, kiss Ma goodbye, and hop into my father's Lincoln. His driver takes me outside the library; I fist-pump my father goodbye and head into the library.

Today, I have no classes, but I want to complete my reading for tomorrow's class, considering I've slept through many and missed a month. Fall is in full action, New York is back to its rainy self, and I didn't mind it, shorter days and colder nights. Immediately, the outside sound drops the second I enter the library. Even nature knows libraries have to be silent. I never pictured myself inside a library voluntarily. I almost laugh to myself, but being here makes me somewhat closer to Amala. I fling open my book, forcing myself to focus on the reading, but I can hear a couple of book nerds whispering about a new book,

"Apparently, it's about a real family in Manhattan." One girl said.
"Have you read the blurb?"

"No, but you never heard this from me, but I overheard my father say it's about the Ali's and the girl that died in a car accident." The other girl said.

Confusion disguised as anger hits me, and I walk over to them, "Hey, I just overheard you guys, what 's the book called?" I ask.

The girl in the cream sweater pulls her phone out, "Urm, it is called A War Against God." She answers.

I know I didn't want to know the answer to this question, but I regrettably ask anyway, "Who is the author?"

"Oh, it's my favorite writer, Ahmed Zidane, as well as urm, an Amala Zidane... oh, you figure they are related."

I storm away, I try telling myself to hear her out and take a moment to calm down, but I can't. I ring Amala-she doesn't answer, I drop her a text to meet me. I'm not angry about what she potentially wrote but at the fact that I hear it from strangers and not the woman I'm marrying.

CHAPTER FORTY-THREE

AMALA.

Ah, forever moments. I clear my throat and think back to when we dropped Amelia off at summer camp and how I envied the joy she felt that day, pure joy, a sense of pride for herself, and I've waited a long time, twenty years to feel a sense of proudness for myself. I run my fingers along the cover of my first published book, *'A War Against God.'* I open my book and glance over the first words: *For Amelia, my forever sister.* I turn to chapter one and quickly return my glance up to the packed-out audience waiting patiently, eagerly for me to start. I look at the first row to see if Aiden is here too, but he's nowhere to be seen. I tell myself to persevere when I see Mimi wink at me. I take a deep breath in and return to reading my first page,

> *'History has compiled mountains of evidence against men with truly opulent wealth, defining themselves as superior. Omitting themselves from the law, proudly declaring a war against God, Mr. Ernst Al-Du Pont and the entire Du Pont family were no different than their long line of brethren. Except one, Mrs. Savanah Du Pont…*

I went on reading my first page, and people were listening attentively. Once finished the people applaud my father and me, and crowds of smiles surround me. The audience, fire up with questions and speculations of who the characters are and who the Du-Pont family could be, took an entire column in the New Yorker this morning. I realized that I wasn't writing for the New Yorker, but the New Yorker is writing about me. The audience threw peculiar questions one after the other; people are naturally and implausibly inquisitive, a desired satisfaction of finding out something you can't know. They also wanted to know if I was in the book, but of course, my father instructed me to keep it light and fluffy. The lead-up to the book has had me on edge, I thought by now I would have heard some black lash from the Ali's or even the mayor, but nothing thus far. My father said,

'They're too smart to draw the attention their way, they'd be stupid to come forward now.' And I believe it...somewhat.

After my reading, I rush out; all I want is to look for Aiden. I know he's angry. I know I should have told him instead of him finding out along with everyone else. I asked myself repeatedly this entire week why, why did I not tell him sooner or from the start, that I was writing about him, about all of it. I think, secretly, I was scared of him getting sad all over again to have all his trauma and sorrow on paper. Making it unescapable for him, and I hate myself for it. I hate that I thought he'd talk me out of it yet again, like all the opportunities before, but most of all, I hate that I can't trust him...after all this time, I still don't know where I stand with him. We take one step forward only to move ten steps back.

"Congrats, Red, you've officially made it on the top five bestsellers list," Zak yells excitedly and shows me the list.

I half smile at him.

"Isn't this what you wanted?" he asks.

"Of course, I am happy. I...thought Aiden would be here," I say.

"Red, he was here for a bit; he dropped flowers off but said he couldn't stay," Zak said, pointing to the flowers.

"Amala," Zak says in his serious voice, "Man, the guy loves you, but are you sure you love him?" I stare at Zak, too afraid to give him an answer.

"I'm sorry, I have to go find him…please tell my father I'll see him at home and that I'm sorry." I walk towards the flowers he brought, a beautiful bunch of roses; I pick them up to notice how heavy they are, a rosebud falls to the floor and crumbles, I look down at the crumbled flowers and notice something strange, I kneel down to pick it up-it's a cupcake. I gasp. Aiden brought me a dozen cupcake roses, I take a bite out of a fresh one- *May's praline cupcake; he* brought me a dozen of May's cupcakes that look like real flowers. Here's a man who knows me and isn't afraid to let the world know, I feel horrible. How could I ever think awfully little of him? My pride turns quickly to disappointment. I call him not a second to waste,

It rings out.

It continues to ring out.

And continues.

Intrigued, fueled people line up near me with their pens ready, cameras ready, and mics ready, and I look out to them, and I think not now. In moments of worry, you feel as if nothing in the world matters other than rushing to the place you need to go to, and the fact that others don't share the same urgency angers me; why can't people feel that I need to rush to Aiden and step aside, clear the human traffic for me and make way for me.

Rushing out the doors onto the wet streets of Manhattan, I didn't care for the rain; I allowed it to wash my pride off until I had nothing but guilt and regret. The sky continued to generously shower us with her currency whilst I continued to ring Aiden,

My ears listened out desperately for the line to connect to his until I heard a,

"Hello." Aiden finally answers, and his voice brings comfort to my heart.

"Hey, Aiden, where are you? I'm so sorry; please don't tell me you left." I ramble on.

"Amala, you're breaking up, I can't hear you." He yells loudly like he's stood near me.

"Hello, Aiden, can you hear me now," I yell, moving around in the rain.

"Amala." He shouts.

"Yes, can you hear me?"

"Amala?"

"Aiden?" I call out.

I hear him laugh, "Amala?"

"Aid!" I move around some more.

"Turn around, Amala." He says, laughing.

Instantly, I turn around, and there I see him standing tall like the day I met him, drenched in the rain as much as I am, in a black suit, bright, yellow sunflowers in hand that have flopped down the side of his hands. His grin peaks through the downpour of rain, my heart immediately feels whole.

"You never left!" I yell over the sound of rain picking up, coming down faster than earlier.

"How could I, May? It was your big moment!" he yells back.

"I'm so sorry, Aiden, I'm so sorry that I never told you." I continue to yell over the rain, which is now dancing with the wind.

"No, May, you had every right to be, I-" The noise of New York flooded his voice out. He points to the shelter near the doorway, and we walk over, harboring ourselves from the cold, sharp rain. "I was trying to say I realized why you didn't tell me."

"Why is that?" I ask him.

"Because of how much I've jeopardized you before," he says quietly.

"That still doesn't give me an excuse, I should have told you what I was writing about."

He sighs deeply, looking out at the rain falling stronger, "Why do we always find ourselves back here."

I knew the answer immediately, but I couldn't find the courage to say it, and I did what I always do: stay silent. Aiden looks at me, and we both face each other, rain drizzling down his face, into the faint scar upon his top lip, getting lost in his small kept beard, his suit clung to him, showing off his new runner physique, his deep brown eyes gently lay on mine but not for long. I see his frustration build up, "May be honest with me."

"I," I filter through all the words my brain has stored and try to find delicate words, but ultimately, he's right, I have to tell him the truth, "I never know where I stand with you, Aiden."

I read his face quickly he looked taken aback, "Why? I know we've both been distant after everything that's happened, but I didn't think that would have changed anything."

"Everything's changed, Aiden. I'm engaged to you, but I feel shy saying it out loud because after everything that's happened, I don't know if you even feel the same about me," I tell him.

The wind sprays our faces with a gentle touch, and the people move off the streets to dodge the rain, to dodge its coldness, unaware she's harmless. Aiden looks frustrated at the both of us, emotions intertwined with each other, each fighting to get on top.

"Amala, I'm sorry that I've lost focus of us at times; *God*, I'm sorry that I've made mistakes that have left you feeling unsure or that you can't trust me, but none of what I did was because my feelings have changed; you are it for me Amala, you... I have been busting my balls to be okay, where I become a man who accepts what's happened and knows that God sends time to make things okay. I'm tired of feeling angry at myself, at Ma, with my father, with the Ali's. It's exhausting; I can only control myself, and I see that now, but do you?"

CHAPTER FORTY-FOUR

AIDEN.

The rain poured over us, my suit drenched, her dress squeezed to her, and New York skyscrapers towered over us like guards; we caught a glimpse of the full moon hiding between the buildings. Everyone else hid inside, but I didn't want to move from this spot. Under the wet night sky, New York City in all her glory next to the woman who mended my heart, every streetlight lit for us a parade of affection, every gush of wind pushing us closer, and every spec of rain washing our frustration away. But none of it makes any sense unless she feels the same way as I do otherwise: wind is just wind, rain is just rain, and New York City is merely just a city. I wait for her response,

"I can't see it, Aiden; how can I when you close that part from me." She responds softly and as gently as she can, and I know she is right, instead, I ask her a question I should have asked a long time ago.

"Amala," I speak over the sound of wind and rain, building up the courage to ask her, and it takes all the courage in me to ask her, "Are you in love with me?" I ask her.

In this very moment, it feels like an eternity goes by; every fiber in me froze, the wind stands still, rain defines gravity, the branches held their breath, and nothing absolutely nothing moved until she did. She stares at me intensely, her face covered in tiny droplets of rain that make her glisten under the lights, "With all my heart, Aiden."

CHAPTER FORTY-FIVE

AIDEN.

I see her again. She looks conspicuously graceful tonight her, in her emerald dress, her smile, and her humility guarding her. It's hard to take my eyes off her.
My wife is nothing like what I've ever read about.

The sky decorates itself for us with a million stars passing by to watch the wedding of the century. I hold my wife, my Amala, under the same sky, in the same spot where I told her that I adored her, and I look at her for a few more seconds. I tuck her hair behind her ear, her rosy cheeks illuminate, and our eyes find each other, her smile enthralls me entirely, and I cannot hold back anymore, the stars shy away as I lean forward and kiss my wife.

MY CARAMEL

Afterword

A letter of love from the author

Dear young readers,

Love isn't defined by a kiss or a hug or anything physical; it's defined by so much more.

Love, is a testimony of your character and your honor. My grandmother has taught me that we must concern ourselves with having the most beautiful characters, and once we've truly learned respect for ourselves, modesty for our bodies and tongues, and honor and through all these intricate lessons, find happiness and be able to stand firm in who we are, will God open doors for us far beyond anything we could have imagined for ourselves.

Don't allow the temptation of lust to allure you in for moments of satisfaction, be true to what you want, and never be shy to ask God, and once you've asked, have a little patience.

We live in a confused world, and we cannot forget what the honor of a woman is because God has placed so much honor in us.

Stay true to yourself, and never compromise your love.

With all my love,
Angely Kahn.

ACKNOWLEDGMENTS

First and foremost, all praise to The Most High, without whom none of this would have been possible.

To my mother, who taught me what selfless love is and wore a brave heart despite not always feeling brave.

To my father, my first and forever love, who taught me to adore my religion and every day told me how proud he was of me even when I didn't feel like I accomplished anything.

To my Mimi, my other mother who believed in me when others didn't, and through her, I witnessed the purest form of love; when times were scary, she turned on the lights for me.

To my Uncle Z, my (second father) who filled my childhood with wild stories, and a flare for drama that etched a passion for storytelling.

To the sweetest two editors who pushed me to keep writing, Aiden and Amala, when I gave up on it. Thank you, Amelia and Eesha. I can't thank you enough for your time.

I saved the best till last, my husband, who without, this book wouldn't be here. For all his patience, for creating a peaceful environment for me to work in, thank you, my love.

ABOUT THE AUTHOR

Angely Kahn spent her young life watching mob movies with her father and reading classics. As a young Muslim she fell in love with all things classical but dreamt of reading a book with relatable characters, and thus set on a journey to combine all her dreams and favorite stories into one.

Angely lives in England with her husband, and is currently working on her second book.

Learn more at:
angelykahn.com
Instagram @angelykahn
TikTok @angelykahn

Printed in Great Britain
by Amazon